TO RENEW
THIS BOOK
TEL 57115

SEP 98

12 APR 2000

01. NOV 88

07. FEB

NELSON

10. FEB
23. MAY 97

10/99

30. AUG 00

-- OCT 2000

21. MAY 0

CLITHEROE
JAN 1998

23 DEC 1999

RENEW
BOOK
92511

22 JAN 2000
F 3 FEB 2000

01. JUN 00

AUTHOR	CLASS
KING, F.	A FG

TITLE	A hand at the shutter

X

A Hand at the Shutter

Also by Francis King

A HAND
AT THE SHUTTER

Francis King

Constable · London

First published in Great Britain 1996
by Constable and Company Limited
3 The Lanchesters, 162 Fulham Palace Road
London W6 9ER
Copyright © Francis King 1996
The right of Francis King to be identified
as author of this work has been asserted by him
in accordance with the Copyright, Designs and Patents Act 1988
ISBN 0 09 4756309
Set in Linotron Palatino 10pt by
CentraCet Ltd, Cambridge
Printed and bound in Great Britain by
Hartnolls Ltd, Bodmin

A CIP catalogue record of this book
is available from the British Library

For

PAUL MICHL

Contents

Acknowledgements

'The Web' was originally published in *London Magazine*, December–January 1995; 'Sukie' was originally published in *Seduction*, ed. Tony Peake, Serpent's Tail, 1994; 'Credit' was originally published in *Best Stories of 1986*, ed. Giles Gordon and David Hughes, Heinemann, 1986; 'Crash' was originally published in *Woman's Journal*, 1992; 'The Interment' and 'A Lost Opportunity' were both originally published in *Winter's Tales*, Macmillan, 1990; 'Beakie' was originally published in *Encounter*, 1983; 'Have You Had a Nice Day?' was originally published in *Telling Stories*, ed. Duncan Minshall, Coronet, 1993; 'The Burning Glass' was originally published in *The Ten Commandments*, ed. Tom Wakefield, Serpent's Tail, 1992.

Even at my advanced age, I wake up each morning eager to get my hand to the shutter and, with luck, to snap something worthwhile.

V. S. PRITCHETT
in conversation with Francis King
July 4, 1989

Thaw

I

Having given Egon Rosenthal hardly a thought for more than fifty years, I have in the past weeks often found him intruding, with a characteristic mixture of hesitancy and persistence, not merely on my thoughts but, on three separate occasions, also on my dreams. However much I try to shut out his ghostly presence, his foot keeps the door between the past and the present, the dead and the living, ajar.

I write of him as 'Egon Rosenthal'. But am I really sure that the Christian name was Egon? No. It could have been Erich or Erwin or Emil – or, indeed, a host of other names not even beginning with E. During those few weeks when I saw him daily, never to see him again, he was always Dr Rosenthal to me, just as to him I was always Mr King. That was a time when there was none of the spurious mateyness between doctor and patient so common in this country today.

I try now to see him as I used to see him then – and as, last night, at last having fallen asleep in the sweltering heat of my bedroom under the eaves, I also saw him, unaltered by the years which have so much altered me. Although he could not have been more than forty-five, he already had the stoop and the stiff walk of a man as old as I am now. The sleeves of his white coat came down too far over those long, blue-veined hands, with the scrupulously manicured nails – 'The hands of a pianist,' I once told him, to receive the gently smiling answer: 'Well, I do play the piano.' (Later he was to tell me that he and his wife, who played the violin, had been attempting to learn the Kreutzer Sonata.) The eyes were a pale, milky blue under eyebrows which, like the close-cropped hair, were already turning grey. He looked, the cheeks sunken and the long neck scrawny, as if he was not getting enough to eat. But that could have been said even of his patients in that hospital, long since demolished, during the War.

[13]

He was a Jewish refugee, who had arrived penniless in England in the middle of the Thirties. He would often say, after examining me, 'You interest me, Mr King, you are one of my most interesting patients.' But I never knew whether it was as a medical case or as an individual that I held this interest for him. Certainly he would spend an inordinate amount of time with me in the little room, not much more than a broom-cupboard, which I had been allotted off a ward crowded with people for the most part much older and much iller than myself. During that period of V1s and V2s, it was a slow, uncomfortable and even dangerous journey for him from the Surrey village in which the hospital was situated to his house in Ealing, and so – since his wife had taken refuge in the country, I have forgotten where, with their three children – it was natural that he would so often doss down on a camp bed in his consulting-room.

When I was not 'Mr King' to him, I was 'Young man'. Accompanied by one of the nurses – usually the sallow, sad one, whose boyfriend, his Wellington shot down over Germany, was in a prisoner-of-war camp – he would sidle almost furtively into the room as though he had no business there, and then, having approached my bed, clipboard in hand, would say, 'Well, young man, how are we today?' Sometimes he would tut-tut as he discovered that my temperature was once more up; sometimes he would smile in congratulation – 'I'm happy to find a real improvement.'

Perhaps we did not really see each other all that often. It may be merely that, in a retrospect clouded by distance, the boredom of those days, during which so little happened other than the regular arrival of medicines and meals, now makes his visits seem so frequent.

On his social visits, as distinct from his medical ones, he would of course not be accompanied by a nurse or be carrying the clipboard. But, oddly, he would still be wearing the white coat with the overlong sleeves. On one occasion I remember that there was a rust-coloured stain on one of its lapels, which I persuaded myself, such was the morbidness of my imagination at that time, could only be blood.

Since there were always books piled up on the rickety table beside me, it was of books that we often spoke, particularly of German ones. I must, he insisted, read Thomas Mann but not, definitely not, *The Magic Mountain*, since in my present condition that would only depress me. *Buddenbrooks* would be a good start.

When he next returned home, he would bring me a translation – wholly inadequate but it was better than nothing – which the translator herself had presented to him. Had I ever read Thomas Mann's brother, Heinrich? I must read him too. And Ernst Jünger – a terrible man but a wonderful writer ... We also spoke of music – in addition to the books, I had brought with me a wireless set and a wind-up gramophone – and of art. It flattered me that this doctor should be prepared to spend so much of his time talking to me.

On one occasion he began to speak about the sanatorium, up in the Harz mountains, of which he had for a brief period been the deputy director until, as he put it, 'the bad times started.' He had been demoted, and then a few months later demoted yet again, this time to the work of laboratory assistant. It was then that he and his wife had opted for a life of exile. During his time at the sanatorium he had had high hopes, he told me, that the sulphonamide drugs – discovered by a scientist friend of his called Domagk, who, a Gentile, had done his honourable best to protect him during 'the bad times' – would prove to be the cure for tuberculosis which so many people had sought in vain for so long. Mysteriously, Egon had experienced what seemed to be some initial successes with their use; but ... He raised his bony shoulders, he sighed.

From time to time he would talk of the other War, the one in which, a man in his early twenties, he had served. The present War seemed to have little interest for him; he seemed to be hardly aware of it – which was odd, since, if the Nazis were to win it, he, his wife and his children would surely be exterminated. But that far-off War, of which I knew so little, was one still vivid to him. Perched on the edge of my bed or on the edge of a chair facing it, he would talk in abrupt sentences, a hand raised, fingers splayed, to his pointed chin or pulling at an ear, of its endless horrors. His face was grey with fatigue, but his manner was animated, even febrile.

It was a Penguin copy of *A Farewell to Arms*, resting on my bedclothes, which once got him started. Hemingway had also been in the Trenta Valley at the time when he himself was there. Strange, they were so close and yet there was no chance that, on separate sides of the conflict as though on separate sides of a chasm, they would ever meet. 'That was when I met my first and only love,' he said. 'In the Trenta Valley.' Then he shook his head and burst into laughter. 'No, no, that isn't true! I also love my wife, I love my wife very, very much. But ... but ... There is no love like first love. As you, young man, will no doubt discover in due course – if you have not discovered it already.'

II

The skies throughout that winter were always a wide, unfathomable blue, illuminated by the brief daylight which bounced off the snow, to impart to them an extraordinary dazzle. The local people said that they had never known so cruel (that was the word they often used) a winter. Fuel and food were scarce; the roads, the snow hacked and scraped off them by weary, frozen gangs of soldiers, glistened like metal, as they might have glistened in a heatwave; it was necessary to use a pickaxe to crack the ice which sealed off even the water in the barns from the cattle.

Yes, it was a cruel winter. The local hospital and the houses requisitioned near it were so full with the wounded and the dying, many of them lying on pallets in the corridors, with the nurses and doctors constantly obliged to pick their way around and even over them, that tents had had to be erected. These tents were heated by huge coke-burning cast-iron stoves, which diffused an acrid smell of sulphur among the other, even more nauseating smells.

As he tended to suppurating wounds, assisted at amputations or attempted to calm some patient convulsed by pain or terror, Egon would experience a loathing not merely of all this suffering and of the war which caused it, not merely of the intense cold, of the premature darkness and of the long nights spent stretched out sleepless on a narrow bed in the attic of a house owned by an elderly farmer and his invalid wife, but of life itself. He would say to himself: It would be better if I were dead! Often, summoned from that attic to the bedside of someone in his last throes, he would feel a sudden, savage envy. But for a punishing sense of duty, he might have picked up one of the hypodermic syringes with which he constantly injected others with morphia and instead injected himself with a lethal dose.

All that changed when Elza appeared as a nurse. Her home was in Ljubljana, where she had trained briefly before volunteering for work in the Trenta Valley hospital. She was painfully thin, with breasts so tiny that they were scarcely visible under her scrupulously starched blouse and with knobbly wrist-bones on arms seemingly devoid of any flesh. Her face was extraordinarily pale, her lips a bluish grey. Was she ill? After a few days he put the question to her. She laughed and shook her head vigorously: of course she wasn't ill! She had always been thin, it meant nothing, nothing at all. Certainly her energy and her high spirits were boundless. That was a period when nurse after nurse went down with a particularly virulent form of influenza, some even dying of it. Elza would replace now one nurse and now another, in addition to performing her own duties. She would work all day and then declare that she was perfectly happy to continue to work all night.

During those nights Egon and she would often pick their way, sometimes accompanied by an orderly but more often just the two of them alone, down the crowded wards. That terrible sulphurous smell from the stoves, glowing through the near-darkness, coiled insidiously through their lungs; and meanwhile in their ears was a constant jumble of sounds: cries, coughs, tears, whimpers, whispers, demented shouts. Yet Egon no longer thought: If only I could end all this. He no longer picked up a syringe and, turning it over and over in his hand as he gazed down at it with fascinated eyes, told himself: 'It would be so easy. Why not?' He was in love with Elza: not so much with her fragile, emaciated body, or with her sharp features, as with that tireless, unbreakable spirit of hers. He did not find it easy to feel pity for his patients, and he never felt love. But as she stooped over this man, smiling down at him, as she supported that one while Egon administered an injection, as she patted a pillow or tugged a blanket straight or put a hand to a forehead, Egon knew that she pitied and loved everyone, however crude or crass or unattractive or ungrateful.

Eventually, they became lovers. At one end of the largest of the tents there was a curtained-off area containing three dilapidated armchairs in which the duty doctor and nurse could rest and even, if lucky, sleep. Here, furtively, terrified that some patient or orderly would intrude, struggling with each other's clothing, his hand over her mouth in case she cried out, their mouths hungry and their eyes brimming with frenzy, they reached their first climax. Many more were to follow. On one occasion, making their way from one tent to another, he drew her, on a rampant impulse, into a shed in which the coke for the stoves was stored. Through the cracks in the wood from which the hut was constructed, he could see the gleam of snow in moonlight. As he hugged her to him, he thought: If I hug her as hard as I wish, I could break her bones.

The director of the hospital, whose name was Nagel, talked constantly of the spring. Why was the spring so long in coming? he demanded. It was already March, by the beginning of March last year the thaw had already started. What had happened? Last year Egon had been not in the Trenta Valley but at medical school in Germany. Nagel spent all his spare time writing long letters to his wife. Few came from her. When one did, the sleepy, sad eyes of this plump, ill-shaven gastroenterologist, later to become world-famous, would briefly acquire a sheen. That evening in the mess, still elated by the letter, he would tell the sort of jokes which disgusted Egon but which would send the other doctors into peals of obsequious laughter.

Nagel, who was observant, teased Egon about 'little Elza'. But he did so only when the two men were alone together. Egon was grateful for that. 'What you see in her beats me,' Nagel declared more than once. 'Making love to her must be like making love to a skeleton.' Nagel's own wife, whose photograph Egon had been shown, was as plump as her husband, with generous breasts, thighs and calves and thick blonde hair encircling her head in tier on tier of elaborate plaits.

One day, as Elza and Egon were running, arms linked, from one tent to the other, the snow crisp under their feet and the bite of the wind ferocious on their cheeks and foreheads, she unconsciously repeated Nagel's words: 'Why is the spring so long in coming?' Then she added: 'I'm sick of this winter.'

But Egon was not sick of it. The snow-capped mountains, glittering with sunlight during the day and luminous with moonshine at night, the ice which veined the paths like iron ore, the cold and the clearness of all sounds and the cleanness of the air as it burned the lungs: all these things seemed to be a part of the unfathomable, inexhaustible love which he felt for Elza.

One afternoon, waking from a long sleep of exhaustion – the previous night had been crammed with dramas and tragedies, so that he had been kept perpetually rushing from bedside to bedside and even from tent to tent – Egon heard a strange, lisping sound outside his attic window. The snow was at last, reluctantly, grudgingly, beginning to thaw. Diamonds of water were scattering from the sun-bright eaves. A tremendous joy surged up in him.

It was that same evening that Elza told him that she had decided not to take the leave due to her. She wanted to see the spring with him here in the Trenta Valley – they could walk up into the mountains; they could see the wild flowers; she did not think that the spring brought so many wild flowers anywhere else in the world.

It was the next day that Nagel told Egon that he had received from headquarters the news that the hospital was to be moved out of the valley and into the plain beyond it. The plan was to requisition a school and a large manor-house next to it, and so to dispense with the tents. 'But I have made a plea. I have asked that we be allowed to stay here until the spring comes. After this winter I want once again to see the valley in all its springtime glory.' So unsentimental about everything else, Nagel was senti-mental about Nature (when he spoke of it, he always seemed to be giving it a capital letter).

Nagel got his way. The departure from the Trenta Valley was delayed by two weeks.

It was Egon's duty to drive each Friday to Ljubljana, there to present to headquarters the list of whatever drugs were required for the hospital. This would be the last such journey before the move. He always wished on these occasions that Elza were able to accompany him. That way, she could visit her family – the father whom she so much hated, the mother whom she so much loved, the siblings who were so much younger than she was – and he himself could meet them. By now, he had decided that he would ask Elza's father for her hand.

Driving back, Egon was buzzing with a quiet, assured exhil-aration. The thaw was accelerating. He could see patches of black on the branches of the trees, and from time to time there was a muffled thud as some snow slipped off them and, in a flashing spume, crashed to the earth. Above the hoarse engine of the car, he could hear the songs of birds. At one point a group of peasants stopped, grinning, and waved to him as the car chugged past them. They had rarely done that during the long, cruel winter. Blinking in the brilliant sunlight, they might have been prisoners suddenly released after months of incarceration in a dark cell.

About three miles from the valley, he felt the car jolt and slither and knew that he had a puncture. Hell! Well, he and the orderly with him would have to change the tyre. The two men got out of the car with extreme reluctance. Neither of them was expert at such a job.

It was as the orderly got to work and Egon, gloved hands on hips, stared down at him, that suddenly they were both startled by a sound. Later, describing it to me, his brows drawn together in a puzzlement that had persisted over more than twenty years, Egon said 'It sounded like something metallic striking a stone. But magnified, horrendously magnified. And it was high, high, up, up in the air.'

That was the first intimation which Egon had of the avalanche which submerged all but one of the tents. That was when Elza, along with many of the patients, had her life crushed out of her.

III

'Are we still in Slovenia?'

'Oh, yes. Yes, of course.'

'Where are we?'

'This is the Trenta Valley.'

That was when, having for so long forgotten him, I remembered Egon. At that moment, the ghostly foot inserted itself into the door of memory where it has remained ever since.

All the time, as we drove on up the valley, it was as though, baffled yet determined, I were retracing some journey taken more than half a lifetime before. Piece by piece, I began to reassemble all that Egon had told me of those months spent working in the military hospital.

'Wasn't there a military hospital here?'

'Here?' Boris had been driving with an intent, even strained expression on his face. No doubt he was fearful of a skid on the slush of the narrow, winding road, between high rocks still shrouded in snow. 'During the last War, you mean?'

'During the War before that.'

In his mid-twenties, Boris pulled a face, then shrugged his shoulders. 'Possibly,' he said. Then he added: 'I remember once hearing that, during that War, the First World War, Hemingway, Ernest Hemingway, was in the Trenta Valley. But what he was doing . . .' Again he shrugged.

'A friend of mine – a doctor, a German doctor – was here then. He used to talk about this valley. He talked about it a lot.'

At the next village we stopped. Boris said that he would ask about the hospital. There might be some old man who, as a child or even an adolescent, had lived here at the time. But when, outside the post office, Boris had accosted such an old man, muffled in a great-coat reaching almost to his ankles and leading a tottering, rheumy-eyed spaniel on a rope, the old man seemed reluctant to stop, let alone talk to us. He had, it seemed, come to live in the valley only some ten years ago. Having told us this, the old man stared disconcertingly at me, his pale blue, watery eyes going up and down me, with what struck me as an amused, slightly disapproving curiosity. Then all at once, to my surprise, he began to speak not merely about the hospital but also about the avalanche. The hospital had been there, there! He pointed up the street, while the dog, eager to resume its walk, set up a high-pitched keening. We would see, he instructed us, a modern church, a supermarket, a school; they were on the site of the hospital. Behind them, on a hill, was the graveyard. That was where the victims had been buried. All this Boris translated for me from the Slovene.

'Do you want to go up there?' Clearly, in this cold which pierced through even the thickest of gloves and topcoats, Boris wished only to get back into the car.

'Well, yes, I'd like to.'

As we tramped through the slush, I could feel icy water seeping through my shoes. Wisely, Boris was wearing boots.

'In the spring it's very beautiful here. You cannot imagine.'

'Yes, that's what my friend used to tell me.'

'Your friend?'

'My German doctor friend.'

Boris was not really interested; and when not really interested, he had a way of asking questions to which, if he had thought about it, he would have known that he already had the answers.

Standing in turn outside the hideous little church, the school and the supermarket, I tried to imagine the hospital building and the huge tents pitched around it. Perhaps where those delivery vans were now parked, there had once been row on row of field ambulances. That gaunt, grey house, with its high, sharply pointed gable, might well have existed even then. And perhaps – the thought suddenly came to me – it was in that house that Egon had lodged, with that elderly farmer and his invalid wife. I almost told Boris that I wanted to call on the occupants; but then I thought: That farmer and his wife must be long dead – and their children, if they had any children, must be dead too.

There was a cobbled lane which wound up the hill to the cemetery.

'Do you want to go up there?' Boris asked dubiously.

'Oh, yes, I think so. But don't come with me. It's far too cold. Why don't you wait for me in that café which we passed – or in the car?'

But dutifully Boris shook his head and set off up the hill ahead of me. Once I slipped and all but fell. The air was like acid in my heaving lungs.

A white-painted wall extended in a horseshoe around the cemetery. The graves, ranged in tiers, one above the other, were all alike, a rectangular granite stone and on it a cross, a name, a date. Boris took out a packet of cigarettes and lit up. He knew that, if he smoked in the car, it made my asthma worse, and so, considerate as he always was, he never did so. He leaned against the wall and drew in the smoke and then, smiling with long-delayed pleasure, blew it out. I left him there.

I began to zigzag up and up, walking along one tier of graves and then mounting to the one above it. All the time I looked for a name among all those names of people, most of them in their twenties and thirties, men and women, who had been crushed or smothered under the avalanche.

Eventually, on the highest tier of all, I came on a grave, no different from all the others, with the name on it 'Elza Mozetič' and the dates 1897–1917. I had no recollection of ever having heard Elza's surname from Egon, or of ever having learned her age. I stared down. Was this Elza Mozetič the Elza whom Egon had loved? Was it? I knelt and brushed away the snow which still lay, dazzling and friable, along the top of the headstone. It was almost as if I thought that something else, a coded message in tiny letters intended only for me, had been carved there too.

Then I experienced an extraordinary moment of terror.

Magnified, horrendously magnified, I heard, high, high, up, up in the air it seemed, the sound of something which might have been metal striking on stone. I cowered, my heart lurched under my breast-bone, everything around me seemed to judder from side to side.

Then I recovered. For a while I stood totally still. Then I walked over to the wall and looked over it.

An old man, in a balaclava helmet and wellington boots, his ragged coat fastened round his waist with a length of twine, had begun to hack at the half-frozen earth of a tiny cottage garden with a hoe.

Suddenly aware of my presence, he halted his work and, hoe clutched in gloved hands, squinted up at me, wary but not unfriendly, from under the wide peak of a soiled forage-cap. Then he lowered his head, extended the hoe again, and went on with his work.

The Web

The portly, bedraggled black mongrel, rheumy eyes half closed, was standing in such a way, her legs with their prominent dewclaws widely splayed for balance, that Liz's first attempt to squeeze past her was a failure. When she attempted the other side, she was barred by the bitch's harness, gripped in the hand of a young man in a dingy cloth cap and dark glasses, who, oblivious of her, was carrying on a conversation with the old woman slumped beside him. 'Oh, she's choosy,' he was saying. 'Amazingly choosy. You wouldn't believe. More like a cat than a dog.' His voice, with its flattened vowels, had a whiny twang to it.

'Excuse me!' Liz said. The young man went on talking. '*Excuse me!* I can't get past.'

'It's no use trying this way, love. Her lead's this side. In my hand.'

'Well, I can't get past on the other side either. I've got to get round her somehow. I can't spend this whole journey standing here by the driver. Can I? And what about other people trying to get on?' Her voice was sharp. 'Please move her!'

The man put out a hand and gave a tug at the harness. Then he transferred the hand to the dog's rump and swivelled her towards him.

Liz edged past, the straps of two bulging bags biting into her palms.

'What a way to speak to a blind person!' the old woman next to the man said in a loud, indignant voice. Clearly she intended Liz to hear.

'Oh, don't let it bother you, love. Happens all the time. One gets used to it.'

Liz wanted to turn and protest: 'He's not blind. I've seen him in the library. Without that dog. In the Reference Room.' But she decided not to do so. She sat down, placing the bags on the seat beside her. She gazed out of the window.

As, minutes later, the bus lurched round the corner from Church Street into Kensington High Street, the man staggered to his feet. He was wearing a grubby anorak with yellow fluorescent bands sewn to it and unpolished brogues worn down at the heels. 'Come on, old girl!' he said to the dog, which, having long since lain down, now stirred from sleep, grunted and eventually tottered to her feet. 'It was nice talking to you,' he told the elderly woman.

'Take care,' she said, and then: 'Bye!' As, followed by the dog, the man slowly edged himself off the bus, she then remarked to no one in particular: 'Poor chap!'

Liz watched him through the window. He and the dog were both peering around them. Then the dog went over to a lamppost and squatted beside it. Urine gushed out of her, flooding over the pavement and splashing into the gutter, where it steamed in the winter air. The man smiled to himself, raising a hand to adjust first the dingy cap and then the dark glasses. A moment later, he looked over at the bus, stuck at the traffic-lights. His gaze locked with Liz's.

She would show him what she thought of him. She put out a tongue.

The man threw back his head and laughed. He had large, white teeth and his neck was thick and strong.

Then, as the bus jerked forward, he raised two insulting fingers.

A few days later, Liz saw the man again. He was huddled in the doorway of a block of flats in Kensington High Street, the dingy cap pulled down low over his forehead and the collar of his soiled, tattered tweed overcoat turned up, his chin sunk into it, so that it was impossible to see more of his face than the eyes, now without the dark glasses, and the nose. His greasy, dishevelled hair cascaded to his shoulders. The dog, who now seemed even more portly than on the previous occasion, was asleep beside him, oblivious of the people hurrying past, often so close that a misjudged step might easily have struck her. The man's hands, clasped around his knees, were grey and waxen with dirt. The laces of one of the brogues were untied and the other brogue had a crack across the instep. Beside him, propped against a chipped enamel mug, was a piece of cardboard, on which he had written in large, straggling letters: 'STARVING. PLEASE HELP.'

The middle-aged woman ahead of Liz put down her Marks &
Spencer shopping-bag, balancing it between her sturdy legs, and
fumbled in her purse. She then dropped a fifty pence piece into
the enamel mug. She put out a hand and patted the dog's head.
The dog made no response. 'Isn't she sweet?' she said. 'It *is* a
she, isn't it?'

The man nodded. 'She'll be glad of something to eat. And so
will I,' he added.

The woman picked up her bag and hurried on. Shoulders
thrown back, her pace was now much brisker. Her negligible act
of charity had clearly exhilarated her.

Liz approached. She stopped and stared down at the man. He
stared up at her. Then she said: 'If you're really starving, why
don't you eat your dog?'

'Cunt!'

As she walked away, she could hear his derisive laughter.

Having finished her shopping, Liz went into British Home
Stores for something to eat before returning home. She picked
up a wedge of quiche, some salad and a cup of coffee, and found
a table in a corner to herself. She folded her *Guardian* at the
crossword and, between mouthfuls, studied it.

Suddenly she was aware that the man was standing over her,
one hand gripping a tray while the other rested on the back of
the chair opposite to her. She scowled up at him.

'May I?'

'Certainly not!'

But he merely set down the tray, pulled out the chair and
edged himself on to it.

'I said No!'

'But you didn't mean it.'

'I most certainly did. There are plenty of empty tables.'

'What's wrong with a little company?'

'I certainly don't want your company.'

'What a lucky coincidence I found you here! I'd have thought
you'd be eating at somewhere much more posh.'

He picked up his knife and fork from the tray. His hands no
longer had that waxen, grey look. They were scrupulously clean.
The dingy cap and the soiled, tattered overcoat had been
abandoned. He was now wearing grey flannel trousers, a white
open-necked shirt, and a sports jacket made of a loosely woven
dark green tweed.

'Where's your dog?'

'In the van. Which is on a double yellow line. I just hope it
doesn't attract the attention of a warden.' This certainly was not
the accent, its vowels whiningly flattened, with which he had
spoken to the old woman on the bus. He might have been one of
Liz's male cousins – except that, with his dark eyes under thick
eyebrows which almost met each other, his aquiline nose and his
strong, dimpled chin, he was more handsome than any of them.

'You have a van?' She was incredulous.

He nodded. 'That's where I change. Out of all that filthy gear.
Into these.' He indicated the clean clothes with a downward
sweep of both hands.

She stared at him with a mixture of amazement and
indignation.

'You're shocked.'

'Yes, of course I'm shocked.'

'It's just another way of ripping people off. Why not? All
business is a process, in one way or another, of ripping others
off. Isn't it?' He pointed at the Harrods shopping bag on the
chair between them. 'If that name wasn't on that bag, you
wouldn't have paid as much money as you have for the things
in it. Would you? Just as, if I didn't look as filthy as possible or
as helpless as possible, no one would bother to give me any
money. It's all a question of appearances.'

'You deceive people – pretending to be destitute, pretending
to be blind. But what of the people who are really destitute,
really blind?'

'You mean I'm in unfair competition with them?' His fork
raised to his mouth and head tilted on one side, he gazed at her
quizzically. He chewed on the piece of chicken. Then he laughed.
'Oh, don't be such a prig!

Later she had difficulty in believing in the reality of what had
happened after they had left the store. Had she suddenly lost her
mind? Or had he, in the course of their increasingly friendly
conversation, exerted some kind of hypnotic power over her? Or
had it all been an extraordinary dream? She had had lovers
certainly, she had even had an occasional one-night stand. But in
retrospect the casual promiscuity of her behaviour on this
occasion frightened and shocked her.

'Let me give you a lift up to Notting Hill Gate,' he had
offered, having already learned that she lived there. When she
had said No, thank you, she needed the walk, he had pushed
that aside: 'Oh, come on!' Uttering no further refusal, all resist-

ance mysteriously disintegrating, she had then followed him down one side street and up another, with an extraordinary mingling of apprehension and excitement.

Suddenly he had turned to her. 'You know what I want, don't you?'

She shook her head. But weirdly, frighteningly she knew, oh yes, she knew already.

'As soon as I saw you on that bus – when I had to pretend I couldn't see you . . . I fell for you at once. You're a class act, you know. So cool, elegant, snooty. And very beautiful,' he added. He put an arm around her shoulder. 'You know what I want, don't you?' he repeated.

Yes, yes, I know! And I want it too! But she did not say that. She said nothing.

'Oh, shit!'

'A ticket?'

He jerked the piece of paper out from under the windscreen wiper, crumpled it up, and chucked it into the gutter. He gave the loud, explosive laugh with which, in the days ahead, she was to become so familiar. 'With any luck that'll be the end of it. They can't chase up everyone. They haven't the staff.'

He had opened first one of the deeply scratched and dented doors of the van and then the other. There was a whimper like a startled, muffled cry. From the darkness within, as from some cave, two points of light gleamed. Then, muzzle lowered, the bitch crept forward.

'No! Go back, back! *Back!*'

The bitch retreated.

When, at a gesture from this stranger – was she crazy, utterly crazy? – Liz had clambered into that cave, she found it unpleasantly damp and hot and full of the smell, not only of the dog, but of what, strangely, appeared to be resin. Her companion clambered in after her and then jerked shut first one of the doors and then the other. A chink of light remained.

'Someone might come. Someone might see us.'

'So what? Anyway, it's highly unlikely.' He pushed away the dog with an exclamation of annoyance, as she began to sniff at his face. The he put out both arms and heaved Liz towards him.

His name was Gavin. His father, who had been a captain in the Navy, was dead and his mother, remarried to an American much older than herself, was living in Florida. He had been educated at a minor public school and at Oxford, after which he had taken up a job with a merchant bank. Ten months before he had been made redundant.

On two more subsequent occasions they made love in the van. Then he persuaded her to travel out with him to his two-room flat in Bedford Park. Norman Shaw had been the architect of the house, he told her with pride. He also told her that none of the other occupants had any idea of how he now earned his living. 'Aren't you afraid that one day one of them might see you?' Liz asked. His reply was once more to give that loud, explosive laugh. 'Too bad if they do! I like to live dangerously. Anyway what could they do about it?'

Holding her in his arms on the narrow, low divan, with the bitch snoring beside them, he told her: 'The odd thing is that, when I'm out on the job, I really do seem to become that blind man, that derelict who's starving . . . Perhaps I'm really an actor manqué. I know all about that blind man. He was an orphan, brought up in a special school. His girlfriend jilted him and he can never settle to a proper job. That derelict is a schizophrenic who was released from a mental hospital now closed. Often he forgets to take his pills – or decides not to take them. Then he suffers horrendous – or, sometimes, wonderful – hallucinations. You see? I know everything about the two of them. That's why I can convince people. That's why they give me money.'

'How much money?'

'How much? Oh, on a good day – well – say, fifty, sixty pounds. But there are sometimes even better days than that . . . And, of course, worse ones. There are certain days – don't ask me why – when everyone is in a giving mood. And then there are other days when everyone is feeling as mean as hell. As soon as I settle at my pitch, I know just how it is to be. I suppose actors feel the same when they first walk on to a stage. Within seconds they know if the house will be a good one or a bad one.'

One day, as she sipped from a glass of wine in his tiny kitchen, Liz mused: 'I wonder if I could do it?'

'Do what?'

'What you do.'

'Why not?'

'Would I have the nerve?'

'Why not?'

The next Saturday afternoon she tried it, close by Earls Court

Station. She had dishevelled her hair under a black crocheted beret and she had made her face, devoid of any make-up, look grubby and greasy. Her tights were laddered and there was a hole in the voluminous, dusty black skirt arranged about her. She earned in that one afternoon as much as he had ever earned in a whole day. 'A pity you didn't have a baby with you,' he commented. 'Then you would have made even more.'

Squatting on the pavement, from time to time extending a hand to some compassionate-looking passer-by, she had felt humiliated. But she had also felt a dizzy exhilaration. Suppose someone she knew saw her there? She now understood what Gavin meant by the excitement of danger. This excitement on the pavement, with the traffic thundering past, was oddly similar to the excitement which she had experienced in the dark, malodorous cave at the back of the van.

Gavin had a number of what he called 'dodges'. Seated on a bench outside the Commonwealth Institute, Liz had watched him 'work' one of these.

He leaned on a stick with a rubber ferrule. He limped, from time to time grimacing with pain, along the pavement. His face – how did he achieve that? – looked grey and clammy.

He approached a distinguished-looking elderly man in a wide-brimmed black hat and a black coat with an astrakhan collar. The elderly man also carried a stick; but, slender with a silver knob, it was clearly decorative, not functional.

Liz knew what Gavin would be saying to him, since already he had told her. 'Excuse me, sir . . . I'm terribly sorry to trouble you, but I wonder if you could help me. I'm in something of a fix. I have an appointment at the Marsden Hospital for a scan and, because I've never been there before and because I'm not from London, I've rather lost my way. If I'm late, I'm afraid I may lose my appointment. If I didn't have this problem with my spine, it wouldn't be all that far for me to walk, I suppose, but as it is . . . I'll have to take a taxi, and the trouble is – well, what with the train fare from Birmingham and so on, I am, well, skint . . .'

The elderly man looked irritated. He sighed and pulled a face. But eventually, with extreme reluctance, he tugged his wallet out of the breast pocket of his suit and removed a five pound note. 'I'm an old age pensioner,' he said in a peevish voice. 'I can no longer afford this kind of thing. But there you are!'

As Gavin limped past the bench, he gave Liz a wink. Then a

moment later he was approaching a young girl strenuously pushing a pram towards the entrance to Holland Park. She listened to him, head tilted to one side and full, moist lips parted. Once or twice in the course of his narration, she said 'Sorry?', not understanding. She was foreign, probably an au pair.

Eventually she produced a pound. 'I have no more,' she said.

Gavin bowed and smiled. 'That's terrific! Bless you, my dear!'

It was Gavin who thought up the idea for Liz. He had been reading the biography of a famous novelist, Julia Granger, who had been the lover of an obscure poet, Gloria Destinne-Franks. Both women were now dead. He had reached out from the bed on which he and Liz were lying and had picked up the telephone book on the floor beside it. 'I wonder,' he said, impatiently flicking over the pages. 'I wonder if there's a Destinne-Franks . . . Yes!' He stabbed with a finger. 'It must be someone from the same family. No two families could share such a silly name. Living in Fulham. We're in luck.'

'What do you mean? I don't get it.'

Gavin explained.

The small, mean house was one of a row of small, mean houses. Gavin had parked the van in Lilley Road. He told Liz that he would wait there for her.

The gate hung askew on a rusty hinge and the small front garden contained a number of straggling hydrangea bushes, the few blooms of the previous year shrivelled and brown on them. Having failed to hear the bell ring, Liz raised the knocker, a rusty metal fish, and let it fall.

A tiny, elderly woman, with unnaturally red hair tumbling in curls around her triangular face and a smear of lipstick across a cheek, put her head round the door. 'Oh!' She sounded disappointed, as though she had been expecting someone else.

'You don't know me,' Liz said. 'Please forgive me. I'm a – a niece of Julia Granger, well, a sort of niece, really a cousin once removed.'

Liz had feared that the woman would not know whom she meant. But, pulling the door wide open, she cried out, her face irradiated with pleasure: 'A niece of Julia Granger! Oh, what a lovely surprise! Do come in. I thought it was my Meals-on-Wheels. One never knows when they'll come.'

'I don't want to waste your time,' Liz said, edging into a

[31]

narrow, fusty hall, a cat-basket, a Siamese asleep in it, all but blocking any further progress. 'It's just that ... I'm in a terrible fix.' Like Gavin when he became the blind man or the derelict, she now felt that she had really become the dead novelist's relation.

'Don't worry about Ming. Just step over him. That's right.'

The old woman preceded Liz down the hall to a tiny conservatory, choked with plants most of which seemed to be dead, at the far end of it. 'Do sit,' she said, carefully lowering herself into one of the two folding metal chairs placed at either end of a wooden table covered with packets of insecticide, bottles of fertilizer, secateurs, bast, string.

Liz sat down on the chair opposite the old woman's. She leaned forward. 'I feel terrible about bothering you – throwing myself on your mercy. But I'm in such a fix, I don't know what else to do.'

Twisting her hands in her lap, Liz told the story of how she had come to London from the Wirral to have an interview for a job as a window dresser at Dickins and Jones. After the interview she had gone into the café of the store for a cup of coffee and a Danish before catching her train back home. And it was then that the terrible thing had happened. Someone had taken her bag, containing everything she possessed. No, she had no idea who could have done it, no one had seen anything. Well, at that hour, just after one, that cafe was *packed*. The staff had been awfully kind about it all, they had told her not to worry about paying, and one of the girls – wasn't it sweet of her? – had even given her a pound. But the problem was that her return ticket to Liverpool had been in her bag. How on earth could she buy another one? Everything she possessed had been in that bag. 'I know no one in London, absolutely no one. But then I remembered that Aunt Julia – I always called her Aunt – had told me that this relative of her great, great friend lived somewhere in Fulham. And so I looked you up in the telephone book. You were my one hope. Thank goodness I found you in.'

The old woman had been clucking, now with sympathy and now with indignation, as Liz had gone through her story. Now she put out a claw and gripped the hand which Liz had rested on the table before her. 'Oh, you poor dear! So what can I do to help?'

'Well, if you ... if you could possibly lend me the money for the ticket ... of course, as soon as I get home, my father will send you a cheque for it.'

It was all so easy – 'How gullible people are!' Gavin was to exclaim derisively when Liz rejoined him in the van. 'Fancy swallowing such a story!' The old woman fetched her bag from upstairs and began to empty it on to the table. 'I just hope that I have as much as you need. If not, we can go down to the cashpoint together.' She looked up and smiled. 'I think my bank balance will just about stand it. I got an unexpected little dividend the other day. I was lucky to get a hundred Powergen shares when they had that issue.' She began to count out first notes and then coins. 'I'm sorry it's all going to be in dribs and drabs.' Then she looked up again. 'I know that Gloria – my sister – would have wanted me to do everything possible to help a relative of Julia's.'

When Liz had eventually pocketed the notes and innumerable coins, she stood at the window of the conservatory, gazing out at the surprisingly large, dishevelled garden, while the old woman, tip of tongue caught between upper and lower lips, wrote out her name and address in large letters on a sheet of writing paper. An ancient hand-mower stood by a flower-bed, so rusty that Liz could not imagine that it had been used for years and years. She could read the name engraved on its cast iron: TURFMASTER. When Liz had been a child, the gardener, a wiry, gypsy-like little man, cut the lawns with a Turfmaster, but one much bigger than this one.

'There!' the old woman said, handing Liz the address. 'But there's no hurry.'

'I'm so grateful to you. I really am. I don't know what I'd have done without you.'

The old woman offered Liz some tea. When that was refused, she asked if Liz would like to see some photographs of Julia Granger and Gloria Destinne-Franks. Liz shook her head. 'I'd love to see them. But I must catch a train back home as soon as possible. Otherwise my parents will be frantic.'

The old woman then kept Liz talking for minutes on end by the front door – the locks and bolts on it had cost a fortune, she said, but these days, with so many burglaries taking place, one couldn't be too careful, could one? People had become so dishonest. It had not been like that when she was young. Then all the family could go out leaving the front door unlocked and even the windows wide open.

Seated in the van beside Gavin, Liz was silent.

'What's up?' Gavin asked.

Liz shrugged. She thought of the old woman, head lowered, counting out those fifty, twenty, ten and five pence pieces on the table with fingers knobbly and twisted with arthritis. She thought of the shabby bag from which she had emptied them. She thought of those Powergen shares. Finally she thought of that Turfmaster rusting away in a corner of the garden, the grass high and silvery around it.

'What's up?' Gavin repeated.

'Nothing.'

But somehow something which had been so swiftly knitted had now, with no less devastating precipitancy, begun to unravel.

Sukie

After the lecture, the dean of the medical school said: 'Maybe you are hungry. Maybe I should take you somewhere out to dinner.'

The apparent half-heartedness of the invitation must, Middleton decided, be due to the fact that, though the Korean had spent a year at Guy's, he still had a shaky grasp of English.

'It's very kind of you. But I think I'll take myself off to an early bed. I still haven't got over my jet lag.'

The dean at once relaxed, he even smiled. His relief was unflatteringly obvious. 'Yes. Yes, I understand, Dr Middleton.' No doubt, Middleton thought, his one wish was to be rid of this dreary old buffer foisted on to him by the British Council. 'Then I will call the car for you.'

'Oh, no need for that! I can easily walk.'

'No, no, Dr Middleton!' The dean sounded shocked. 'You must not walk.'

'The hotel's so near.'

'It is late. You are tired. I will call the car. The driver is waiting for you. University driver,' he added. 'It is his job. He is paid to drive guests.'

As Middleton was about to dive into the back of the cumbersome, black saloon, the door of which the driver was holding open, the dean gave a deep bow. 'We are very grateful,' he said. 'That was quite an interesting lecture. Our students learned much.' *Quite* an interesting lecture? Then Middleton reminded himself that foreigners tended to be confused about when 'quite' qualified praise and when it intensified it.

Middleton's first thought was to go straight to bed. But then an embarrassing rumble of his stomach just as he was leaning forward to take his key from the desk clerk, reminded him that he ought to eat. Perhaps he would try the Café Good Luck, which he could see at the far end of a foyer crowded with the suitcases of a party of French tourists. These tourists had kept him from approaching the desk for several minutes, as they had elbowed each other, filled in their reservation cards and then, in many cases, argued about the rooms allotted to them.

The head waiter's English was far superior to the dean's. He was also far more welcoming. Having bowed repeatedly to Middleton, the sleek back of his head reflecting the light above him, he had asked: 'Alone, sir?'

'Yes, alone. I'm afraid so. All, all alone.'

'No problem.' He smiled and extended a hand in invitation. 'Please, sir.' As he led Middleton through a long, cavernous room, he would from time to time swivel his head, flash a smile and, with a strange bobbing motion of his body, almost a bow, repeat: 'Please, sir. This way, sir. Please.'

The room was full of unoccupied tables, laid with glistening white cloths, glittering cutlery, and vases with artificial flowers sticking out of them like feather dusters. Why could he not sit at one of these tables? Middleton wondered.

Now they were passing a horseshoe-shaped counter, at which half a dozen or so people were seated. Then they moved into an area behind it, invisible to anyone at a table in the main room.

Here, in contrast to the main room, hardly a table was empty. There were a surprisingly large number of women either alone or in pairs, each with a cup of coffee or a glass of Coca Cola or orange juice in front of her, and there were some couples, male and female. The women were, almost without exception, young, elegant, attractive. Middleton guessed that the men, mostly middle-aged or elderly and wearing sombre dark blue or dark grey suits with ties no less sombre, must be drawn from the Japanese businessmen who made up a major part of the hotel's clientele.

'This OK for you, sir?' the head waiter asked, yet again bowing and yet again flashing his brilliant, vacant smile.

'Fine, thank you.'

On Middleton's right were two attractive young women; on his left a far less attractive older one, in thick glasses with huge, diamanté-encrusted frames, which glittered in the light from the chandelier above her as she turned her head to look him over. A moment later, the two attractive young women also turned their heads. One of them smiled at him. Then she leaned across the table to her companion and whispered something. Both of them giggled, then again looked at him, then again giggled. What did they find comic about him? he wondered.

As he waited, in growing weariness and vexation, for the waitress to bring him the *spaghetti al sugo* and green salad of his order, Middleton surveyed the crowded scene. But he took care not to glance at the two women on his right, or at the solitary woman on his left.

All at once, an elderly, goblin-like Japanese, with thick, silvery hair brushed back over pointed ears, rose from his table and walked awkwardly, as though afflicted with arthritis of the hips, towards a table at which, stirring her coffee, a young woman slumped alone. Her triangular face had on it an expression of sullen weariness. But, as soon as it was clear that the Japanese was approaching her, it was as though a bright light had been shone on it. The Japanese pointed to the vacant chair opposite to the girl and said something, inaudible to Middleton. *'Dozo, dozo!'* the girl replied, in what Middleton recognized as Japanese, not Korean, nodding vigorously and smiling. The Japanese lowered himself gingerly into the chair, as though any quick or abrupt movement would cause him pain; took up the menu; then put it down and leaned towards her, elbows on the table. He extended both his small hands. With a laugh she took them in her even smaller ones.

A short while later a couple, man and woman, arose from their table and decorously, she following behind him, wove their way between the tables to a door – not the one by which Middleton had entered – marked EXIT, below Korean characters which presumably said the same thing. Middleton turned to watch them as they passed through to the lift.

Soon after this couple had vanished from sight, two young men jumped up from their table and then, as though deliberately restraining their eagerness, sauntered, hands in pockets, to another table, in a distant corner, where a couple of young women in large straw hats were seated before long, empty glasses.

Suddenly it became clear to Middleton why the head waiter had brought him, past all those empty tables, to this crowded area out of sight behind the horseshoe-shaped bar. But he felt no gratitude to him. The years when, on a trip abroad, away from his wife, he eagerly sought out some adventure, were now far behind him.

[37]

He picked up his glass and drained the last of the wine in it. Then. as he tasted the sour liquid on his tongue – he would have done better to order sake or beer – he heard a high, metallic voice: 'Excuse me, sir. Excuse me!'

It was the woman in the thick glasses at the table to the left.

He turned his head, the glass still in his hand. 'Yes?' His tone and expression were both deliberately unfriendly.

She smiled, revealing good teeth. 'May I . . .?' With a hand raised palm upwards, she indicated the copy of the *Financial Times*, bought at huge expense from a stand in the hotel, which he had placed on the chair next to his own.

Reluctantly he nodded. Then he said grumpily: 'I can't imagine that it'll be of much interest to you.' It was not even of much interest to him. He had bought it only because it was the sole English newspaper on offer.

She half rose from her chair as he passed the paper over to her. 'Thank you, sir.' She gave a little bob, not dissimilar to the one given by the head waiter.

For a time she put on a show, lips pursed, of reading the front page. Then she looked up at him and laughed. 'You are right! Not very interesting. Or maybe it is interesting but my English is too poor.' She lowered the paper on to the table beside her. 'You are American?'

'No, I'm not American.' He hesitated. 'I'm English.'

'Ah, English!' She squealed with delight. 'English gentleman!'

Middleton went on with his eating.

'I love Englishmen. At university I had one English teacher. Professor Rhodes. Real English gentleman.'

'I'm not sure that I'm a real English gentleman.'

'You like Korea?'

'I don't know. I haven't been here long enough.'

'You have only just arrived?'

'Yesterday evening.'

Suddenly she was over at his table. 'May I please . . .?' But even as she said the words, she was lowering herself into the chair opposite him. 'It is easier to talk if I . . .'

Unsummoned, the waitress was coming over. She addressed the woman, who consulted the menu and then, tilting her head upwards, ordered one of the ice-creams so resplendently illustrated on its cover. As soon as this had arrived, she dug her spoon into it, a ferociously determined expression on her face, and then, sucking noisily on it, looked up with a smile. Well, she had an attractive smile, there was no doubt of that.

Between further spoonfuls gouged out of the towering edifice of multicoloured ice-cream cemented with frozen chocolate, she continued with her questions: about where he lived; about his wife and children and grandchildren; about what he was doing in Korea. When she learned that he was a doctor, she let out another squeal of delight. 'You are not businessman! That is good, *good*!'

'Oh, I'm not sure about that.'

So it went on. Middleton was offhand, unwelcoming, eventually even brusque. But nothing would deflect her, as she now put some intrusive question to him and now vouchsafed something about her own life. Eventually he wanted to shout at her: 'Oh, for God's sake shut up, *shut up*! I don't want to talk, not to you, not to anyone. I'm old. I'm jet-lagged. I'm tired after having given far too long a lecture. I want to finish this soggy spaghetti and this vinegary salad and whatever is left in the carafe of this disgustingly acid wine, and then I want to trudge up to bed and swallow a sleeping-pill and sleep and sleep and sleep. Alone.'

But he had never found it easy to be discourteous. For the past forty or so years his wife had been telling him that people imposed on him and used him, that he was far too gullible and accommodating, that for God's sake he must learn to be tough.

Eventually he called for the bill. Waiting for it, he stared in moody silence, his head turned away from her, at the horseshoe-shaped bar. Then all at once he felt her hand on the sleeve of his alpaca jacket. She tweaked it gently. 'Are you angry that I speak to you?'

'No, I'm not *angry*.' He all but added: 'Merely bored.'

'I must explain.' She placed her elbows on the table and then leaned across it. 'May I tell you story?' She did not wait for an answer. 'I am country girl. Father was farmer.'

Although her English was so poor, she told her story well. His bill now clutched in a hand, Middleton was first impatient, exasperated. Then, as though he were a child coaxed into swallowing some strange medicine against his will, he began to listen, became interested, eventually was moved.

She had been born when her numerous brothers and sisters – there were eight of them in all – were nearing adulthood and had most of them left the family farm in a remote cranny of the island of Cheju. Her parents had doted on her; but they had also been extremely strict, as they had never been with any other of their offspring. They had lavished money which they could ill afford on her education at private school. They had been determined that she should eventually go to university.

The farm sloped down to a river; and it was there that, one day, as she was watering the cows, she had seen a figure seated at an easel. He was wearing crimson trousers, high black boots, a black shirt and a black beret, tipped jauntily over an eyebrow. He had called out to the fourteen-year-old girl and reluctantly she had gone over to him, a bucket full of water in each hand. Slim, his narrow back erect as he sat on a canvas stool at his easel, he had, when seen from a distance, struck her as young; but now she saw that he was an old man, even older than her father, almost as old as her grandfather. He had held out a thermos flask. He was thirsty, this heat made one thirsty, he wanted to brew some ginseng tea. Could she possibly bring him some hot water?

Fortunately her mother and father were out. She filled the thermos with hot water and then, on an impulse, took one of the rice cakes which her mother had baked the day before and carried that too down to the old man by the river. He offered her some ginseng tea but she refused. She did, however, remain with him, squatting on the bank, while he drank his. In answer to her at first shy and then increasingly bold questioning, he told her that he was not a professional painter, only an amateur, even though he sometimes managed to sell his paintings. For many years an accountant in Seoul, he was retired now, living alone, a widower, in a one-room flat in Cheju City. His only son was in America, working in a Korean restaurant. The son was so busy that he seldom wrote and then only briefly.

She was touched and attracted by his loneliness. What had brought him to the river? she asked him. He shrugged. Chance, he said. He pointed to the ancient motor-bike which he had propped against a tree. He explained how, without any plan, he mounted the motor-bike and kicked it into life. Then he let it – he laughed, displaying uneven, brown teeth and purple gums – take him where it wished. Today it had taken him here. Again he laughed. For once the motor-bike had shown good sense, he said. It had brought him to a kind and pretty girl.

From then on she would each day listen, wherever she was on the farm, for the roar and rattle of the motor-bike. As soon as she heard it, she would find some excuse to go down to the river. The man was a wonderful talker, she said; he could have been a writer, he had many, many stories, some funny, some sad.

'Then we are lovers,' she said. 'Maybe you think that, because I am very young girl and he is old man, he . . . he . . .' She sought for a word.

'Seduced me?' he supplied.

'Seduced me,' she repeated dubiously. 'But he is not bad man. He loves, I love.' She sighed. 'For me, first lover, first lover of my life. But he – he has many lovers before me.' Suddenly her round, pudgy face looked attractive, as she tilted her head sideways and away from Middleton, to stare across the room.

All at once he was reluctantly drawn to her, no longer feeling any exasperation or even weariness.

In a copse by the river they would make love – 'wonderful, wonderful love,' she sighed. 'I am happy, happy, happy. I do not care if mother and father find out. I care about nothing, nothing.'

One day she waited for the roar and rattle of the motor-bike, waited all through a long summer's day, waited in vain. He never came. Nor did he come the next day. She thought, in despair, that perhaps he had tired of her. Then, after many anguished days of waiting, she saw, tucked away in the bottom corner of her father's newspaper, which she was using to light the kitchen fire, a brief paragraph about the old man's death. In Cheju City a motor-bike had suddenly careered off the street into some pedestrians, killing a woman and seriously injuring a child. The driver, an old man, had apparently suffered a heart attack. He too had been killed. The paper gave his name.

Her eyes had by now filled with tears. 'I could not stop thinking of him, day after day. Dead. I still think of him. I cannot love young man. I am not interested in young man. I want only man like him. Old man.' She placed her cheek, head turned sideways, on the arms which were resting on the table. She drew a deep sigh. 'Strange,' she said. 'Sad. Why do I love only old man? What am I to do?'

That was how Middleton eventually agreed to meet her the next day. He would be free in the afternoon, he told her; and she then said that she would show him over one of the palaces – 'Very historical, very beautiful.'

Before they said goodnight, he asked her for her name.

'Sukie,' she said. 'That is my name in English. In Korean it is Sook-hee.' She spelled it out for him very slowly, frowning as she did so, as though in an effort to remember the sequence of letters. 'S-O-O-K-H-E-E.'

After his lecture the next afternoon, the dean said to Middleton: 'Maybe we have some ginseng tea or a drink together? I am not busy – ' he looked dubiously at his watch – 'for forty, forty-five minutes.'

'Oh, that's very kind of you. But a friend has promised to take me sightseeing.' As he said the word 'friend', Middleton felt a sudden, unexpected explosion of joy within him.

'A friend? I thought you have no friends in Seoul.'

'Well, not really a friend. An introduction. Some friends in England gave me an introduction.'

'Korean introduction?'

Middleton hesitated. 'No. An, er, American businessman.'

Sukie was waiting for him in the lounge of the hotel. She was wearing a shiny purple dress, tight across the stomach and breasts and so short that it revealed her knobbly knees, dizzily high-heeled shoes, and a yellow straw hat, the brim of which flopped over her forehead as she jumped up from a bench to greet him with a shrill: 'Dr Middleton!' She looked unappealing, vaguely absurd. But yet again he felt that sudden, unexpected explosion of joy within him.

Joy soon turned to irritation. 'I will carry briefcase,' she said, putting out an arm.

'Why should you?'

'It is heavy for you.'

Of course it isn't. Anyway, I can leave it at the desk. I don't need it. It has nothing in it but my lecture notes '

When, in the garden of the palace, they came to a steep flight of steps, she solicitously took his arm in order to support him. He pulled away. But as her body touched his, he breathed in deeply the scent, muskily heavy, with which she must have drenched herself.

Constantly she asked him: 'Do I walk too fast?' Constantly she urged him: 'Let us sit here for a moment.'

Did she imagine that he was so old that he needed repeated assistance, repeated rests? For God's sake, did he look like an invalid? But as well as being exasperated by her concern for him, he was also moved – as he had been moved, in the Café Good Luck, by her grief for her dead lover.

[42]

That evening she took him to a small Korean restaurant, owned by cousins of hers. Still she fussed over him. Was he able to sit on the floor? Maybe it was too uncomfortable for him? Maybe he would like another cushion? Maybe he would like a back-rest? Would *kimchi* – the revolting pickled cabbage which Koreans seemed to devour at every meal – upset his digestion? Did he need a taxi to take him back to the hotel or could he manage the five-minute walk? Throughout that walk, she held on to his arm with both her hands, from time to time placing her cheek against his sleeve in what appeared to be both love and submission.

They were together again the next afternoon and evening, after he had first lectured at another university and then endured a tedious luncheon party given for him by its president.

This time it was in the Japanese restaurant of the hotel that they ate dinner. Sukie laughed at his clumsiness with chopsticks. 'No, no! I will show you, I will show you!' She took his chopsticks from him, picked up a piece of raw fish and then held it out to him. As she inserted it in his mouth and he then forced himself to swallow, he felt acutely embarrassed. He was sure that all the people around them, some of them Westerners, were watching them. 'Now you try! Try again!' She spoke to him like a schoolmistress to a pupil. Reluctantly he tried. The piece of fish fell off the chopsticks on to his shirt. She shrieked with laughter. 'Oh, Sam, Sam!' By now he had persuaded her to call him, not Dr Middleton, but by his Christian name.

When they left the restaurant, Sukie again took his arm; and again she pressed her face against the sleeve of his alpaca jacket. Then looking up at him, her eyes huge behind their glasses, she asked with simple candour: 'I come to bedroom now?'

Middleton hesitated. He shook his head. 'Better not, Sukie.'

She looked like a small child from whom an expected present has been suddenly and unaccountably withheld.

'Better not? Why better not?'

He did not answer.

Later, lying sleepless in his air-conditioned bedroom, he thought: You fool! You bloody fool!

The following day, they had luncheon together in the Café Good Luck. When, at one moment, laughing at something which he had told her about his favourite granddaughter, she leaned across the table to put her hand over his and then gently to squeeze it, he suddenly found that he was getting an erection. Now he wanted only to finish the meal and to take her upstairs.

'Will you come up to my bedroom now?' he leaned over to whisper to her, as she passed out ahead of him through the glass door which he was holding open for her.

Her smile was radiant: 'Of course! Yes! Yes!'

Clearly she knew the hotel well. It was better, she said, for them first to walk down to the basement, where the lavatories and telephones were situated. If they took the lift there, then no one at reception would see them. 'For me it does not matter,' she said. 'I do not care. But you are famous man, famous doctor. Maybe for you it is better not to be seen.'

In the lift she suddenly lowered a hand to his crotch, disconcerting him by her boldness. 'Why you refuse yesterday evening?' she asked in a teasing, coaxing voice.

'Because I was a fool.'

When she had undressed, he was amazed by the beauty of her breasts: large, rounded, firm. He had heard that silicone implants were far more common in the countries of the Far East, where breasts were naturally small, than in Europe. Could she have had such implants? He was no less amazed by the ferocious skill with which she made love to him. He rarely now made love to his wife and, when he did so, the love-making all too often ended not in ejaculation but in a weary: 'Let's just have a cuddle.'

Later, washing himself while, in the bedroom next door, she sang what he guessed to be a Korean folk-song in a high, clear voice, he remembered an incident from the previous year, when he had attended a medical conference in Bangkok. One of his colleagues, a young North Country gastroenterologist, had told the story, in the crowded bar of their hotel, of how he had picked up a Thai girl – 'She couldn't have been more than eleven or twelve. But God – her technique was terrific! It was the fuck of a lifetime.'

At the time Middleton had been disgusted both by the story itself and by the crudity of the final phrase.

But now he thought: The fuck of a lifetime.

Yes, that was what it had been.

After they had dressed, Middleton said that he must buy his wife a present.

'You buy present because you feel bad?' she asked.

He was angry. 'Certainly not! I always take a present back for my wife after a trip abroad.

'I come shopping with you?'

'Yes, of course! You can help me choose – and bargain for me. I can never bargain.'

Beneath the streets around the hotel, there stretched a subterranean labyrinth of stores. Her arm in his, Sukie led him from one to another. Clearly an experienced shopper, she repeatedly dissuaded him from this or that purchase. 'No good!' she would say. 'Look at stitching here!' Or: 'Too much, too much!' after she had failed to strike a bargain. Eventually, at amazingly low prices, he had bought a fake Longines watch for one of his two daughters, a silk nightdress for the other, and a fake Cartier handbag for his wife.

'This is beautiful bag,' Sukie said, as the shopkeeper rummaged for some wrapping paper. She picked it up and clicked it open. 'Beautiful. Like real Cartier.' She put it down and then picked up her own bag from the chair where she had placed it. She smiled down at it ruefully. 'This bag very old,' she said. 'Look.' She held it out to him.

Suddenly, on an impulse, he stretched across the counter and took another of the fake Cartier bags off it. 'For you,' he said. 'My present for you.'

She clapped her hands together. 'Oh, Sam, Sam!' she squealed. 'Truly for me? A bag like you give your wife?'

They returned to the hotel and once more made love. Then, while she was in the bathroom washing – once more he could hear her singing that Korean folk-song in her high, clear voice – Middleton got off the bed and tiptoed across to the chair on which the new bag was resting. Sukie had already transferred to it all the contents of her old one. He clicked the bag open, pulled two fifty dollars bills out of the back pocket of his trousers, and then inserted them in the purse inside the bag.

He would say nothing to her; he would let her find the money by herself.

The next morning the hotel restaurant was unusually crowded for breakfast, because of the arrival of a party of Germans. Middleton searched in vain for a table, walking up and down now one aisle and now another. Then he felt a tweak at the back hem of his jacket.

'Why not sit here?'

It was a sixtyish Englishman, with sparse greyish hair and a luxuriant greyish moustache cascading over his long upper lip, who had addressed him in the bar on the night of his arrival. Employed by a computer firm, he had already spent several weeks in the hotel.

'Oh! Oh, thank you.'

'What a row these Germans make! They never *say* things. They have to shout them.' The Englishman had a hoarse, nasal voice. On the table beside him was a rumpled paperback thriller. 'I'm a great reader,' he had confided to Middleton at their first meeting.

When Middleton had returned to the table from the buffet, the Englishman chewed on some toast and said, a malicious glint in his eyes: 'I saw you yesterday with our Sukie. In the Café Good Luck.'

Our Sukie? 'Yes, we were having lunch together.'

'No doubt, as usual, she chose all the most expensive things on the menu!' The Englishman's laugh snorted down his long nose. It sounded as though he were blowing it.

'Actually she ate very little.'

'That girl certainly gets around.' The Englishman leaned across the table. 'Did she feed you all that crap about the aged artist boyfriend, the one and only love, and about needing an old man to turn her on?'

Head lowered, Middleton began deliberately to scrape butter over a slice of toast.

'Well, I suppose if a tart is that unseductive, she has to have some gimmick for seduction. A successful one, a very successful one, one gathers. It flatters all us geriatrics. The other girls say she's never short of a client – or money. Men of our age are much more generous, I imagine, than young ones. We want to be, if only out of gratitude. And usually we can afford to be.' He sighed. 'Ah, well! She gave me a good time – until I got bored with her. She certainly knows her stuff. And – as you no doubt noticed – she has the most terrific tits!'

That afternoon Middleton almost did not keep his appointment with Sukie in the foyer.

When she thanked him effusively for the money placed in the handbag, he merely shrugged and snapped: 'Oh, forget it!' When

[46]

she now took his arm to assist him down the steps into the labyrinth of underground shops, he pulled free with an exasperated 'Oh, for God's sake!' When she once again asked, in one of the museums, 'You are tired? You wish to sit down?', he retorted angrily: 'No, I am not! And no, I do not!' At one moment she addressed him as 'Daddy' – 'Why is Daddy so cross with his little girl today?' Then he really exploded: 'What did you call me? Why the hell did you call me that? I am not, repeat not, your Daddy, and you are not, repeat not, my little girl. Thank God!'

She bit on her lower lip; her eyes blinked rapidly behind their thick glasses. 'Sorry.' She looked as if she were about to burst into tears.

'And whatever possessed you to choose those awful glasses?'

'Sorry?'

'If you have to wear glasses, why draw attention to it by choosing ones so large and ugly?'

'Sorry.' She repeated it: 'Sorry.'

They parted in the foyer of the hotel only a few minutes after nine. He was tired, he told her; he had to make an early start for the airport.

'Maybe I come up to bedroom just for short time?'

He shook his head.

'Just for few minutes. Yes?'

'No! I've told you, I'm tired, I have an early start. I must get a good night's sleep before that hellish journey.'

'As you wish.' She shrugged, clutching the fake Cartier bag tight against her stomach as though as a shield. Then she said: 'I will come to airport with you. What time you leave?'

'No, I'm afraid that won't be possible.'

'Not possible?'

'No. You see the dean of the medical faculty will be coming to see me off. He'll be coming in his car. It would be difficult to explain if you . . .' Suddenly he felt ashamed of his cruelty.

'So I say goodnight.' Her voice was weak, drained. She put her face up, as though for a kiss.

But he merely extended a hand, took her limp, reluctant one, and shook it.

'Goodbye, Sam!' she called after him.

He pretended not to hear her, as he continued to walk towards the lift.

When, shortly before seven o'clock, Middleton was about to

clamber into the dean's car, he suddenly became aware that Sukie was standing, in her tight purple dress and dizzily high heels, the 'Cartier' bag under an arm, at the far end of the forecourt. He knew that she knew that he had seen her; but, getting into the car and slamming the door, he behaved as though he had not done so.

The dean was fiddling with the door of the boot. He seemed to be unable to lock it. Middleton drew a handkerchief out of a trouser pocket and mopped at his forehead. The sun was already high enough to make him sweat. Then, suddenly, he was aware that Sukie was racing towards him.

Her heels rattled like hail on the cement of the forecourt, louder and louder. Having reached the car, she stooped at the window, hands on knobbly knees, to stare in at him with an extraordinary mixture of grief, panic and anger.

Briefly Middleton stared back, then looked away.

But almost at once he was overmastered by a mysterious compulsion to look again at her. He could not help it, he had to do so. As their gazes locked, she put up a hand and tore off those hideous glasses. Her eyes, huge and dark, were gazing into his. Her mouth stretched and crumpled. Then tears welled out from the eyes and rolled down her cheeks.

That could not be acting, could not!

The dean clambered into the seat beside Middleton. He peered across, bewildered, at the stooping woman. He seemed about to say something, then clamped his mouth shut.

The car began to move.

'I hope you have enjoyed your visit,' the dean said.

'Yes. Yes. Oh, yes. Thank you.'

Middleton twisted his body round, to look over his shoulder, out of the rear window.

'Is everything all right?' the dean asked.

Sukie had vanished.

'Yes, thank you. Yes. Everything is fine.'

The Tradesman

An energy as vibrant and forceful as the screw of a liner propelled her through that day. The weeks of inertia, propped up in bed, slouched in the armchair or reclining on the sofa, the television only half watched or the book or newspaper only half read, might never have been. She had so often said: 'I no longer seem able to take anything in,' and now, as she hobbled on the zimmer frame room to room, she could take in everything with a speed that both delighted and frightened her.

She wrote the letters which she had for so long been merely writing in her head. She went through the drawers of her kneehole desk and her old-fashioned, crocodile-leather writing-case, a twenty-first birthday present from her father long before the War, and tore up other letters, bills long since receipted, and ancient brochures from that far-off time when she had been well enough to travel and her beloved Harry had still been alive. She sorted out clothes, cheque-book stubs and even, in the kitchen – breathing heavily as, propped against the dresser, she strained to reach upwards – old packets of Smash, Bisto and Bird's Custard. Miraculously, she felt none of the usual giddiness, dull aching of the limbs, or that sensation of sweat pricking through the skin of her forehead like needles of ice.

The telephone rang. It was Ida, spinster friend of her spinster niece, Julia. 'Oh, Mrs Masterman, I didn't want to drag you to the phone. That was the last thing I wanted. But I promised Julia to give a call to see that all was well with you.'

'Yes, dear.'

'*Are* you all right?'

'Yes, I'm fine, Ida.'

In her tense, secretive way, Ida resented the amount of time that her best and almost only friend had to spend on this aunt. Such a disagreeable, demanding old woman, and so obstinate in her refusal to go into that home in Torquay which she and Julia had spent a whole broiling summer's day finding for her, Ida's feet swelling in a new pair of shoes and Julia complaining that the glare off the sea had given her a migraine.

'I'd like to come by to see you,' Ida lied. 'But we're so busy with our annual stocktaking all through this week. And this evening I must pop over to the hospital to see how Julia's getting on. Perhaps tomorrow evening . . .'

'No, dear, it's sweet of you to offer, but there'll be no need for that.'

Ungracious old slug! 'Oh, I'd be happy to come if I can manage it. It just depends on what time I get off.'

'There'll be no need, Ida. Really.'

'At all events it's good news that Julia came through the op so well. And nothing sinister found . . .'

'Yes, that was good news.'

Soon after that chubby, cheery Mrs Gore, a navy blue headscarf tied low across her forehead so that she looked like an overgrown child disguised as a pirate for a fancy-dress party, was ringing at the door.

'Well, you opened up very quickly today! That shows you must be better.' Mrs Gore had a way of waddling from side to side, as though on a deck in a rough sea, as she transported the food into the sitting-room. She looked around her. 'Julia seems to have had a regular tidy-up in here, I see.' Mrs Gore must have forgotten that for the past three days Julia had been in hospital. Mrs Masterman did not reveal to her that it was she who had done the tidying. 'Toad-in-the-hole,' Mrs Gore announced enthusiastically. 'I know that's one of your favourites.'

Mrs Masterman, who liked Mrs Gore but disliked toad-in-the-hole, did not correct her. 'You're a great reader,' she said.

Mrs Gore, who had been English mistress at a girls' school before her marriage, said: 'Well, yes, I do read a lot. Much more than I ever watch the telly. That's a bone of contention between Jack and me – the telly, I mean.'

'Well, I put aside this edition of Joseph Conrad for you. A little present. You've always been so kind to me. It belonged to my late husband.' ('My late husband' – that was how Mrs Masterman always referred to him.)

'Oh, but I couldn't accept such a beautiful edition. Really, Mrs Masterman. Honestly. It must be a – an heirloom.'

'I can only manage large print now.'

'But oughtn't Julia to have it? Or at least someone far more deserving than myself?'

'Julia's not a reader, I'm afraid. Or, at any rate, not a reader of Conrad,' Mrs Masterman added drily. 'And there's no one more deserving than you.'

Mrs Gore's plump cheeks flushed. She shook herself like a dog after someone has patted it, her rump swaying from side to side. Head tilted, she asked: 'Do you really want me to have it?'

'Of course. Otherwise I shouldn't have offered them to you.'

Mrs Gore often told her husband that she liked Mrs Masterman's 'straightness'. She liked it now.

'Well, in that case . . .'

Mrs Gore began to gather up the books. 'You'd better start on that – ' her head indicated the toad-in-the-hole – 'before it gets cold.'

But Mrs Masterman never started on the toad-in-the-hole. Although usually she looked forward so eagerly through the long, empty day for the arrival of Mrs Gore in her little Meals-on-Wheels van, the colour of an overripe cherry, today she had no appetite. When, as a child, her parents would order her to eat, she would complain: 'But I don't feel hungry! Today's a special day.' Today was once more a special day.

She wondered whether to attempt to mount the stairs. But it was years since she had managed to do that, so that upstairs had long since become Julia's kingdom, to which she and Ida would retreat ('You won't feel lonely, will you, Auntie? It's just that Ida and I have some things to discuss in private'), after they had done their duty (they often used that phrase) with the often gruff and grumpy old woman, who appeared to be so much deafer with them than with anyone else. There were things gathering dust in the little guest-room which was now never used, and even more things gathering dust in the attic. 'One day we really must have a turn-out,' Julia would say, after she had gone into one or the other. Well, one day she could have it.

Soon after four, little Molly arrived, so neat and so bright, with her shoulder-length hair glistening in the slanting October sunlight as Mrs Masterman opened the door to her. She too remarked on how quickly Mrs Masterman had arrived at the door. She held her bag before her, in both her small, plump hands, as she stepped across the threshold.

'Aren't you cold, my dear?'

'I never feel the cold. I walked all the way here, since the bus took so long in coming. I hope I'm not late.'

'Not so that it matters.' Mrs Masterman was always truthful.

'Why did you decide on a week instead of a fortnight this time?' Molly asked as she began to set out all the tools of her trade on the table in the bedroom. 'Are you expecting someone special?'

Mrs Masterman gave a small smile, without answering the question.

Molly crossed over to the basin and began running the water, fingers fluttering under it. 'It's coming hot more quickly than usual.'

'Is it?'

'Usually it takes quite a time.'

'That's such an old boiler. Should have been replaced years and years ago. But since it does its job – after a fashion . . .'

'It's probably not very economical . . .'

As she first washed and then set Mrs Masterman's hair, Molly chatted away, as she usually chatted away, about her boyfriend, who was in the Army in Germany. He had been promised leave and then, for a variety of reasons, he had not received it.

'How disappointing for you!' Mrs Masterman sighed. 'You should get married and then you could be out there with him.'

'But the thing is – I'm not yet really *sure*.'

'Yes, one must be sure. That's always important.' She herself had been wholly sure. She was wholly sure now.

'What fine hair you've got! Like a baby's.'

At each of her visits Molly said that.

'Too fine. So difficult to keep in place.'

'And how's your niece?' Molly, who did not care for Julia – she spoke in such a hard, bossy way – always asked that too.

'Well, she's in hospital. A little operation. Just one of these women's things. Nothing serious.'

'Oh, I'm glad – that it's not serious, I mean!' Molly, who often blushed, blushed now.

When Molly had finished and was carefully putting all her things back into the bag, Mrs Masterman said: 'Oh, Molly, I have a little present for you. I was tidying up my drawers and I came on it. It's over there, on the dressing-table. The cameo brooch. On the little china tray.'

Molly was astounded. She also felt uneasy. She went over to the dressing-table and put out a hand and touched the brooch, without picking it up. It was carved with the head of a woman. 'Oh, but Mrs Masterman . . . I *couldn't*!'

'It belonged to my mother and to her mother before that. It's early Victorian. Nothing special,' she added quickly, afraid that its antiquity might make Molly even more reluctant to take it. 'You've always been so kind to me, I've always so much enjoyed our meetings.' Then, seeing that Molly was still hesitating, she said: 'Take it, dear! Unless, of course, you don't like it. Unless you feel it's something you'd never wear.'

'Oh, I *love* it! It's – it's ever so elegant!'

'Then take it. Take it!'

'But wouldn't your niece . . .?'

'Oh, she has a lot of jewellery – her mother's, mine. And she never wears it. She doesn't care for jewellery. Not as I used to do at her age.'

Molly at last picked up the brooch, with a strange mingling of pleasure, foreboding and guilt. 'I'll wear it now.' She pinned it to her pink blouse, high up, almost under her small, pointed chin.

'Lovely!' Mrs Masterman exclaimed. 'It suits you. Just right.'

Molly looked at herself in the dressing-table mirror. 'Just right.' She nodded. Her fingers rested on the cameo, feeling now its smoothness and now its roughness.

When Molly moved away from the dressing-table, Mrs Masterman then looked at her own reflection. 'Oh, Molly, you've excelled yourself!'

'Well, it seemed to go exactly right today. Don't ask me why! I've noticed that. Sometimes, however hard I try, it doesn't go right, not really right. And then one day . . . I've never seen it look nicer.'

'I wanted it to look nice.'

Who could the old pet be expecting? Some boyfriend from the past? Or just the doctor or her solicitor? Molly wanted to ask but did not dare to do so. If Mrs Masterman wanted her to know, she would tell her. If she didn't want her to know, she would merely smile and ignore any direct questioning or indirect probing, as she so often did.

'Dear Molly!'

Mrs Masterman put up her hands from the chair and, as she did so, Molly found herself lowering her head, the golden hair falling forwards. The hands rested one on either of her cheeks. Then the lips, unexpectedly warm, moist and soft, touched

Molly's mouth for a brief moment. The old woman had never kissed her before, but it seemed perfectly natural and in no way surprising that now she should do so.

'I'll show myself out ... Oh, the cameo is lovely! Thank you, thank you! Bob will never believe that *you* gave it to me. He'll think some other boy gave it to me and he'll be terribly, terribly jealous!' She laughed. She liked the idea of his being jealous of old Mrs Masterman.

When Molly had gone, Mrs Masterman sat on for a while in the bedroom, gazing at her reflection in the mirror. Yes, her hair, silvery and thin, had never looked better. The hair of a baby, the hair of a very old woman. She stroked it gently and briefly with the palm of a hand. Then she hauled herself out of the chair and made her way into the sitting-room. She looked at the watch which she wore pinned to her cardigan, peering down to do so. Nearly five. Well, he'd be here soon.

But five passed and then quarter-past five and still he didn't come. These days one could never rely on anyone to come on time to do anything for one. Last week it had been the gasman to repair the heater in her bedroom. Each day she had telephoned and each day she had been told that, yes, he would be with her that morning or that afternoon. Finally, when he had turned up, he had told her that the fire needed some new radiants, which he had omitted to bring with him. The week before that, it had been the man to measure the sofa in Julia's 'den' (the word that she herself used for the little upstairs sitting-room to which she and Ida would retire) for some loose covers. 'One hears so much about unemployment,' Julia had grumbled, 'but when one *does* have a job to be done, there's no one in the least interested in doing it.'

At half-past five, Mrs Masterman went to the window and, propping herself against the wall beside it, gazed out into the already darkening street. Two of the children, a boy and a girl, who belonged to the Irish family next door – Julia was constantly complaining about their noise or the squalor of the garden from which that noise so often emanated – raced along the pavement, their faces screwed up with effort. No doubt they were afraid of missing something on their television. Mrs Masterman could often hear that television through the wall, as she could often hear the father and mother shouting at each other.

A car passed and then another. She thought that the first, a battered Peugeot, might be his. That swish white Mercedes couldn't be. Oh, it was too bad! Perhaps he was not going to come after all today. And she'd gone to so much trouble to prepare everything.

The light of the bicycle, faint and wavering from side to side in the dusk, was the first thing that she saw. Then she saw the bicycle itself, an old-fashioned one with high handlebars, and then she saw the figure sitting erectly stiff on it. He did not look as she had expected him to look and yet she knew at once that, yes, this was he. He was wearing a rubber cape and a cap pulled down low over his forehead and – she screwed up her eyes – brown boots, highly laced, not shoes. All at once she was reminded of the man who used to come each week, on a bicycle not unlike this one and in a similar rubber cape, similar cap and similar boots, to wind the clocks of her grandfather's house in Norfolk. That man and her present visitor shared the same benignly gnome-like appearance.

She had opened the door before he had had time to ring the bell.

'Is it all right if I leave my bike here – behind these bushes? Don't want anyone to see it.'

'Yes, of course.'

'Lucky no one saw me approaching.'

At that he scuttled into the house. Once in, he pulled off his cap to reveal that it had left a mark, red and raw-looking, across his forehead. His hair fell long and greasy over his pointed ears, but the baldness at the back of his skull suggested a tonsure. Next he removed the rubber cape, with a swishing, sucking sound, and placed it, over the cap, on the hall chair.

'Sorry to be late,' he said, rubbing together hands mauve with cold. 'But the last job took longer than I'd expected.'

'It doesn't matter. You look cold,' she added.

'Should have brought some gloves. But early this afternoon . . . An Indian summer.'

They went into the sitting-room, she hobbling ahead of him on the zimmer. Once in, he hurried over to the windows and pulled the curtains across. 'You should have pulled the curtains. Hope no one saw me.'

'Yes. Yes, I'm sorry . . . Can I offer you anything before – before we begin?'

'No. Thank you. Nothing. As a matter of fact, I never drink tea or coffee or, indeed, any alcoholic beverages. My body doesn't need that kind of stimulus. In fact, it rebels against it.' On the telephone, she had thought his way of speaking old-fashioned. She thought so even more now. Yes, he was uncannily like that man who used to come to wind the clocks and about whom there was some mystery, dark, sad and perhaps even disreputable, never to be revealed to her.

'You'll want some water.'

'Yes, I have it. Here.' She pointed to the carafe set out, a glass beside it, on a lace doily, worked by her mother, on a silver tray which she herself had polished at the start of that long day.

'Fine. You'd be amazed how many people expect *me* to do everything. I can see that you're an independent spirit.'

She liked that. 'Yes, I've always been an independent spirit. All my life.'

He felt in a pocket of his loose-fitting cardigan and drew out a beige envelope.

'They're in there?' she said.

'That's right. Now you make yourself comfy, there's a good girl. Lie down on the sofa, put your legs up.'

'No. I'll sit here. That's how I planned it.' She placed herself in the armchair by the window, settling her head back on the pillow in its white linen cover fringed with lace.

'That's fine,' he said. 'If that's how you want it.'

'That's how I want it.'

He was about to pour some of the pills out of the envelope into his own cupped palm, but she stopped him. 'Give them to me here.' She held out a hand.

He tipped the pills into her palm. Then he went over to the carafe and poured water out from it into the tumbler.

'I've always been bad at swallowing pills.' She smiled up at him placatingly, as in recent years she had so often smiled up at nurses and doctors.

'Take your time.'

She swallowed three of the pills, one after the other. It was far easier than she had ever supposed. She pointed. 'Later – I want you to use that ribbon over there. You won't forget, will you?'

'I'll make everything as nice as possible. Don't you worry.' He picked up the pale blue ribbon and began to wrap it round his right forefinger. The finger was long and bony, the nail had a ridge of dirt under it.

'Your – your envelope is on the mantelpiece.'

'Oh, don't worry about that, dear! Don't worry about anything!'

She smiled. 'You're very efficient, I must say.' Nowadays one didn't expect people to be efficient when they came to do things for one.

'Go on swallowing those pills.'

She went on swallowing them. Eventually, her breath became shallow, there was a blue tinge to her lips and her eyelids. The eyelids fluttered, fluttered again, closed. From a pocket of the cardigan he drew out a transparent plastic bag. Gently, kneeling now beside her, he placed it over her head. He took the length of ribbon and stretched it taut between one hand and the other. Then he circled it loosely around her throat and tied it in a bow.

Through the bag, he saw her lips moving. She was saying something or trying to say something. What, what? Then he realized. She was saying 'Thank you, thank you, thank you.'

Credit

That was the day when the cable, four days old, caught up with them in the hotel in which, as though in some long since abandoned palace, they had the freedom to wander from dusty, cavernous bedroom to dusty, cavernous sitting-room, to a bathroom always susurrant with the lisping of a cistern hung askew on the peeling wall, to a terrace on which some ferocious emerald green vine had all but suffocated the rose trained along its trellis. 'We'll have to return as soon as we can,' Bill told Alice, holding out the cable to her, although he had already read out its contents. 'Is that necessary?' she asked perversely, even though she herself had for days now been wishing to put an end to what had become for her a secret martyrdom of greasy, unclean food, rickety and lumpy beds, maimed and suppurating beggars, and children as exasperatingly persistent as the omnipresent flies. 'Yes, it is necessary,' Bill answered. 'The funeral is on Monday.' 'Won't that be a little premature to try on Mac's shoes for size?' Bill did not answer that. Instead, he said: 'It's probably just as well that our tour has been curtailed like this. We've been spending an absolute fortune. Far more than I'd expected.'

That was also the day when Bill discovered that their driver, an Indian Christian called Joseph, could only, for all his interest in the museums, temples and ruins that they visited, be illiterate. Joseph was a daily, living contradiction of all that they had been told, even by the Indians themselves, about Indians being inefficient, unpunctual and dishonest. 'Oh, if only we could take him back to England,' Bill exclaimed more than once, looking out of the grimy window of some hotel to see the ramshackle car, newly washed yet again, waiting for them, half an hour before they required it, in the drive, with Joseph bending over it solicitously, a shammy-leather cloth in his hand, to add a final polish. Joseph would jump out with alacrity to open the car doors for them, would haggle for them whenever they made a purchase, and would insist each day that they should check the mileage, so that there was no possibility of his tampering with the clock.

Bill made his discovery of the illiteracy when – Alice having taken to her bed on the pretext of a migraine – Joseph was driving him out, on the last of their days in India, to some Jain temples perched on an island in the middle of a turbulent river. Joseph, hundreds of miles from his northern home, had never been there before. As they lurched and bumped over a road that was often little more than a dusty track, he kept shaking his head to himself and frowning at his reflection in the driving mirror. 'What's the matter?' Bill eventually asked. Joseph shrugged his bony shoulders. 'Do you think we've lost the way?' It seemed kinder to Bill to say 'we' than 'you'. Joseph shrugged again. Then, at a crossroads, he stopped the car. 'Maybe we have taken the wrong direction, sir,' he said. 'Oh, no – look!' Bill exclaimed, leaning forward from the sagging back seat and pointing ahead of them. Joseph squinted through the windshield at the signpost, its English and Hindi emerging uncertainly through a film of ochre dust. He looked profoundly unhappy. 'Yes, sir,' he said, his voice rising in what was a half-interrogation. 'To the left,' Bill said. 'It says to the left, doesn't it?' 'Ah, yes, sir, to the left!'

That was also the day when Bill saw his first white hitchhiker. In a village strung out along the road, he stood, blond, close-cropped head bare, outside a shack that seemed to be a petrol station, vegetable and fruit store and café all in one. A rucksack on his back, he wore what had clearly once been an elegant blue and white seersucker suit and had a no less clearly once elegant attaché case beside him. On his feet he had the kind of wooden clogs usually worn on beaches. He smiled ruefully as he raised his thumb, as though to tell them, 'Yes, I know you won't stop.'

Joseph, who had already shown that he had no use for Indian hitchhikers, now made it plain that he had no use for white ones either, as he accelerated. 'Stop, Joseph, stop!' Bill cried out, leaning forward and putting a hand on the driver's shoulder. 'Stop! We might as well give the poor beggar a lift. Plenty of room – and it can be no fun standing around in this heat.'

'That's very kind of you, sir,' the hitchhiker said, as he clambered into the front seat beside Joseph. Frowning and pursing his lips, Joseph had already disposed of the rucksack and attaché case in the boot. The youth's accent was American.

[59]

'It's lucky we're bound for the same destination.'

'On this road there's probably no other. A truck took me as far as that village. The driver said I'd catch a bus. That was at least six hours ago.'

Bill leaned forward to see the newcomer better. Big-boned but pitifully emaciated – the knuckles looked huge on the sunburned hands, the nails far from clean, that he had placed behind his scraggy neck as though to ease away some ache – he would have been handsome if the sun had not stripped the skin from his forehead and nose, as though some searing flame had passed across them. An acrid odour emanated either from his body or his clothes.

Bill fumbled in the breast pocket of his safari suit and took out a packet of the lemon glucose sweets that he and Alice had been advised to carry around with them to combat thirst. He held the packet out: 'How about one of these?' The boy took three, digging into the packet with a forefinger. 'Thanks. I've had no breakfast, except some tea. No supper either, for the matter of that.' He put all three sweets into his mouth simultaneously and began to suck voraciously.

'Have you been in India long?' Bill asked. He did not really wish to know or even to talk at all, so intense had become the midday heat, but he felt obliged to make an effort.

The youth swivelled round in his seat. 'Well, I suppose the price of a ride like this is always to tell one's life story.' He smiled. He was not being offensive.

'No need for that.'

But the youth went on. 'I came here for a vacation – my godfather, he's English, is with the United Nations in Delhi. Then, instead of going back to the job that's awaiting me as an accountant in a bank in Philadelphia, I decided to bum my way around for a while.' He paused. 'Now I don't think I'll ever go back home.'

'Never?' Bill had begun to think, as the boy spoke, of his own imminent return: the funeral, the protestations about the 'tragedy' of Mac's early death, even though few people in the office had liked the sour bastard, the subsequent jostlings for his job.

'Never ... probably,' the boy added in sudden qualification, as though he had now for the first time realized the full implications of that 'never'.

'Then what will you do?' Bill wanted to add: 'You can't bum around forever.'

'I hope my visit to the temples will decide for me.' The youth fell silent for a moment, chin on chest, his eyes fixed on the grey road ahead of them. Then he swivelled around again in his seat. 'There's an ashram there,' he said. 'I'll stay there awhile. Maybe I'll stay there for the rest of my life.' He gave a little, choking laugh. 'Who knows?'

'Who knows?' Bill echoed. Secretly he was thinking: What an idiot!

'They have something,' the boy said meditatively. He did not specify who 'they' or what the 'something' were. 'Yep, they have something.'

'Haven't you got a family – a girlfriend – back in America?'

'Had.' To Bill the monosyllable was chilling.

After that Bill made no further effort to prolong the conversation, until, after a series of precipitous hairpin bends, negotiated by Joseph with a blithe insouciance, they arrived at the village caught, like a random scurf of rocks, wood, corrugated iron and thatch, in an elbow of the wide, turbid river. As, his body aching and stiff as though from a fall, Bill clambered out of the car, a number of men in nothing but loin-cloths, some of them daubed with ash, clustered around with begging-bowls outstretched in claw-like hands. The boy laughed: 'I'll probably soon be holding out a bowl myself.' Bill had taken out some loose change from his trouser pocket, with Joseph looking on benignly, as he always did when Bill or Alice gave anything to a beggar.

'Do you want me to hire a boat for you, sir?' Joseph asked, when the coins had been distributed.

'Is that how one gets across?' It was a stupid question, Bill realized as soon as he had asked it. How else would one get across to the island, since there was clearly no bridge?

'There is also a public boat,' Joseph said meaningfully, looking at the American. He clearly thought that the youth should travel on it, instead of with his master.

'Get us a boat,' Bill said, with unwonted sharpness. Then he turned to the American, who had taken off his seersucker jacket and was now carefully folding it up, as though it had just been washed and ironed, instead of being creased and saturated with dust. 'I take it you want to cross over at once?'

'Fine. Thanks.'

Joseph found a boatman, a white-haired man, with a lean muscular body, naked, like the beggars, but for a loin-cloth. He and Joseph both extended hands to help, as Bill and the American clambered aboard. Bill placed himself gingerly on one of the two narrow, horizontal slats that served as seats, put up a hand to shade his eyes and looked across the river to where the temples rose up, shimmering like a mirage in the afternoon glare. The American made his way, the boat tipping perilously to now one side and now the other, up to the prow. Joseph hesitated and then walked over to join him. From the stern the boatman propelled them with a single oar that looked like a vast wooden shovel.

'Beautiful,' the boy said, smiling out towards the temples, his eyes half closed against the slanting sunlight.

'Beautiful,' Bill agreed. 'But you should get yourself some sunglasses,' he added irrelevantly. 'This light is dangerous.'

The boy laughed. 'Too late now.'

'I have a spare pair in the car. I could have let you have those.'

'Too late now,' the boy repeated with a kind of suppressed joy.

Its opaque, brown waves edged with a yellow froth, the water swirled around them. At one point, as Bill peered down at it, he was disgusted to see the swollen carcass of a dog, one side showing a purple gash. Briefly it surged into sight and then was plucked away by one of the criss-cross currents. On the far shore, three thin, tall men were bathing. Some white lengths of cloth – Bill assumed them to be loin-cloths – flapped out like sails from the rocks to which they had somehow been fastened.

The American, standing motionless at the prow, once again smiled into the dry, hot wind. Then he shifted his stance, swinging his seersucker jacket, which had previously been dangling from a forefinger, up on to his shoulder. Something glittered momentarily in the sunlight, as Bill glanced over. The youth let out what was more a scream than a shout. 'My credit cards! My credit cards!' He pointed downwards into the swirling water. 'My credit cards have fallen in!'

With extraordinary speed Joseph tore off his clothes, revealing, to Bill's amazement, long cotton drawers reaching to his bony knees and a long cotton vest. Shouting something to the boatman he jumped over the side of the boat. After a second of hesitation, the boatman jumped in after him, but prudently held on to the side of the boat with one hand, so that it should not be swept away on the flood. The river at that point was sufficiently shallow for both of them to stand. Joseph disappeared under the murky waters again and yet again. The American, kneeling in the boat, leant over and peered down. From time to time he shouted: 'There! *There!* No, not there! I think that I can see it.'

'See what?' Bill asked. Receiving no answer, he repeated, 'See what?'

'The wallet. The crocodile-skin wallet. My godfather gave it to me. For my birthday. Oh Christ! Christ! All my credit cards! All of them!'

The two Indians eventually clambered back, dripping, into the boat. Joseph picked up his shirt and began to dry himself on it. The boatman threw back his head and unaccountably laughed, showing a few teeth stained with betel-nut. 'Gone,' Joseph said. 'Impossible to find.' He sounded breathless after all his diving. 'A lot of money?' he asked.

'Not money. My credit cards. All my credit cards. Fortunately any money I have – and there's not much of that – is in another pocket.'

'You can always get the credit cards replaced,' Bill said, as the boatman once again took up the shovel-like oar.

But stricken, his bony hands clasped around his knees as he huddled in the bottom of the boat, oblivious to the bilge that was staining his clothes yet further – he might be some sack thrown down there carelessly, Bill thought – the American made no answer.

When they had reached the further bank with a scrape and a jolt, Joseph elbowed aside the boatman to help Bill ashore. He made no attempt to help the boy, who jumped free clumsily, all but falling over on the mud flat. 'I will tell the boatman to wait for us, sir. He says that it will take about an hour and a half to see the temples.'

'Which way is the ashram?' the American asked, struggling back into his jacket despite the heat.

Joseph turned to ask the boatman. Then simultaneously the two of them pointed. 'That way, sir,' Joseph said. 'You walk straight ahead. Not far.'

'That way?' the boy asked dubiously. It was as though he imagined that they might be misdirecting him.

Joseph nodded. Then he said to Bill: 'We go this way, sir.'

Suddenly Bill felt an unreasoning sadness at saying goodbye to the boy. 'Are you sure you don't want to change your mind and come back with us?'

'Quite sure.' It sounded ungracious, even angry.

'I'm sorry about those credit cards.'

The boy shrugged and began to walk away with long, effortful strides, mumbling, 'Well, maybe . . .' He reached some steps, halted, turned half round. What he said next Bill could barely catch, but in retrospect he decided that it was 'Maybe it was a sign.'

The boy hastened up four or five of the steps. Then again he turned, raising a hand in a final salutation as he called out: 'Thanks! Thanks a lot!'

At the hotel desk when they were paying their bill, in the car as they drove out to the airport, at the airport itself – Joseph saw to all the interminable formalities for them, queuing patiently and persistently, while they sat silent and motionless under a slowly churning fan – Bill's hand would keep straying in near-panic to the breast pocket of his jacket. Eventually, as they shuffled on to the tarmac, Alice noticed the repeated gesture. 'Why do you keep touching that pocket?' she asked sharply. 'Have you lost something? Are you frightened of losing something?'

'Of course not! What *are you* talking about?'

He only stopped touching the pocket when they were safely aboard the aeroplane.

Wanting

Yearningly myopic, Anna's mother leaned forward, hands pressed between her knees, to ask: 'Are you sure you really want it?' In the same tone, as though resigned to the instant infliction of yet another wound, she would ask Anna back home: 'Are you sure you really want some rhubarb?', 'Are you sure you really want a game of Scrabble?', 'Are you sure you really want to come to church with me?'

'Oh, yes, Mother!' But Anna was not sure about really wanting the cat any more than all those other things.

'It is rather a pet,' Mrs Stafford said, her head on one side, as she gazed down at the lanky, black-and-white animal crouched beneath the frayed valance of the sagging sofa. 'I was so afraid you'd get lonely, all by yourself in this flat.' Bereft of husband and children, Mrs Stafford was far more likely to get lonely in Eastbourne than Anna in Maida Vale.

'Why do you call him "it"?' Anna asked.

Her mother gave a nervously defensive laugh. 'Oh, I don't know. Silly of me. He has a right to a sex as much as anyone else. Your father always used to refer to babies as "it". Remember?'

'He's a tom,' Anna said. 'I wonder if I ought to get him fixed.'

'Oh, much better.'

'But cruel.'

'Do you think so?'

Anna rose and scooped up the cat in her arms. As he struggled, she thought for a moment that he would scratch her. 'He's awfully ugly,' she said.

'Oh, I think him rather sweet. I like that white patch over his eye. Dashing.'

'It was precisely that patch, Mother dear, that made me decide that he is ugly. That and those huge paws of his. If he were a human, he'd be taking size eleven shoes.'

[65]

'I wonder who owned him. It was so odd his turning up like that at the back door. Well-fed, wearing that smart collar with the bell on it. I asked around everywhere and even put a notice on the gate. *Someone* must have missed him.'

'Perhaps his owner moved house. Or died,' Anna added brutally, knowing that, since she had lost her ailing husband, her mother hated the mention of death.

'Oh, I do hope you really want him, dear. If you don't, I could always take him back home with me. Though Trixie, having queened it so long in the house, doesn't care for him at all.' Trixie was Mrs Stafford's Yorkshire terrier.

Anna allowed the cat, wriggling again after some seconds of resigned motionlessness, to flop out of her clasp. It rushed to the closed door and pressed itself against it, its triangular head, long ears pricked, oddly raised, as though in expectation of some titbit. 'Yes, I do want him,' she said almost crossly. But she still was not sure.

'You mustn't let that cat become a burden and tie,' one of Anna's boyfriends, a student of engineering, told her when she said that, oh dear, she was afraid that she could not possibly make the weekend in Paris, the couple upstairs had sprung it on her that they were going to be away themselves, and there was no one else she could trust to feed Prince.

'Surely you could leave out enough food for three days?'

'Oh, he won't touch *stale* food,' Anna said, as though this was something of which to be proud. 'He's terribly fussy.'

'Cats are only fussy if people make them fussy,' the boyfriend retorted. He hated Prince, who brought on his asthma and left hairs on his suit.

More and more Anna's life was centring itself on the cat, so that, as she was typing some invoice in the office, strap-hanging in a clogged underground train, or gazing at her own reflection in the mirror of the Greek unisex hairdresser's round the corner, she would all at once think with a surge of joyful anticipation, as though a lover were expecting her: Prince will be waiting for me. When she was out shopping, it was often of his food – chicken, mince, melts, liver, or the hard, dry nuggets, labelled 'Lamb and Beef flavours', mysteriously his favourite form of sustenance – that she would consider before her own. Returning home from this shopping or from work, she would neglect the post – a letter from her mother, a postcard from abroad from the boyfriend who hated Prince – in order to go at once to the window of the kitchen, throw it open and call out in a high-pitched, clear, eager voice: 'Prince, Prince, Prince!' Over one of the walls of the garden that no one in the house, amateurishly converted into four flats, bothered to tend, Prince would eventually appear in answer to her summons, his eyes glinting like topazes if it were sunny, his coat beaded with what looked like tiny fragments of glass if it were raining. 'How that cat adores you!' one of her women friends remarked as Prince, jumping over brambles and tufts of weeds, raced towards her down the garden; and the boyfriend who hated Prince then put in: 'Oh, he knows Anna's going to feed him. Cupboard love. That's the only love that cats ever feel.'

In the house next door there lived a middle-aged German businessman, owner of a Mercedes car, and his wife. Anna called them 'the fascist couple', not because she knew anything of their political views but because they so often complained about Prince. First, he had been digging among some recently planted seedlings of lettuce. Later, during a heat wave, when it was impossible to keep windows closed, he had managed to sneak into their kitchen and make off with a slice of tongue from a plate set out for their evening meal. When the diminutive, demure tabby in the house on the other side of them came into season, he spent each night howling in anguished frustration outside the back door behind which her owners had confined her. 'Beastly people,' Anna said of these Germans, and even 'Nasty little brats' of their two immaculately dressed, impeccably behaved, blond-haired children.

'I'm surprised you've never thought of having him doctored.' the German businessman said to Anna, after he had yet again been complaining about the all-night howling. The cheek of it! Anna felt like saying that she was surprised that his wife had never thought of having *him* doctored.

Anna's mother, wrinkling up her nose at the peppery odour that now hung about the cramped flat, also annoyed Anna by saying on one occasion: 'I know it's not really my business, but don't you think that in a flat of this size, in the heart of London, it would be kinder to have him fixed?'

'Kinder? How kinder? Why kinder?'

Mrs Stafford quailed under the onslaught. 'Well, more convenient,' she amended weakly. 'For you. For him.' She wondered whether to mention that nasty smell but then decided not to.

Since Anna had left home, she had grown increasingly afraid of her.

Anna gathered up Prince into her arms, taking a voluptuous pleasure in his fatness and sleekness. She put a cheek against his coat. 'I don't think you'd find it very *convenient* to be fixed, would you, darling?' she said.

One July day Anna come home hot and dishevelled from her rush-hour journey and her walk to her flat, hurried into the kitchen and threw open the window that she had been obliged to keep shut even during this day of heat wave for fear of the burglars who had been preying on the neighbourhood. Fortunately, Prince by now owned a cat-door, installed by a red-faced handyman, clearly the worse for a drink, whom one of her boyfriends had recommended to her. 'Prince, Prince, Prince!' Anna called out over the waving grass and the tangled brambles of the garden that no one wished to tend. 'Pri-ince!' The call became a yodel. When Prince did not appear, she took his tin plate, held it up before her, leaning out of the window, and banged on it with a knife snatched up from the draining-board. But there was still no sign of Prince.

Later, in the garden, she called and called again. Then, noticing that the Germans were reclining in deck chairs in their garden stripped to the waist – the husband looked as if he had an even larger bosom than the wife – she crossed over to the low wall between them and asked, 'You haven't by any chance seen my Prince, have you?'

The German shielded his forehead with a pudgy hand, as he looked over at her. 'Prince?' She was sure that he was only pretending not to know whom she meant.

'My cat.'

The German shook his head. Then he looked over at his wife and she shook her head too. 'Yesterday he was in our garden – I am afraid that I had to chase him away, you understand ... But today, no.' Again he looked across at his wife. 'Inge?' Inge again shook her head, hitching at one strap of the bathing-costume that she was wearing.

'I expect he'll come back.' Pursing her lips, Anna spoke the words as much in defiance of the Germans as in reassurance to herself.

But Prince did not come back, either that evening, during a night in which Anna kept waking up to turn on the light, to look around the bedroom, to search in the sitting-room and kitchen and even to pad in slippers and night-dress out in the garden, or with the early break of another day that Anna's boss, mopping his forehead with a grubby handkerchief, would describe as 'a scorcher'. Anna felt reluctant to go to work. Indeed, she was late in doing so, as she wandered up the avenue, peering into other people's gardens, and then returned through the mews on to which her flat backed. 'You haven't by any chance seen a cat, have you?' she asked a black man in grease-stained overalls kneeling before the bonnet of a car in the otherwise deserted mews. 'There are many cats here, lady,' the man replied. 'A black-and-white cat,' Anna said. 'A tom. A large tom.' The man shrugged and returned to his kneeling posture before the car. Then, wishing to help this tall, blonde girl in a blue cotton frock and flat-heeled shoes, he called out after her, 'If I see your cat, where can I find you?' Anna was not sure whether to tell him. She hesitated, turned round, then at last gave him the address – not that he would remember.

Work that day was a prolonged agony. She had planned to go home during the lunch-hour but her boss had loaded her with so much typing – all of it 'absolutely urgent', he maintained – that she could not do so. Then there was a hold-up on the underground – apparently someone stupid had fallen or jumped in front of a train – so that it was almost seven o'clock before she was once again at the kitchen window, calling out, on a note of increasing despair, 'Prince, Prince, Prince!'

In the next few days, Anna scarcely slept, so frequently did she get up in the night to wander out into the eerily silent garden. There were other cats, creeping among the murderously trailing brambles or squatting on the walls, often face to face, mirror-images of each other. Sometimes one of these cats would flop down from its perch, sidle up to her and rub itself against her bare legs. But 'Oh, go away!' she would say crossly. None of the cats was ever Prince.

When Sunday came, she went from house to house in the avenue, asking after him. Some of the people who opened their doors responded to her questions with an air of long-suffering politeness. 'Silly woman!' she heard an etiolated middle-aged man in a silk dressing-gown remark to an unseen companion, no doubt male, before he had even shut the door on her. Others, usually women, were eager to be of help, asking all kinds of irrelevant questions and promising to keep a look-out.

At the suggestion of her boss – 'What a fuss about a cat!' he exclaimed to another of the girls in the office – Anna put an advertisement in the local paper, offering a reward of twenty pounds (her boss had proposed five pounds). Various people rang up, leaving Anna in some doubt as to their ability to read, since the strays of which they spoke turned out to be wholly different from the cat that her advertisement described – female cats, neutered cats, Manx cats, Siamese cats, white cats, tabby cats, tortoiseshell cats, cats with only one ear or only one eye. There was a moment of extreme excitement when a breathless woman with an uncertain command of English rang up to report that she had seen a cat in the street in which she lived, two underground stops away from Anna. It sounded exactly like Prince. But when Anna hurried round, the pallid, moist-eyed Spanish woman, a minute child of indeterminate sex hiding behind her, could only say: 'Now he has gone.' Clearly she expected the reward and no less clearly she was disappointed when, instead, Anna handed the child, now venturing out from behind its mother, a fifty pence piece.

Anna often thought balefully about 'the fascist couple'. Was it possible that they had done something to Prince – removed him to some distant place in their large Mercedes car, poisoned him or sold him for his fur? The boyfriend who had always hated Prince scoffed at the last idea – 'For his *fur*!' 'It happens,' Anna insisted. 'Well, yes,' the boyfriend acknowledged. 'But Prince . . .' He gave a rueful smile. 'Prince has – had – a gorgeous coat,' Anna told him crossly. This was the last time she saw that boyfriend.

'Well, I suppose I'll have to accept the fact that he's gone forever. I only hope he's got a good home.' Now Anna found herself constantly repeating these words – to her mother, when she rang up to ask exasperatingly 'Any news, dear?', to her boss, who could never mention Prince without an odd smirk, to the Indian at the local late-night store, puzzled by this devotion to a mere cat, and to a neighbour, never encountered before Prince's disappearance, who herself had eleven cats and offered to let Anna have the next kitten that, as she put it, 'came along'.

Anna still kept the packet of hard, dry nuggets, 'Lamb and Beef flavours', and the chipped Wedgwood saucer and the tin plate. But increasingly, as the days of that summer passed, she looked down at these objects meditatively, set out on their rubber mat in a corner of the kitchen, and wondered if she ought not to throw them in the dustbin. Without Prince she did not now hurry home from the office, but instead would accompany colleagues to the pub round the corner or accept an invitation from one of her boyfriends to go straight from work to a theatre, a cinema or a concert. She began to forget her previous bondage to the cat.

'Would you like me to get you another cat?' her mother asked on one of her visits. 'I could ask Miss Castle.' (Miss Castle was her Eastbourne vet.) 'I could even *buy* you a cat, I'd be happy to do so. A pedigree one, I mean.'

'Sweet of you, Mother,' Anna said. 'But another cat wouldn't be Prince, would he?'

Mrs Stafford sighed. 'No, dear, I suppose not.'

More than five weeks after Prince's disappearance, Anna rushed home from the office to have a bath and a change before going on to a party. She was going to be late, because yet again her boss had loaded on to her a pile of 'absolutely urgent' letters.

It was as she was scrubbing one leg in the bath that she saw the dark form against the frosted window and heard the persistent miaowing. Jumping out of the water, she snatched up a towel, wrapped it around her, ran into the kitchen and flung open the window. 'Prince, Prince, Prince!'

One moment the cat was on the sill. Then it flopped down on to the linoleum and hurried over to the rubber mat in the corner of the kitchen. Finding nothing there, it looked up at her and let out a squawk. Oh, the poor thing! One eye was half closed with a greenish mucus, he was terribly emaciated. What could have happened to him? (Later, when she found that his claws were worn down, she decided that he must have been stolen and then had somehow found his way back to her across the city.) 'You're hungry, darling! You're hungry! Just wait a moment.' But he did not want any of the hard, dry nuggets that she feverishly scattered into the tin plate nor any of the tuna fish that she no less feverishly emptied out over the chipped Wedgwood saucer. All he wanted at first was water. Endlessly he drank, moved away and then, as though on second thoughts, returned to drink even more. After that, at long last, he ate.

Anna telephoned. 'I'm terribly sorry ... Prince is back ...
Prince ... You know, my cat. Yes, *cat*, the cat I lost ... so you
see I'll just have to give your party a miss...' Then to the
boyfriend who was taking her to the party: 'It's not silly at all ...
No, not sentimental ... After all, on his first night home ... Well,
think what you bloody like ...'

Anna and Prince lay out on the bed as the light of the late
summer evening faded across the overgrown garden and, slanting through the window, made the back of Anna's hand gleam
as she ran it through Prince's coat, tugging at burs and knots of
fur. Sometimes Prince let out a protesting squeak and once he
even tried to scratch her with those blunted claws of his.

'Prince, Prince, Prince!' Anna crooned. 'Where have you been?
What have you been *doing*! Oh, if only you could tell me!'

Darkness closed in, but Anna continued to lie there by the cat,
until a sudden pang of hunger, followed by the thought of
supper unprepared, forced her up and over to the light switch.
From the door, she looked back at Prince; and, as though
conscious of her scrutiny, he suddenly opened his eyes, raised
his head and looked back at her.

They stared at each other for several seconds.

Then all at once, as though something huge and amorphous
had moved within her with a terrible displacement, she thought
of her mother saying, so long ago it seemed now: 'Are you sure
you really want it?'

Foreign Friends

I lowered my newspaper at the sound of the gate screeching open and watched as the two Japanese women – the mother whom I had known more than twenty years before and the daughter whom I had glimpsed only once as a diminutive bundle of brightly coloured clothes held close against her father's chest – made their way up the steps. The daughter was still diminutive and still brightly clothed, in a crimson wide-shouldered coat and a matching Robin Hood hat stuck with a jaunty feather. Mrs Ishiyama's shoulders were still narrow and rounded and her tiny feet still turned inwards as she carefully raised first one of them and then the other to make her ascent. More surprisingly, her bare head showed the same stiff, lustrous black hair – it might have been made of lacquer – and the plain, flat face remained as unlined as in the past.

The daughter, Keiko, translating for her mother, who still spoke not a word of English, reminded me in her joviality, her loquacity and her directness – none of them traits usually to be found in Japanese men, much less in Japanese women – of her father, now dead. Her accent was American, her voice self-confidently loud – in contrast to her mother's, which was little more than a whisper as she spoke with her head turned away from me and a small, useless-looking hand covering her mouth.

'My mother says that she hopes that we do not waste your time. You are a busy man, yes? We have read about you, in the newspapers, when you are lecturing in Japan two years ago. My mother wished to see you again, but she thought that maybe you are too busy.' Keiko kept leaning towards her mother, to hear what she was whispering behind that raised hand, and then eagerly leaning towards me. Embarrassed, I eventually gazed down at the hem of Mrs Ishiyama's skirt. The material might have been the same costly raw silk, a dull, dark grey, as of the kimono that she had worn on the one occasion when I had met her before.

'My mother says that you were my father's closest foreign friend. He had many foreign friends, she says, but you were his closest.' I felt embarrassed. I had heard Ishiyama say on more than one occasion, all those years ago, that I was his closest foreign friend, but Ishiyama, so crude and domineering and even then so powerful and rich, had never been my closest Japanese one. Mrs Ishiyama had lowered her hand, she was at last looking directly at me. She was nodding, smiling. 'My mother says my father admired King-san, liked King-san very, *very* much.'

Why he had liked me and why he had admired me were things that had always puzzled me. Our lives, mine as a British Council official whom he approached to help him with the composition of an English speech to be delivered at some kind of economic conference to be held in Ottawa, and his as the boss of one of the most successful industrial cartels to emerge in post-war Japan, were remote from each other. All that we had in common was a love of the Noh theatre, to which he would often take me.

The two women and I began to talk of 'the old times' (as Keiko called them), since there was little else about which to talk, once I had ascertained that they were staying at Claridge's, that they had been to see *Cats*, and that they had been 'doing shopping, lots, lots of shopping.' While her daughter translated something said in a near-whisper, Mrs Ishiyama would raise her teacup and sip delicately from it or nibble at a biscuit. With her small, limp hands, grey face and narrow, rounded shoulders, she reminded me now, as she had reminded me on the only occasion when I had met her in Kyoto, of some furtive, harmless rodent, a mole or a field-mouse.

In the manner of Japanese men, Ishiyama did not take his wife around with him. If anyone else accompanied us to the Noh theatre, it would be some male relative or friend. In the narrow sake bar in which, perched on a high stool, he would joke crudely with the two bar-girls while his face got redder and redder and shinier and shinier, there would always be customers known to him. But it was inconceivable that any of them would bring along a girlfriend, much less a wife, to such a place. 'I've never met your wife,' I used to say to him. Nor indeed had I ever been inside his house, although he had often been inside mine. To that he almost always gave the same answer: 'The time will come.'

I thought that the time had indeed come when, one night, at an hour closer to two o'clock than one, I was roused from a deep sleep and, having gone downstairs, my two massive Akita dogs growling behind me, opened the door to find him standing there, his face flushed with drink, with a beautiful young woman in a shimmering kimono standing behind him.

But the woman – I realized as soon as she had stepped delicately into the hall, so that I could see her properly – was certainly not his wife. In her high lacquer clogs, her hair piled elaborately up on her head and her face a smoothly enamelled pink-and-white mask, she was all too clearly a geisha. I had never seen one more beautiful. As I stared at her, Ishiyama said: 'This is Takiko-san,' and she at once gave me a deep bow.

Takiko-san had no English other than a few phrases, learned no doubt for visiting businessmen, like 'Please', 'Thank you very much' and 'Beautiful'. She said the word 'Beautiful' more than any of the others, as she examined my shabby sitting-room, as I handed her a drink – 'Scotch on rocks, please,' she said – and as she nervously patted the dog standing closest to her.

Ishiyama gulped at his whisky as though it were water. He smiled across at me and winked. 'A beautiful girl, King-san?'

'Yes, a beautiful girl.'

'All my friends are jealous. She is the most beautiful girl in the whole of Kyoto. Also the most expensive! But I do not mind. I can afford the most beautiful girl in the whole of Kyoto. I can afford the most beautiful girl in the whole of the world!' As he spoke, the girl, understanding nothing, was glancing about her. He went on to speak about her even more crudely. Her talents, he made all too clear, extended far beyond playing the *samisen* and looking beautiful.

Soon I was longing for them to leave. That the girl was totally unaware of what he was saying seemed to make the whole conversation even more degrading. After a while she yawned, raising her open fan to her open mouth. Then she looked across at me and smiled. Again she yawned. Perhaps she was deliberately giving me my cue? At all events, I remarked: 'Your friend is getting tired, I think.'

When at last I had them on the doorstep, I could not resist saying: 'Next time, please bring your wife, Ishiyama-san. I so much want to meet your wife.'

'Yes, yes,' he replied, clearly irritated. 'The time will come.'

The time came some two weeks later. Again it was very late, at an hour nearer to two than to one, and again I was in bed. As I opened the front door, the two Akita dogs were again growling behind me; and again, behind Ishiyama, was a woman. But this woman was small and insignificant, in a dark grey raw silk kimono – I had by then lived long enough in Japan to know its cost – with a silver-fox fur draped over her narrow, rounded shoulders. 'This is my wife,' Ishiyama said, as soon as we had entered the hall, and the wife then gave me precisely the same low bow that the geisha had given me. 'No English,' he added.

Mrs Ishiyama asked for orange juice, at which she sipped as delicately as, twenty years later, she was to sip at my tea. Ishiyama stretched out his short, muscular legs ahead of him and rested his head far back in his chair, his glass of whisky balanced on his chest. 'You asked to see my wife, King-san,' he said. 'Here she is.' Mrs Ishiyama's small eyes darted back and forth between us, with an occasional nervous smile. 'Now you will understand – there was no reason for you to wish to see her. She is not beautiful. Not at all. She is not young, she is older than I am.' I stared at him, willing him to stop, but heedlessly he continued. 'She comes of a rich family. I was poor boy when I married her, without help of her money maybe I do nothing. She give me daughter but so far no son. Maybe one day she will give me son. Son is important.' He sounded far drunker now than when he had arrived. 'She is good woman. But for sex – ' suddenly he burst into rowdy laughter – 'she is no good, no bloody good! King-san, you can see.' He indicated her with an open hand, the palm upraised. Her face broke into a smile. Clearly she thought that he was saying something complimentary about her. 'But girl who come here last time – Takiko-san – fan-tas-tic!' He had learned that last word from an American businessman whom he had brought along to the sake bar a few days before. He began to tell me precisely how the geisha was superior in bed to his wife. Mrs Ishiyama peered in turn into our faces, smiled from time to time, nodded from time to time. She looked happy, even elated.

I began to hate him. I wondered how I had been able to endure his company for all the past weeks.

Now, in London so many years later, Mrs Ishiyama whispered to her daughter. 'My mother says that we have taken up too much of your time. You are very kind. Now we must go.'

In the hall Mrs Ishiyama opened the Harrods bag that her

daughter had left there with their coats, and took out a small package wrapped in Japanese paper. *'Dozo,'* she said, handing it to me with a deep bow. Her daughter added: 'Please.' Then the daughter translated something else whispered by her mother: 'Perhaps you will think the present strange. It is my father's watch. His gold watch. Patek Philippe.' Again Mrs Ishiyama whispered, and the daughter translated: 'You were my father's closest foreign friend.' Mrs Ishiyama was staring at me with a famished, straining, beseeching look on her face. 'You know what a good man my father was. Many Japanese do not understand him. You know. Like my mother, you know.'

'Thank you,' I said. I did not open the package. At that moment it seemed terribly heavy in my hand. 'Thank you.'

No longer in a whisper but in a voice clogged with tears, Mrs Ishiyama said something else.

'She says it is difficult to live without my father. She says that now she is always sad. She miss my father, always, always. She says King-san will understand that. King-san also love my father.'

I nodded mutely, the package like a lump of lead in my grasp.

Crash

In a Brighton neighbourhood as graceful as that, Number Eleven was generally thought to be a disgrace. A weeping eczema perpetually eroded a façade from which, on a still evening of the long, hot summer, part of the cornice suddenly slipped sideways, an erratic meteorite, and crashed downwards into the basement, where its rubble lay neglected for weeks and weeks on end.

On the first floor, its curtains never drawn together, a young Israeli student prowled about a room as naked as himself, until he temporarily disappeared out of sight on to the floor on which he slept, worked and ate. When he emerged on to the street, by now fully clothed, those who had merely seen him up in the house would experience surprise and even, in some cases, disappointment: the noble head and torso dwindled, tadpole-like, into legs so short and thin that they appeared almost to be deformed.

From the basement flat two youths with orange hair and tight leather trousers would bound up early each morning, a Dobermann gagging on a leash held by one of them. Neither the Dobermann nor they were seen for the rest of the day, though the throb, as persistent and sickening as a migraine, of their stereo playing pop music and an intermittent baying from the Dobermann when footfalls clacked in the street, proved that they must be at home.

The second-floor tenants were a wan, disconsolate girl, little more than a child, often to be seen wearily pushing a pram with twins in it up the hill from Western Road, and a man – husband or boyfriend no one knew – who, when not working as a jobbing builder, spent all his time painting a ramshackle Standard Vanguard, at least thirty years old, in swirling, psychedelic colours. Apparently this pair had no refrigerator – even though, like the two youths in the basement, they certainly had a hi-fi – since on their window-ledge high above the street bottles of milk, packets of butter, cartons of eggs and even dishes of left-over food could be glimpsed.

Alison, who lived in the first-floor flat in the neat house opposite to Number Eleven, often found herself looking out of her bedroom window. Through that late dusk the naked young Israeli moved about his melancholy errands, passing and repassing, the hair thick on his chest and even on his shoulder-blades. In the basement, the curtains would already be drawn across as the music thumped on and on and the dog bayed eerily. On the second floor – Alison would have to tip up her sleek head to see – the pale, thin-chested girl would be nursing one or other of the twins, a mulberry-like nipple plugging its greedy mouth, while below, out in the street, her beaky-nosed partner, his hair thinning at the crown, carefully loaded his brush with paint like molten silver. Mysterious, terrible, fascinating lives.

At the check-out at Marks & Spencer, money, two pence, five pence, ten pence pieces, rolled out of the wan girl's purse, its stitching unravelled at a corner, while the twins, tethered at either end of the pram, threw themselves about and screamed and screamed.

'Cheers,' the girl muttered when Alison had stooped and, with the assistance of a boy who happened to be passing, had collected all the coins and tipped them into the outstretched palm. Strange word that 'Cheers', as though Alison had bought her a drink. Did one say 'Cheers' back? The girl did not look at Alison, her eyes on the cash-register as though in terror that, if she glanced away for a moment, something extra might be dishonestly rung up. Clearly the girl did not realize that she and Alison lived opposite to each other and that, on those late summer evenings, Alison would stand behind her net curtains and watch her as she held one or other of the twins to her breast by the open window.

After that, in St Anne's Well Gardens, exercising her Yorkshire terrier, Snuff, Alison had once ventured a smile as the girl had passed, leaning against the pram as though she were some nineteenth-century woman pit-labourer pushing a truck almost too heavy for her to shift. But the girl had merely gazed at her, with a dazed, moony expression on a face gouged with deep shadows under high, hectic cheekbones. Mysterious, terrible, fascinating lives.

The Israeli student vanished – Alison could not remember who had told her that he was Israeli and a student, perhaps it was the Robinson-Beaumonts, they seemed to know everything about the tenants of that house, since they made a point of chatting to the elderly, dapper Pole in a pork-pie hat each time that he walked up from Brunswick Terrace, silver-knobbed cane in hand, to collect his rents – and he was succeeded by three Iranian ones, who were suspected of daubing the neighbouring walls and even a pillar-box with their slogans, anti-Khomeini or pro-Khomeini no one knew or cared.

One of the Iranians, pockmarked and with a moustache straggling untidily on either side of his full-lipped mouth, whistled at Alison in Western Road as she hurried off a bus thinking only, in a heat wave, of the cool water in which she would soak her body as soon as she had put out Snuff. When she made no response, he doggedly followed her, still hissing from time to time, to her front door. How old did he think she was, for Christ's sake? A woman of thirty-six, almost old enough to be his mother! The discovery that she lived opposite clearly caused him no embarrassment.

That was a particularly difficult summer in the firm in which she worked as an economic analyst. Old, easy-going Tommy Fairbairn retired, a dry, shrivelled leaf swept off the tree to which it had hung on so long, and eager, ambitious Eric Kloster, with his sweating, strangely pink palms, his limp and his stammer, had taken his place. Then Lettice, who shared Alison's office, had left to have her baby and the baby had had to have some dangerous operation because of a congenital defect of the heart and Lettice's leave had then been prolonged on and on, with Alison having to cope with her work as well as her own. 'Now don't you go getting married and having a baby,' Eric told her with his usual tactlessness. 'We can't do without you, as we can do without Lettice.'

Alison's widowed mother decided to leave one Kensington flat, because it was so noisy, and to move into another, no less noisy, not far from it. Alison had to help her. Her mother said, 'Oh, do let me get on with that, you've no idea what I want to keep and what I want to throw away.' Her mother said, 'You might not be here, for all the use you are to me.' Her mother said, 'Really, Alison, you always were the impractical one, weren't you?' The practical ones, her two older sisters, were both married with children and so of course they could not be expected to come and help.

In the flat below hers there was an elderly widower, a retired

Army officer. He and Alison had got on well for a number of years; but then suddenly he had become obsessed with 'that beastly little dog' – as he called Snuff even to Alison's face. 'That beastly little dog has deposited a turd just outside the gate.' 'That beastly little dog has brought in some mess.' 'This whole house is beginning to smell of that beastly little dog.' Beastly little man. But Alison, who was noted for her self-control both in the office and at home, did not say that to him, any more than she said what she wanted to say to Eric or her mother.

At her bedroom window, wishing that the Israeli student had not gone and that those dark, dwarfish Iranians had not taken his place, Alison heard a shrill voice: 'You bloody well leave that car alone and come and see to it yourself!' See to what? Alison had no idea. From the street the young man in the grease-smeared overalls shouted up to the girl in the pyjamas, leaning out of the window, 'Oh, fuck off! Do me a favour, will you? Just fuck off!' He disappeared under the car, only his legs protruding. The girl peered down, one of the twins in her arms. For a dreadful moment it seemed to Alison as though she were going to hurl the child down on top of him.

Alison and the Robinson-Beaumonts were having a drink in the pub on the corner where their street debouched into Upper North Street. Mr Robinson-Beaumont, who was an estate agent, told Alison that she was a fool not to have bought her flat when she had the opportunity. It was too late now, she would never manage to get a foot on the property ladder, not in a district like theirs. As a statutory tenant, he had been able to buy the freehold of his house for a few thou. (He liked to tell people, even strangers, about his good fortune.) Mrs Robinson-Beaumont remarked that she thought the beer was 'off'. 'Well, then, don't drink it,' her husband brusquely told her. 'Don't be daft!'

The wan girl came in, in slippers downtrodden at the heels. 'Have you seen Roy?' Alison heard her ask the ladylike barman who came from Perth. The barman shook his head: 'No, love. sorry.' 'Oh, sod him!' the girl cried out, seemingly on the verge of tears. She rushed out of the pub. 'Who'd want to be married?' the barman asked Alison. 'Night after night I go on my knees and render thanks to the Great Bachelor in the skies that at least he has saved me that. Don't you agree with me?' Alison smiled bravely: 'Oh, yes, yes.' She was in the habit of agreeing with people. That was why she was so often referred to as 'good old Alison' in the office, even if her promotion was long overdue.

The girl stood, hands on hips, on the pavement that Sunday morning and screamed at the pair of legs protruding from underneath the banger: 'You promised! You bloody well promised! Just as you promised last Sunday and the Sunday before it!' A voice, oddly high-pitched for a man so tall, emerged: 'Just as soon as I've fixed this oil-leak, I'll take you.' 'You've been working at that bleeding wreck for the best part of this year. Oh, sod it – and sod you!' Alison retreated from her open window. She did not want to hear any more. All that raw aggression made her feel sick, as steak tartare made her feel sick.

Alison's mother rang. What she said, when not interrupted by gulping sobs which made it sound as though she had whooping-cough, was that she hated the new flat, she would never be happy in it, it was even more noisy than the other one and there was this terrible stink, there was no other word for it, this terrible stink from that take-away on the corner. Alison should have dissuaded her from moving. 'Why did you let me come here, why did you let me? Don't you care about me at all?' Alison said soothingly that she was sure that her mother would get used to the flat, it was such a lovely flat, so much roomier and lighter and in every way more convenient than the other.

The wan girl, hair flopping loose, ran down the steps, a child in the crook of either arm. Tears were streaming down her cheeks, though, oddly, her face did not move. One of the Iranians was perched on the balustrade, hissing from time to time at outraged or secretly flattered women, and as she pushed past him, she almost kicked him. He asked. 'Is there something wrong, lady?' She stopped, she stared at him. Then she shouted at him, 'You bet your bloody life there is!' She raced off down the road, jerking the children up and down. Alison let the net curtain fall. She picked up Snuff, pressing a cheek to his wiry coat. Then the telephone began to ring. It was Eric. There was something he had to clear up, he hated to ring her at this hour, it was about that report, that report from Sussex University.

*

The pram was empty of the children but loaded with groceries. Hair stuck in damp wisps to the girl's forehead and in no less damp tendrils to the vulnerable back of her neck. Where were the children? Alison did not dare to ask. Presumably their father was with them. 'Good morning,' she said. The girl stared fiercely at her, as though the greeting were an insult. In the pram there was a cardboard case, then another piled on top of it, and three full plastic bags. Later, Mrs Robinson-Beaumont, having also seen the girl, was to say to Alison that she could not imagine where these people got their money from – pram piled high with shopping, that hi-fi booming away all day, the husband more often tinkering at that unsightly wreck of a car than doing a decent day's work. She went on, 'Mr Robinson-Beaumont has had such a piece of luck. He's just put through a deal for that lovely old house in Montpelier Road, the one that was just collapsing from neglect. Arabs, from one of the Emirates. They've set their hearts on chopping down the old sycamore. There's a preservation order on it, as he's told them. But what's a fine of a thousand or so to people as rich as that?'

The old colonel was in the hall, turning over a pile of letters for tenants long since vanished, with blue-veined, arthritic hands. The letters accumulated there, week after week. No one bothered to forward them. This time he merely scowled at Snuff, he made no comment about him. But his small eyes blazing and a choleric flush spreading up from his pointed chin to eyebrows that looked as though he had singed them when lighting his pipe, he complained to Alison: 'My pension has got lost. Cheque.'

Alison smiled placatingly.

'Someone must have taken it,' he pursued. 'Stolen it.'

Alison began to mount the stairs to her flat.

'Haven't you seen it?' He craned his neck upwards.

'No, I'm afraid I haven't.'

Her heart was thumping in time to the thumping from across the way, as she stooped and removed the delicately plaited lead from Snuff's collar.

That night, as she sat reading a book, Snuff in her lap and a towel wrapped round and round her head – she had just given her hair its weekly wash – Alison heard an explosive crash. Her first thought was that the IRA must have let off a bomb, but when she had hurried to the window and peered out into the street, she realized that there had been a collision between two cars. She raised the net curtain to see better through the late dusk. It was the Standard Vanguard, in its screaming, psychedelic colours, and the almost new Volvo which belonged to the Robinson-Beaumonts. Mrs Robinson-Beaumont ran out of the next-door house, all but tripping on her high heels, and began to yelp, 'What are you doing? What are you doing?' People began to race up the hill from the pub, some of them with glasses or tankards still in their hands. Three moustached faces appeared at the first-floor window opposite and the Dobermann Pinscher began to bay. The Standard Vanguard rocked backwards and then, with a screeching of its tyres, lurched away from the pavement, grazing the Volvo with its bumper. Mrs Robinson-Beaumont put plump hands to her quivering cheeks and let out a piercing scream. The Vanguard zigzagged down the road, making inquisitive drinkers leap for safety. Then the ancient car shot sideways and banged another parked car, a Jaguar belonging to the young couple, barristers both, with the twin brass carriage lamps and the foot-scraper outside the twee-est house in the row, inflicting a long graze. Alison now leant out of her bedroom window. 'What's going on?' she heard someone ask and someone else then shouted, 'Ring for the police!' Mrs Robinson-Beaumont pointed: 'Look what she's done to our Volvo 267! It's not even a year old!' 'Hey!' someone bellowed and someone else, leaping in front of the Vanguard and then leaping back again as it bore down on him, emitted a feeble 'Stop!' A woman screamed as the car lurched towards her on the pavement, took a sharp turn away from her and then crashed into the side of a car on the opposite corner. It backed, shot forward, rammed another car. 'Where the hell are the police?' Mr Robinson-Beaumont demanded, arriving in pyjamas and dressing-gown.

A muscular, hirsute young man, whom someone had once identified to Alison as an actor on television, ran down the steps of the house in which he lived with his mother and father. In track-suit and sneakers – he jogged late each evening – he ran after the car and tried repeatedly to wrench open the door beside the driver. But the car bounded off – that was the only word to describe it, it seemed to Alison to leap into the air – and the young man bounced off it, rolling over and over in the road. 'Are you hurt?' A girl stooped over him, a glass in her hand. He rose groggily, eyes screwed up in manifest pain and a hand pressed to the small of his back. 'Seem . . . to have . . . have . . . twisted something . . .' he gasped.

The Vanguard had turned to the left and vanished from sight. But Alison could still hear repeated detonations as it crashed into one car after another. The crowd were in pursuit, with the exception of Mr and Mrs Robinson-Beaumont, who were circling their Volvo in stricken disbelief, and the actor in his track-suit, who was now seated on the steps of his parents' house, with the girl stranger beside him.

Police cars suddenly arrived, sirens squealing and lights flashing, and men in uniform began to race up and down the street. 'Where's the husband then?' one of the policemen asked, and the bald man who owned the local paper-shop answered, 'Gawd knows!' 'She must have gone berserk then,' the policeman said, hurrying off.

The crowds were soon drifting back to the pub, in a state of garrulous exaltation reminiscent of the aftermath of some bomb incident in the War. Some of them once again examined the damage, pointing out to each other some particularly vicious dent or laceration. Eventually, policemen began to ring at all the houses. One of them, a pink-faced youth with a girlishly dimpled chin and a helmet seemingly far too large for his long, narrow head, pressed against all three bells of the house in which Alison had her flat. Alison went downstairs – there was no intercom – and found herself in the hall with the retired colonel. The colonel pushed officiously past her and opened the door. 'Yes, officer,' he said.

The policeman asked if either of them had seen the young lady who had been in charge of the car.

'Hardly in charge, officer,' the colonel said. 'What a bust-up! I always thought there was something unsavoury about that pair. Where's he got to?'

The policeman shrugged. 'You haven't seen her then? She's not on your premises?'

'Not on mine unless she is hiding in my dustbin.'

'Nor on mine,' Alison said.

The policeman asked about the other flat. Alison explained that its owners were in Vermont for the summer. 'Lucky beggars,' put in the colonel. 'Pots of money. Yanks.'

The policeman thanked them and left.

The colonel, more affable than he had been for months,

chuckled and said to Alison, 'What a rum show!' In his slippers, he padded down the corridor to the entrance to his flat. 'Bloody rum.' Again he chuckled.

Eventually there was a silence in the neighbourhood. The people had all left the narrow street to go their separate ways: Mrs Robinson-Beaumont shepherded indoors by her husband, a consolatory arm around her shoulder; the young actor suggesting to the girl that she should pop in for a nightcap; the Iranians returning to their room, their figures monstrously misshapen as the unshaded overhead light silhouetted them against the bedsheets which did them service for curtains. Alison read for a while, but her attention would not focus. She was reading a detective novel by a colleague but it might have been some file or report, brought home with her, for the difficulty she had with it.

Eventually, around midnight, she aroused Snuff, who had been snoring and twitching in her lap, attached his collar and coaxed him down the stairs. Like Alison's mother, he had come, with advancing years, to loathe any kind of exercise.

As she passed one wrecked car after another, Alison was first appalled and then exhilarated by the extent of the damage. Here fragments of orange glass littered the road – 'Take care, Snuff! Don't go there! You'll only cut your paws' – and here a bumper hung askew. A couple, only just returned from a social at the Conservative Association, were staring at the damage to their Cortina. The man moaned, 'Christ! Oh, my Christ! How could – how could . . .? Oh, no!' Alison tried to explain to them what had happened but they seemed to be incapable of taking it in, the man repeating, 'Christ! Oh, my Christ!' in awe-struck disbelief, while the woman drawled in Mayfair Cockney, 'But how are we to get home, Bunny?'

Round the corner, the damage was even worse, with cars with huge lacerations along their sides or spilling their guts into the road, their bonnets shattered. Snuff slipped between a once jaunty MG, now lying on its side, and a dented Rover with a numberplate consisting of two letters and a single figure, and cocked a leg on a discarded carton. That a dog so small could contain so much – 'Multum in parvo,' Eric had once quipped – was amazing. He gazed up at Alison for approval but she was too busy examining the cars about her to say her customary 'Good boy.'

Then, by the pillar-box at the far end of the road, she saw, half on the pavement and half off it, the Standard Vanguard. One bumper was dimpled, the other had been torn off. The windscreen was criss-crossed with a glittering cobweb of fractures. A door hung askew. One tyre was flat. The psychedelic swirls at which the beaky-nosed man in the grimy overalls had worked so patiently and persistently evening after evening and Sunday after Sunday all through that summer were now chipped and gouged. But where was the girl? Where could she have vanished?

Snuff, an aristocratic dog with all the scavenging instincts of a pariah, tugged at his lead in an attempt to investigate an abandoned McDonald's packet lying crushed – no doubt by the Vanguard – in the centre of the road. Alison fastidiously tugged him back, all but choking him as he persisted in straining stubbornly in the opposite direction. A young couple passed, arm in arm, and then paused, gazing in amazement at the line of wrecked cars. 'What on earth's been going on here?' the woman asked the man. Alison felt no temptation to tell them, though they both looked at her enquiringly.

She turned up the next street in order to make the usual rectangle of Snuff's late-night walk and passed under a straggling honeysuckle before a derelict house now in the untidy process of being converted into flats. The scent was heavy, sickly. Snuff again tugged at his lead, managed to jerk it from Alison's grip, and disappeared under a van so ramshackle and rusty that it could only have been abandoned.

'Snuff! Come out of there! Snuff! Here!'

Invisible, Snuff was snuffling. Then he began to emit a series of high-pitched yelps. Alison stooped and peered under the van. She glimpsed something white, then the outline of a shoe. Her first appalled thought was that the van must have run over someone, before its driver had abandoned it. But then she heard a wail: 'Oh, shit, shit, shit!'

She knew that voice. 'What's the matter? Are you hurt?'

'Can't you get that bloody dog of yours away?'

'Snuff! Come here! Come here at once!'

The body beneath the van began to shift; the shoe emerged from under it.

'Have they gone?'

'Have who gone?'

'The coppers. All that mob.'

'There's no one here but me. They were looking for you.'

'I bet they were.' The girl slid herself along the tarmac and eventually emerged, dishevelled and dust-covered, on hands and knees, with Snuff beside her, sniffing at her lank hair. There was a dark smear over one of those hectic cheekbones, which Alison realized, with a shock, could only be blood.

'Are you all right?' Alison put out a hand.

The girl did not take it as she staggered to her feet. 'What a lark!' she half giggled and half gasped. Then she screwed up her face and, bending over double, clutched at a knee with both her hands. 'Ooh, my knee!' Snuff began to jump up around her, squeaking shrilly. 'Can't you keep that dog of yours off?'

Alison stooped and picked up the trailing lead. 'Have you broken anything?'

'Only a lot of glass. Though it feels as if I'd broken every bone in my body. What a lark! What a lark!' She surveyed the wrecked cars around them.

'Would you like to come back to my place? I can give you a drink and – and help you to tidy up.'

'Where would your place be?'

Alison was amazed that the girl should be so unobservant. 'Opposite yours,' she said.

'OK. Why not?' The girl pulled a handkerchief out of the pocket of her skirt and began to wipe at her face.

'Where's your – your husband?' Alison ventured, as the girl limped along beside her, from time to time still rubbing at her face with the handkerchief.

'At the in-laws. The twins are with him. I wasn't going to take any more of that crap from him – or from that mother of his. I blew my top – just ran out of the house and jumped on the first 38, as it happened to stop at the traffic-lights.' She laughed to herself. 'Well, he's in for a nice surprise! Wouldn't take the banger – said some paint had to dry.'

Alison found herself laughing too, at the thought of the beaky-nosed young man gazing in consternation at the wreck of the car which had absorbed all his attention and energies for so long.

'Nice place,' the girl said, gazing around her, when they had mounted to the flat.

'Not too bad.'

'D'you live here all alone then?'

Alison nodded. 'All alone.'

'Lucky you.'

Was she lucky? Alison wondered.

The girl gave a little whimper when, in the bathroom, Alison dabbed at her lacerated cheek and knee with cotton wool soaked in Dettol. Then she put out a still grubby hand and took up the tumbler of whisky she had placed on the lowered cover of the lavatory bowl. She gulped. 'That'll go straight to my head,' she giggled. Then she added, 'Though all those cops and people would say I'd lost it already. Wouldn't they?'

Seated opposite to Alison in the sitting-room, now wearing a pair of Alison's tights in place of her own torn and soiled ones, the girl said, 'God, if you could meet that mother of his! You'd think I'd neglected those twins instead of sweating away to look after them properly, hour after hour, day in and day out. And you'd think I'd neglected him too. He's so fussy, you'd never believe. Finicky. It's his mother, of course. Spoiled him rotten.'

Later, the girl lay out on the floor, a cushion behind her head – 'Mind if I stretch myself out? I'm aching in every joint' – and puffed contentedly at one of the cigarettes that Alison had offered her from a box kept for visitors. 'What d'you think they'll do to me?' she asked dreamily, without any trace of worry. 'Put me away?'

'Oh, no, I don't think so.' Alison could foresee the remand for medical reports, the visits from officials, perhaps even a spell as an out-patient.

'One thing's for sure – we'll never be able to pay for all that damage. Not in a thousand years.' Clearly the girl derived pleasure from that thought. She laughed, raising her head off the cushion and holding the rim of her third glass of whisky against her lower lip. Alison had never seen her so animated. Thrusting the pram up Montpelier Road or scrabbling in her purse for coins at the check-out at Marks & Spencer, she had always looked so tired and discouraged. 'We've no savings,' she said. 'Not a bean. It's all we can do to pay the rent, I can tell you that.'

Eventually the girl got up unsteadily off the floor and said she ought to be on her way. 'He's staying overnight with his mother. She gets nervous on her own when his father's away. Lorry-driver.' She grinned. 'Well, the two of them can bloody well mind the twins between them, can't they? I'm not going back there – even if I could find the transport. I'm going to have a good kip. My first for months, what with the kids crying.'

On the doorstep Alison said, 'If there's anything . . . anything I can . . . if you should need . . .'

'You've been sweet.' The girl skipped down the steps, her bruises and lacerations all forgotten. Then she turned. 'I can't tell you, can't describe. It was that exciting. Bang, bang, bang! Crash, wallop! Glass everywhere! Like the dodgems, only much better. Oh, I can't wait to see his face!' she cried out. 'I can't wait!' She ran towards the gate, opened it, waved a hand. 'Anyway cheers! I'm ever so grateful! Truly!'

Alison remounted the stairs, Snuff behind her, and went back into her flat. She picked the cushion up off the floor of the sitting-room and, as she replaced it on the sofa, noticed that there was a smear of blood on its turquoise damask. But, usually so house-proud, she now did not care. She next took up the half-drunk third glass of whisky, put it to her lips and drained it at a gulp.

She went across the landing to her bedroom. The curtains were undrawn from that time when she had stood in the darkness, listening to that banging of metal and screeching of rubber and that uproar of voices, and looking down on to the Vanguard as it lurched and bounded hither and thither on its destructive last journey. She again went over to the window and again stood, silent and motionless in the darkness, gazing first down into the street below her and then across at the opposite house. There was no one about, everything was still.

She felt a mounting excitement and, with it, a mounting joy. An incandescent wire seemed to vibrate on and on, higher and higher, brighter and brighter, at the centre of the dimness and dependence of her life. She knew that she would not be able to sleep that night. Perhaps she would not even go to bed.

The Burning Glass

My father was loosening his Leander Club tie as, charcoal pin-stripe jacket already removed, he stepped out through the french windows into the garden. All that summer of 1939 we had seemed to be living under a gigantic burning glass. As he approached us, where we lolled out in deck chairs, I inwardly shrank from the peppery smell of his sweat. He was a man who sweated a lot, so that even in winter his forehead and nose would glisten and that peppery smell would seep out of him after he had done nothing more strenuous than sweep up leaves or mend a fuse.

'This'll tickle you all,' he said, not realizing that we were all far too hot and lethargic to wish to be tickled. 'On the way home I dropped in on Lucy.' Lucy was his unmarried, older sister, a gynaecologist, who shared a flat with Ruth, a physiotherapist. 'She told me an absolutely priceless story about Ruth.' He dragged a deck chair out of the sunlight into the shade beside us. With a groan and a sigh he lowered himself into it. Ruth, like Lucy, was a pacifist. 'It seems that she was at Speakers' Corner last Sunday, giving her support to that Donald Soapbox creature, who was spouting there. There was some woman present – a sensible body by the sound of it – who kept heckling him. Ruth told her to shut her trap or to put a sock in it or something equally inelegant, and the woman then lost her rag and answered back in kind. In no time at all, the two of them were screaming abuse at each other. And then our Ruth, our peace-at-all-price Ruth, disciple of John Muddleton Merry and the Great Mahatma, socked the other woman, socked her not once but twice, knocked off her hat and began to pull her hair. So she got herself arrested – aggravated assault, was it? – something like that. And had to pay a whopping fine. Or, rather, Lucy had to pay it, since Ruth, as we all know, gives so much money to charity that Lucy's only charity has now become Ruth.' My father laughed. 'Isn't that just

marvellous? I love the idea of a pacifist being had up for assault.'
He laughed again. 'Don't you love it, Deirdre?'

My mother, who had been gazing at him with a characteristi-
cally rueful, bemused expression over the top of one of the
detective stories which were now her staple reading ('I'm afraid
I'm letting my mind go,' this former teacher of English would
often sigh as she asked me to bring her back yet another from
Mudie's Library), twitched her mouth in an effort at a smile.
'Yes,' she said. 'Yes. Marvellous!' She began to fan her face with
the book. 'It's so hot. Why does it have to be so hot?'

I got up from my chair and began to wander across the lawn
towards the house. I somehow knew that my father would be
scowling at my back. At any moment he would be shouting after
me: 'Doesn't anything ever amuse you?'

But fortunately my sister, Ivy, then distracted him. 'I can't see
what Lucy sees in Ruth. I mean, they seem so incompatible.
What *do* they have in common?'

Yes, people could be as innocent as that then.

I went up to my little room under the eaves of the house,
crossed over to the window and stared down. My father had
now got up from his deck chair and was leaning over my mother.
He put out a hand and eased her book away from her. He turned
a page, read out something from it, and then laughed. He often
mocked at this addiction of hers – 'Here we all are, preparing for
Armageddon, and there you are interested in nothing but
mayhem in vicarages, country houses and gentlemen's clubs.'

I thought again of Ruth's conviction for assault.

Bloody fool!

Have you never been inconsistent? You're always talking
about honesty but only yesterday – no, the day before – you
showed me the change the girl at the Gaumont had handed you
and said: 'Look what she's given me! Ten shillings too much!'
You didn't go back. You just walked on. How is a man who calls
himself honest but goes off with change not due to him any more
consistent than a pacifist who commits assault?

Answer that!

But how could he answer that when, as so often, I'd lacked the
courage to put the question?

Instead of putting the question, I'd merely run away.

*

As we walked along the towpath my father detonated one of his puns, as noisome and as unfunny as a fart, burst into laughter, and then threw his arm around my shoulder and briefly hugged me to him. There were often such moments, islanded in a sea of disapproval, irritation and sarcasm, when I thought, both astonished and guilty: He's fond of me, he's actually fond of me! Strangely, although it was obvious that he was far fonder of my elder brother, Giles, I had never seen him put his arm round Giles and hug him in that same fashion. Perhaps Giles's bulk made it more difficult to do so. I came up only to my father's shoulder.

My father breathed deeply three or four times, in through the nose, out through the mouth. ('Fill up your lungs! Fill up your lungs!' he would sometimes admonish one or other of us. 'You don't know how to breathe.') Then he squinted at an eight scissoring its way up the river. 'Dreadfully ragged,' he said.

When I coxed, did I sound as girlishly shrill as that diminutive figure, a pink-and-white cap making it difficult to discern his features, perched up in the stern? I hated coxing. I coxed only to please my father, a former Oxford Blue, who now coached a crew from his stockbroking firm, with the addition of myself.

'There's going to be a war,' my father said apropos of nothing.

'Do you think so?' I still believed that war could be averted.

'I'm sure of it. And it's not going to be any more of a picnic than the last one.' My father had won a DSO in the trenches. 'I wish you and Giles were five years younger.'

Oh but, Father, I'm not going to fight in this war.

Instead of saying that, I merely stared out over the river at the gardens of Fulham Palace. Suddenly I was once more aware of that peppery smell.

'What's the betting one of them is late? If I can be on time, then why can't all of them?' He quickened his pace as though to ensure for himself the satisfaction that at least one of the crew arrived after we did.

I unloaded from the back of Lucy's box-like Morris, dating from the Twenties, the platform which I had constructed, using a folding step-ladder as its base. Leah, a fellow art student, whose sturdy bare legs, strong bare arms and thick black hair filled me with a palpitating excitement, hauled out the copies of *Peace*

News which she had made into two untidy bundles held together by lengths of hairy green string. The string had come from a ball used by Ruth to tie up plants in the narrow tongue of garden which stuck out from the rear of the cramped basement flat which she and Lucy shared.

'Are you sure you can manage that, Noel?' Ruth always asked that question of me, without ever actually providing any assistance. 'Would you like a hand, Leah?' She always also asked that question of Leah, without ever actually providing any assistance to her either. Lucy herself never once made such offers. Perhaps, as speaker, she felt that she was doing enough for the cause already.

'I do think it's clever of you to have made that platform,' Leah said over her shoulder as she strode out ahead of me. Lucy had been less complimentary about my handiwork. 'It seems awfully rickety. I hope it's not going to collapse under me. I'd look a real chump.'

Leah favoured a porridgey impasto, grey, beige and white, for the huge non-representational oils which she dashed off with so much speed. Lucy had bought one of them as a birthday present for Ruth, and it now hung, slightly askew, like so much else in their lives, between their two beds. She had never bought one of my meticulous watercolours. That hurt me.

Perhaps because of the heat, the crowd at Speakers' Corner was large but unusually lethargic. Sweating people, some of them trailing cowed dogs or fractious children, drifted from group to group. There was little of the usual heckling until Lucy, dressed in a crisp white linen dress, with a belt woven of small green, red and yellow beads, began to speak. I had made a wooden railing for the platform and she gripped this in both her strong, square hands. Her voice, so low in conversation, had a remarkable carrying power on these occasions. What she said, about the immorality of killing, about the devastation of air raids, and about the futility of imagining that a war could ever solve anything at all, I had heard often enough before. But once again I thrilled to it, as did Ruth and Leah. Ruth and I were stationed behind the platform; Leah beside it, with one of the bundles of *Peace News* on the ground at her feet and the other, its string removed, over an arm. Round her neck she wore a leather purse on a strap.

At that period of simultaneous dread of the war which most

people now regarded as inevitable and guilt at yet another ignoble postponement of it, any pacifist could be sure of a rough reception at Speakers' Corner. But the rougher the reception, the more Lucy came to resemble some medieval saint, her eyes closed in ecstasy and a seraphic smile on her lips even as her torturers inflict the most refined atrocities on her.

The chief of the hecklers was, as so often, a plump middle-aged man in a bowler hat, rakishly tipped over a sparse, sandy eyebrow which looked as if he had drawn it there in pencil; a grey pin-stripe suit, the trousers so short that they revealed the grey woollen socks which he wore even on a day as hot as this; and a grey-and-white striped shirt surmounted by a stiff collar into which the hard, unmoving little knot of his tie seemed to have been screwed. Every Sunday afternoon he was there; always unaccompanied, always in that same garb, and always propping himself negligently sideways on an unfurled umbrella, its black cotton bleached at its struts. Sometimes he would content himself with a derisive 'Oh, I say, I say, I say!' in what he saw as an exquisitely funny imitation of Lucy's lah-di-dah voice. Sometimes he would shout out something like 'That's rich, that really is rich!', 'You can't expect anyone to swallow that!', 'Trust you to make a meal of that argument!', 'Well, that finally takes the biscuit!' or 'Aren't you rather over-egging the cake?' It was Ruth who first pointed out how so many of his metaphors seemed to derive from food. Mightn't he be a cook? she sometimes surmised. But I preferred to think of him as a bank clerk, swallowing back all the aggression which he felt against tiresome customers weekday after weekday, only to void it, an explosive, bitter vomit, on Saturday and Sunday. There was only one mystery: why, when there were so many other speakers on such a variety of topics – naturism, Buddhism, Marxism, vegetarianism, spiritualism – did he always choose Lucy for his target?

That day he was particularly vehement. 'You ought to be locked up!' 'If you love your chum Adolf so much, why don't you take yourself off to live with him in Germany?' 'Haven't you any shame?'

A small, wizened woman, standing beside him, her near-toothless jaws chomping – I imagined her, for some reason, as running a small sweet-shop or drapery store – would from time to time vehemently applaud these remarks: 'Yes! Yes! ... That's right! ... That's the whole point! ... Answer that one!' Might it have been she whom Ruth had assaulted? I had been too embarrassed to ask Ruth about that incident or even to refer to it.

Lucy spoke of turning the other cheek, as she often did.

The heckler let out a derisive cackle of laughter. 'Just listen to that!' He turned to the people on either side and behind him. 'Turn the other cheek! Haven't you realized, darling, that if someone slaps one of your cheeks and you then present him with the other, then the likelihood is that he'll slap that one too?'

Most of the others greeted this observation with approving jeers and hoots of laughter.

'Yes, of course I've realized. *Darling*,' Lucy added, leaning forward on the platform. (Oh God, don't let it collapse, don't let it collapse!) 'But that doesn't alter what I was saying. Not one bit. You get one slap and you turn the other cheek. You get a slap on that cheek, and you turn the original one. And so on. And on. Eventually it will work. Eventually.'

'Sounds a mug's game to me,' the near-toothless woman cried out. One could imagine her husband returning drunk from the pub and giving her a cuff. She would certainly not turn the other cheek, she would go for him, spitting and scratching like some famished alley cat.

'I dare say that, when Christ preached the Sermon on the Mount, there were a lot of people who thought him a mug.' The reference was too arcane, the sarcasm too lofty for Lucy's riposte to impress such an audience.

When Lucy had clambered down from the platform – Ruth and I both held out hands to support her but it was only Ruth's that she took – she had that dazed, exalted look which she always had after one of her speeches. She drew a lace-edged handkerchief out of a pocket and began to mop her wide, low forehead.

The crowd was beginning to drift away.

'*Peace News*! *Peace News*!' Leah began to call out, in that loud, clear voice so different from her usual soft, husky one.

'You were marvellous,' Ruth told Lucy. 'As always. That goes without saying.'

'*Peace News*!'

As I folded the platform, I caught a forefinger in a hinge. Ouch! I pulled a face.

'Have you hurt yourself?' Leah sounded genuinely concerned.

'No, no. Not really.'

The heckler, who had been chatting to the near-toothless woman, now approached Leah. He pointed with his umbrella at the copy of *Peace News* which she was holding out to the indifferent people hurrying past her.

'I'm truly amazed that you should be selling that rag.'

'Are you? Why?'

'Well, it's easy to tell from your looks that you're one of the long-nosed fraternity. And if Hitler were to come over here, you'd be one of the first to suffer, now wouldn't you? I shouldn't care to be one of your lot if Hitler were to come.'

Slow in her responses even in the course of an ordinary conversation, Leah at first merely blushed, frowned and shifted as though her body were itching in its clothes. But I knew that really she was furious. 'Well . . .' she eventually said. Then: 'Do you have to talk to people in that – that very rude way?'

It was then that I intervened. I was even more furious than she was. I hated that voice which, snootily drawling, did not even have the courage of its own commonness; I hated that pudgy, pink face; above all, I hated that bowler hat tilted over one sparse, sandy eyebrow. I advanced on him. I could understand how Ruth had committed her assault.

It was, however, in a quiet, reasonable voice that I forced myself to speak. 'Yes, you're right. My friend is Jewish. So there's absolutely no self-interest in her pacifism, quite the reverse. If one holds a belief which, so far from benefiting oneself, is likely to do one harm, isn't that an indication of how sincere one is? Yes?'

The man stared at me, umbrella at half-mast, as though he were about either to poke me or strike me with it. Then, in a strident, crude voice – now it certainly had the courage of its commonness – he said: 'Oh fuck off, you self-righteous little prick!' He turned on his heel and strode off.

'Charming! Charming, I must say!' Ruth called after him.

'Did he say prick or prig?' Lucy asked.

'Prick, dear. *Prick!*'

Then we all burst into laughter.

Later that afternoon the four of us sat out in the garden, sipping at the iced lemon barley water which Ruth had twice told us that she herself had prepared. One of her patients – 'absolutely *twisted* with spondylitis, like a tree really, poor creature' – had given her the recipe.

'When are you going to tell your father?' It was a question which Lucy often put to me. Since I could not answer it, it always irritated me.

I shrugged.

'Sooner or later, you'll have to tell him,' Ruth said. 'If war comes, then conscription's certain to come with it.'

'Your brother's in the Terriers, isn't he?' Leah said. She had never met any of my family.

'Well, kind of. He's training as a pilot.'

Oh, why couldn't they leave the whole subject alone? Why couldn't they mind their own business?

'If you liked, I could tell him,' Lucy volunteered, discreetly spitting out a lemon-pip into her palm and then dropping it to the ground.

She had made this offer before. Oh, no, no, *no!*

I said: 'No, I must tell him.'

'Yes, you *must,*' Ruth said.

'The longer you delay it, the worse it will be,' Leah opined.

Why did she have to gang up with the others?

'It's a question of choosing the right moment.'

'You've been waiting for the right moment for an awfully long time,' Lucy said.

The moment finally came some months after the outbreak of war. It came because, on the evening before my brother left home to join the Air Force, we had a party for him, and in a mood compounded in equal measure of isolation, guilt and despondency, I had managed to drink too much.

There were many girls at the party, since Giles had many girlfriends; and there were also cronies of my father, sleek men in well-cut suits and handmade shoes, with jovially booming voices, and their elegant, self-effacing wives. My sister Ivy's boyfriend, a handsome, vacuous lieutenant in the Coldstream, soon to be killed in an accident on Salisbury Plain, was there; but Leah, although I had invited her, had failed either to put in an appearance or to excuse herself for not doing so.

Soon after eleven, the 'grown-ups' (as I still thought of them) began to drift off; and it was then that Giles had suggested, 'How about going on to Skindles?' Eventually all the young people without cars were crowding into the cars of those with them. 'It's all right if I take the old bus, isn't it, Dad?' Giles said. The 'old bus' was an Armstrong Siddeley. 'Yes, go ahead, go ahead!' Ivy's boyfriend had a long, low, open, powder blue Lagonda with crimson upholstery.

I made no move to accompany them; and none of them, not even Giles or Ivy, urged me to do so.

Our maid, Betty, and the hired waiters began to clear up the mess. My father sank into a chair and my mother into another.

'Well, that was a very successful occasion,' my father said.

'Even if rather a sad one.'

'Sad?'

'Well, Giles going off to the war tomorrow.'

My father laughed. 'Well, you *are* a gloomy one! He's not going all that far, you know. In fact, only as far as Norfolk.'

That did not console my mother. She looked despondent, as she got up off the chair into which she had so recently sunk, picked up her latest detective story off the top of the piano, and said: 'Well, I'm off to Bedfordshire.'

'Oughtn't you to . . .?' My father's voice was low as he indicated the two members of the temporary staff who were loading a trolley with glasses. 'Oh, I can leave everything to Betty.' My mother usually did leave everything to do with the household to Betty, who had been with us for as long as I could remember.

'Another swig?'

'No thanks.' I placed my glass on the floor beside me. I'd already had at least one swig too many.

'Can't do you any harm.' My father was in a jovial mood. 'It's not as though you had any classes tomorrow.' I had just gained my diploma at the Byam Shaw School.

'No thanks.'

'What happened to your girlfriend?'

I never thought of Leah as my girlfriend. She had too many boyfriends for that.

'She didn't come.'

'Yes, I know that, I know that. The question is – why didn't she come?'

'Search me.'

'Not an altogether reliable young miss. Eh?'

I did not answer.

Ruminatively my father sipped at his neat whisky and sipped again.

Then he said: 'Well, I suppose you'll be getting your own call-up soon. Any day now. And then it'll be your turn for a farewell party.'

'No.'

I amazed myself as much as I puzzled him with the monosyllable.

He stared at me. 'What do you mean No?'

'No.'

'I don't get you.'

'When I get my call-up papers, I'm planning to register as a conscientious objector.'

'*What? . . .* Bloody hell!'

He was not as amazed as he pretended to be or as he would have been if my brother and not I had made that confession.

I forced myself to look at him, as into a painfully dazzling searchlight. I nodded my head. 'I've thought a lot about it.'

Suddenly he exploded: 'This is Lucy's fault!'

'I told you, Daddy – I've thought a lot about it.'

'She's got an excuse of a kind. You haven't.'

'What do you mean?'

'Well, her fiancé being killed in the last show. Though I'm convinced that, if he'd come back, he'd have changed his mind about her.'

'I don't think her pacifism has anything to do with that. She's far too rational, unemotional.'

He seemed not to have heard me. He gulped at his drink. 'How am I going to explain this? Tell me that! How am I going to explain this?'

'Explain it? Explain it to whom'?'

'To everyone!'

Of course he meant, to those sleek, loud-voiced cronies of his and their elegant, self-effacing wives.

'I'm sorry, Daddy. But there it is.'

'There it bloody well is! Fucking hell!'

After I had registered as a conscientious objector, many weeks passed before my tribunal. During that period, I suffered a paralysis of will, such as I had never known before and have never known since. For much of the day I lay out on my bed, sometimes listening to music on my portable gramophone, sometimes reading one of the detective stories which I brought back for my mother from Mudie's, and sometimes merely staring up at the ceiling. From time to time I used to drag myself out to visit Lucy and Ruth. At weekends I also still accompanied them to Speakers' Corner. The heckler had disappeared – evacuated, called up, too busy? – but in his place I was from time to time conscious of two men in dark suits and grey trilby hats who, Lucy assured me, must be from MI5. Leah was no longer with us. Having accompanied her doctor father and her mother to Wales ('Trust them to skedaddle to the safest place they could find,' my father commented), she was teaching art in a school for mentally retarded children. From time to time she wrote me letters which appeared to be composed of lengthy extracts from her diary, totally devoid of any affection for me or, indeed, of any interest in my doings.

'Why don't you get on with your painting?' my mother asked.

'Because it's no good.'

'But you've done some lovely things. You've so much talent. Everyone says that.'

'Only your chums. Who want to be kind or polite.'

'Why do you have to be so cynical, darling?'

My father was far less tolerant. He would come home exhausted either from his office – where, he would often proclaim, he was doing the work of three other people in addition to his own – or from his duties as an Air Raid Warden. 'So what have you done for the war effort today?' he would ask me over supper.

'Oh, Jack, do leave the boy alone!'

'I'm only asking. I'm interested.'

On one such evening, he suddenly leaned across the table, his face grey with fatigue and ugly with resentment: 'Why don't you get yourself a job?' He might have been asking, 'Why don't you get lost?' or 'Why don't you drown yourself?'

'Oh, Jack, you know he's waiting for his tribunal.'

'Just as the rest of us are waiting for a possible invasion.'

'Oh, Jack!'

But even my mother, so impractical and seemingly so detached from the world drama exploding all around her, was now putting in several hours each week with the St John Ambulance Brigade.

Two days later I roused myself to call in at an academic

agency, to ask if there was any temporary work available for an art master. Yes, certainly there was – 'They're digging seventy- and even eighty-year-olds out of mothballs,' I was told by a pale, wrinkled, wizened man who looked as if he had just been dug out of mothballs himself.

I wrote off a number of letters of application; but they received either no answers or else rejections discouraging in their polite formality.

'I can't describe to you the things I saw last night. Horrific. There was this old girl, one of your true East Enders ... No ...' My father broke off. 'Better not to dwell on it ... I don't seem to have any appetite. What I think I need is a drink!'

'Oh, not at breakfast, Jack!'

But my father lurched up from the table and fetched himself half a tumbler of whisky. It was during those days that he began the heavy drinking that was eventually to cause him to die of liver failure several years later.

Betty, still with us, came in with the post. No longer bothering to place it on a silver salver, just as she no longer bothered to address my mother as 'Madam' or my father as 'Sir', she merely extended it in a hand: 'I forgot to bring these in, I was having so much trouble with that stove.' The hand was streaked with coke dust, and there was a smear of it on her forehead.

'For you.' My father spun the thick letter across the table towards me. 'From your girlfriend. And this!' He spun another at me. Perhaps it's from that agency of yours – Grabbitall and Thingummybob.' Having opened two bills and gulped at his whisky, he eventually looked up: 'Well, is it from the agency?'

'No.'

'An answer to one of your applications then?'

What business was it of his?

'Yes.'

'Any luck?'

I shook my head, humiliatingly conscious that my hand was trembling as I pushed the letter back into its envelope.

'I don't understand it,' my mother said. 'We keep hearing of this manpower shortage and yet you can't get a job – in spite of all those letters.'

'I can understand it.' Again my father gulped at his whisky. His face, so grey when he had first come into the room, was now unnaturally flushed. I suddenly noticed that he had not yet shaved. In the past, he had often ticked me off for coming down to breakfast without shaving.

'What do you mean?'

I wished my mother had not asked the question. I felt a totally unreasonable fury against her for having done so.

'Well, look at it this way. Suppose you were the headmaster of a school and you knew that at any time, day or night, there might be an air raid. Well, mightn't you hesitate about employing a conchie?'

My father now often used that word. Each time that he did so, with a scornful distaste, I felt as if he had spat on me.

'I don't see why,' my mother said, frowning in genuine puzzlement.

'Well, there'd always be the possibility that the conchie would rush into the air raid shelter ahead of the pupils. He might even knock them down in doing so.'

'Oh, I don't think . . .' my mother began.

She looked at me, eyes wide and lips parted. Her hand, holding a piece of toast, was half raised to her mouth. She was imploring me: Say nothing.

I said nothing.

Later, after my father had set off for his office, my mother knocked on the door of my little room.

'Don't be upset by Daddy. He's living under a terrible strain at present. The office. His ARP work. And of course his worry over Giles.'

By then the Battle of Britain had started. Giles was a fighter pilot.

'Yes, I know, I know.'

Suddenly she sat down on a corner of my unmade bed. I was lying on it, my hands clasped behind my head. 'Darling, I'm being awfully stupid. But explain to me. I've never really understood. This – this pacifism of yours . . . Do you mind my asking this?'

'Not at all.'

'Is it – is it something religious?'

'No.' I spoke up to the ceiling. 'I don't really think so. I'm not sure that I even believe in the existence of God. At least, there are times that I don't.' I felt no resentment at her question, since there was, I knew, no malice in it, only a hurt, bewildered wish to understand. 'It's just that I couldn't kill anyone. I just couldn't. Even if someone were going to kill me – even if a German entered the room at this moment to kill me I somehow couldn't . . . absolutely couldn't . . .'

'I see.'

But of course she couldn't see.

She placed a hand over mine. 'I think you'll feel better when your tribunal is over. It's the waiting that's . . . demoralizing.'

I had come up for the weekend from the Cambridgeshire farm at which I had now been working for several weeks as a cowhand. I had one weekend in every four off.

For that same weekend Giles had been allowed out of hospital. Having been shot down in his Hurricane over the Channel and then been miraculously rescued, he was one of what were called 'McIndoe's guinea-pigs' in the burns unit at East Grinstead.

As always with the mutilated, the disabled or the deformed, I found that the problem was: To look or not to look? If I forced myself to look at that skull over which the skin was here stretched unnaturally taut and there wrinkled like soiled tissue paper about to peel off, would not Giles be aware of my horror, however much I attempted to conceal it? But if I did not look, would he not say to himself: 'He can't bear to look at me. That shows what a sight I am'?

'What's the news of Marianne?' my mother asked him.

'She's still in Portsmouth. Still in the Wrens.'

'I mean – have you seen her recently?'

How could she be so maladroit? How could she, how could she?

'No. Not recently.' He answered in a totally even voice. 'We've rather – drifted apart.'

'Oh, dear!' My mother could not conceal her shock and pity.

'We never had much in common.'

Giles and I had never had much in common either. But now he was at pains to ask me about myself. Was the work on the farm terribly boring, terribly exhausting? What exactly was it that I did? Had I made any interesting friends? What sort of accommodation did I have? I had never known him so gentle, sweet and friendly. In the past he had so often ragged me, bullied me or merely ignored me.

He reminded me of some giant bird. The face was bird-like: the nose small and hooked; the almost lidless eyes constantly blinking, blinking, blinking; a sparse coxcomb of hair sticking up from the crown of the otherwise bald head.

Sorrowfully my mother waited on him; even more sorrowfully my father also did so. I guessed that Giles hated this attention – after all, he was perfectly capable of looking after himself; but with a calm forbearance he submitted to it.

On the Sunday afternoon my father decided that he would accompany Giles on the train to East Grinstead. The next day he would be having yet another skin-graft, his eleventh.

'Your father's taken Giles's accident very badly.'

Accident! It was a strange word for what had happened to him.

'Yes. Yes, I'm afraid he has.'

'Once he's passed fit, he wants to return to his squadron. I can't understand it.' My mother's upper lip trembled as though she were about to sneeze, tears formed along her lower eyelids.

'Oh, Mummy, don't, don't!'

'It's easy enough for you to say don't, don't!'

She had never before spoken to me with that harsh, contemptuous bitterness.

Because of a cancelled train, it was past eleven when my father returned. He had had to stand in the corridor most of the way, and he had had nothing to eat since luncheon. Entering the sitting-room, he was oddly hunched over to one side, a hand pressed against his right ribs, as though he had a fracture there. His face was as grey as I had ever seen it.

My mother had already gone upstairs – 'I think I'll prepare for Bedfordshire and then read in bed until your father gets back.'

'Where's your mother?'

I told him.

He began to speak of the trials of his journey, as though I were to blame for them. Then he crossed over to the drinks cabinet. 'What a world! What a world!' I realized that, even if he had found nothing to eat on the train, he had somehow miraculously found something to drink. Or could it be that he secretly carried a flask around with him? 'Christ!' He turned round, a half-full glass of whisky in one hand.

Suddenly I was overwhelmed by his pathos. He was like some huge, heroic statue suddenly beginning to crumble. I realized that I not only hated him, I also loved him.

'Shall I get you a sandwich?'

He gazed at me, stunned. I had never offered to do anything of that kind for him before. 'A sandwich?' He might have been trying out a foreign word.

'There's some cheese. There's also some ham left over from supper.'

He nodded. 'Thanks. Thanks.' Then, in a ludicrous approximation to an American accent, he added: 'That would be dandy. That's mighty kind of you.'

Clumsily I made the sandwiches, cutting the bread too thick and using up far too much of what was left of our week's ration of butter.

My father bit into one of the sandwiches and chewed for a while in silence. I sat opposite him, watching.

Then he burst out: 'What a thing to have happened! I never thought that a thing like that could have happened to my Giles. He was so – so bloody handsome. And now! And that bitch of a girl has dropped him. Oh, Christ, Christ!'

Suddenly, without any effort at concealment, he was crying. His mouth was half open, screwed up to one side, and a soggy fragment of the sandwich slipped out of it and stuck to his chin. He made no attempt to wipe it away. Huge tears ran down his cheeks.

I jumped off my chair and hurried over to him. I stooped, put an arm round his shoulders, then put a cheek to his. 'Daddy! Don't! Don't! Please!'

Suddenly I felt an extraordinarily violent shove. I all but fell over. 'Oh, get away! Leave me! Leave me alone!' Then he swivelled round in the chair. There was no grief now in his expression, only a malevolent fury. 'Do you know what I was thinking in the corridor of that bloody train throughout that bloody journey? I was thinking: Why him? Why, why, why? If it had to be someone, why couldn't it have been you? And then I answered myself. Because it's the best who always carry the can. And it's the sneaks, the cowards, the shits . . .'

I snatched at the knife on the plate beside the sandwich. I raised the knife. I lunged out with it. I stabbed. I stabbed a second time. I stabbed repeatedly.

My father was wearing a hairy Harris tweed jacket. The blade of the knife buckled and buckled again and again, until it was twisted up around my hand.

My father jumped to his feet. He snatched the knife from me.

He raised a fist, preparatory to hitting me. Then lowered it. Burst into laughter.

'You feeble little idiot! You can't kill a man. You haven't the guts or the strength or the savvy to kill anyone or anything.'

Later my mother came downstairs in dressing-gown, hairnet and slippers. She had finished one detective story and was fetching another.

She stared at me, where I sat slumped in an armchair before the dying fire.

'Your father came up in such an odd mood. Did you say or do something to upset him?'

'No. Nothing. Nothing at all.'

Time

Justin was obsessed with time, as others are obsessed with God, a beloved or a political cause. During the day, as he was dealing with the enquiries of a customer, drinking with colleagues in the pub nearest to the office or sitting opposite his wife at the kitchen table, supper set out before them, he would surreptitiously push back the cuff of his shirt and glance down at his Rolex watch. During the night, he would wake and peer over the intervening darkness at the glowing dial of the alarm clock on the bedside table, to tell himself something like: 'Twenty-three minutes to four. That means that I have two hours and thirty-seven minutes before getting up.' His wife hated this obsession, which so often caused him to exclaim in exasperation to her: 'Late, as per usual!'

Now his wife had left him, to share the flat of a widowed sister – typically quitting the house not early in the morning, as she had originally planned, but several hours later in the afternoon. 'I just don't see it,' he had repeatedly told her, when she had announced her departure. 'What have I *done*?' 'Oh, I don't know. I suppose it's the endless fussing,' she had replied. She did not want to put into precise words that she was jealous not of another woman, of his work or of a hobby, but of something as abstract as time. It would sound so foolish.

After she had gone, taking with her both the dog and the cat, Justin began to glance at his watch even more frequently during the day and to peer over at the alarm clock even more frequently at night. Repeatedly he would turn on the wireless or the television set not to listen to something or to view something, but merely to check that neither watch nor clock was slow or fast. It was then that he began to write the first of innumerable letters of complaint about the irregularity of bus and train services and the lateness of the post.

*

That day he had feared that he would arrive at the house in Kew – located the previous evening in his A–Z – many minutes after the agreed time of eleven. He had fumed when one Wimbledon train had succeeded another and no Richmond train had appeared on the indicator board. It was lucky that he had allowed himself so much time – as he always did. Then, idiot that he was, he had turned right instead of left when emerging from Kew Station (yet another hurried glance at his watch), until he had suddenly realized that he was not in North Road but in Station Approach. He reversed, quickened his pace and then (again a glance at the Rolex) began to jog. Oh, thank God – there was the number he wanted, and the minute hand of the Rolex, always infallible, was now just about to touch XI on the dial. He paused, breathless; then at the precise moment when the hand reached its goal, he pressed a finger to the bell.

When the door creaked open, the first thing that he saw was a diminutive child of indeterminate sex standing before him, thumb in mouth. Behind the child was a plump, red-headed girl in an apron and clogs.

'Mrs Abercrombie?'

'Sorry,' the girl said in a foreign accent, which he thought must be Swedish or at any rate Scandinavian. 'She had to go out to see the doctor and has not come back. She telephoned just now. There are many people at the doctor, she is waiting. She asked you to come back about eleven thirty maybe.'

Justin did not at all care for that 'maybe'. He jerked back his cuff and peered down at the Rolex. Then he said: 'Let's say twelve. Would you tell Mrs Abercrombie that, please? Twelve. Noon. Precisely,' he added. 'I'll be back at twelve precisely.'

The girl nodded, at the same time putting out a hand and drawing the child, who was edging out of the door, towards her. 'I hope that she is back by then,' she said.

'I hope so too. It's appalling how doctors constantly run late.' He might have been complaining yet again about the buses and trains. He peered into the interior of the house. At the far end of the hall, he could make out a grandfather clock. 'That clock there is slow – four minutes slow.' He held out his wrist, to show her his watch in confirmation.

She shrugged. 'Old clock,' she said. Then she laughed: 'Sometimes it wakes me up at night. Terrible noise! Bang, bang, bang!'

The child yelled out after her: 'Bang, bang, bang!' Then it burst into laughter, in which the girl joined.

I have an hour, well, not precisely an hour, in fact I have fifty-nine, no, fifty-eight minutes, Justin thought, as the door closed on him. It was odd that the girl had not asked him to come in and wait. But perhaps, alone with the child, she was nervous of a stranger. So what was he to do now? How was he to kill fifty-eight, no, fifty-seven minutes? Well, Kew Gardens were near, no more than six or seven minutes' walk away. Why not? On a Saturday or Sunday, during the few months between their first meeting and their marriage, he and his wife – who had the same sort of passion for gardening, albeit in a muted form, as he had for time – would often travel out to Kew. 'These weekend trains are an absolute disgrace,' he would protest; and she would then reply: 'Oh, what does it matter? We have all the time in the world. Why fret yourself?'

It was exasperating to discover that it had now become so expensive to enter the gardens. He consulted the map handed to him in lieu of a ticket, located the Tropical House on it, and decided to go there. He had often thought, when listening to *Desert Island Discs*, how wonderful it would be to be marooned on a tropical island. But when he had confessed that to his wife, she had replied contemptuously: 'But time would not matter there. So what good would that be to you?' Then she had added: 'I suppose your luxury would be a watch that ran for ever and ever without ever being even a second out.'

At such an early hour on a weekday, the gardens were almost empty. As, sweating more and more profusely, he strode towards the Palm Houses, he worked out precisely how much time he had at his disposal. It had taken him eight minutes to get from the house to Cumberland Gate and he had therefore better allow nine minutes to make the same journey back. After all, crossing that busy main road might not be so easy on his return. That meant that he must reach Cumberland Gate at ten to twelve at the very latest.

The Palm House itself appeared to be totally deserted – not surprisingly on this day of heat wave. Justin slipped off his jacket and, having carefully folded it, carried it over an arm. Suddenly he remembered the sundial in the formal garden of Kew Palace.

That was where he should have gone! Too late now. There was a sundial in the small garden of his own house in Barons Court; but, since the sun rarely reached it because of the high blocks of flats all around, it as rarely told the time.

Ahead of him he heard a metallic scraping sound. But so thick was the foliage that he could not at first make out what caused it. Then he saw the girl – at first he mistook her for a boy – with the close-cropped blonde hair and the bare freckled arms and the bare freckled legs. He could see both arms and legs because she was wearing a pair of khaki shorts and a khaki short-sleeved shirt, its top two buttons unfastened. Justin had been about to glance at his watch to check on the time. But now he forgot to do so. The girl was stooping over the base of a banana-tree – Justin could see the clusters of fruit, one above the other – while doing something with a trowel.

The girl looked up at the sound of his approach. She had green eyes, slanting upwards at each side, a wide mouth and a snub nose covered in freckles. Her hands were small and strong, the fingernails caked with soil. 'Have you got the correct time on you?' she asked.

Justin tweaked back the cuff of his shirt. 'The *correct* time? Does anyone knowingly have the *incorrect* time?' He laughed. 'Yes, I have – as always – the correct time. It is now twenty-two, no, twenty-three minutes past eleven precisely.'

She laughed. 'You say that like the talking clock.'

Justin suddenly realized how attractive she was; and since she had not returned to doing whatever she had been doing, he surmised – with a sudden elation – that she found him attractive too. 'I love the Palm House,' he said. 'My parents used to bring me here as a child. And my wife and I used to come here.'

'Why did you stop?'

'Why did I. . .?'

'Why did you and your wife stop coming here?'

'Oh, you know how it is. When you're young – before you're married – or when you're just married . . . But then . . .'

'No, I don't know. How could I know?' She laughed. 'I'm not married yet.'

'No, of course not. You look very young.'

'I'm a student. Of botany. This is just a summer job.'

He was enchanted by the faint down on her bare legs and arms; by the gleam of her prominent cheekbones; by the glimpse

[111]

of her small, firm breasts as she bent over to pull at a weed and the khaki shirt fell away to reveal that she was wearing nothing beneath it.

They went on talking. Justin felt the sweat breaking out under his arms and gluing his shirt to his back; a bead of moisture trickled down his forehead and into his left eye, stinging it with its saltness; along his upper lip there glistened other beads of sweat, which, at last becoming aware of them, he wiped off on the back of his hand.

Eventually, after they had talked about the Gardens, about her university course and about the planes which, every few minutes, roared overhead, she asked: 'Aren't you working today?' He looked like someone who would be in a regular job.

'Oh, yes. Yes, I'm working. Very much so.' He went to explain that he was a house-agent, a house-agent with one of the largest firms in London, and that he had travelled out to Kew to look at a house for someone who could not make up her mind whether to put it on the market or not. 'We have a lot of people like that – people who want to sell one day and not to sell the next.'

Abandoning all pretence of weeding, the girl now stepped out from under the banana-trees and perched herself on some railings. She swung her bare legs back and forth, as those green eyes peered up at him. Justin felt a mounting excitement. He knew that, with his height, his muscular build, his regular features, his olive complexion and his shiny black hair, he was attractive to women; and he knew now, knew with an absolute certainty, that he was attractive to this particular woman.

She continued to ask him about his work. Then she said. 'You might be able to help me.'

'To help you? How?'

She explained that she had recently inherited some money from an aunt – 'not a fortune, far from that, but, well, a nice sum – what people call a *tidy* sum.' She thought that the most sensible thing to do with it was to buy herself a flat, instead of, as now, paying out a fortune in rent. Did he ever deal with property of that kind in, say, Fulham or Battersea or even Acton?

'Well, yes . . . Often . . . I'm sure . . .'

It was at that moment that, far off, he heard a clock striking twelve. He often heard far-off clocks striking when other people were unaware of them. Oh, God! He looked at his watch. That clock was fast, eleven minutes fast, but if he was not to be late for his appointment with Mrs Abercrombie, he would have to leave now, at once, with not a second of delay.

'I'm afraid I must dash. I've just noticed the time. I must see this client at twelve o'clock, you see. Forgive me.'

At that he hurried off down the aisle between the towering trees, many of them trailing fleshy lianas, and began first to walk and then to run towards the gate. Another despairing look at his watch convinced him that he could not possibly make it, until – a miracle! – he was all at once aware that a bus was bearing down on him just as he was scuttling across the road in the face of a stream of traffic. A 291, that rarest of buses! It would take him past Mrs Abercrombie's door. He had noticed the request stop just beyond it.

Gasping, streaming with sweat, he flopped down on the seat nearest the entrance. Again he consulted his watch. Yes, with luck, if the traffic were not too heavy and if there were not too many people boarding at the next two stops . . .

At exactly twelve o'clock he once again rang the bell of the house.

The au pair squinted in distaste at the damp stains of sweat under his armpits. Then she said: 'I am sorry, very sorry. Mrs Abercrombie has still not come back. But if you like to come in . . .'

'But we said twelve o'clock. We agreed on that. Twelve o'clock precisely.'

The girl shrugged. 'Doctors have no idea of time.'

Mrs Abercrombie, when she eventually returned, made no apology for her lateness of seventeen minutes. All too clearly she was more eager to talk about her hay-fever than about selling the house; and when she did talk about selling the house, it was with an exasperating vagueness. On the one hand, she said, she would like to be nearer the centre of London, but on the other hand for a young child it was essential to have a garden – wasn't it? She had briefly considered the option of a move into the country, but then . . . From time to time she spoke vaguely of 'Mr Abercrombie', but it was clearly with her, not with him, that any decision lay. Meanwhile, Justin became increasingly aware of a smell of cooking. A bolognese sauce? A stew? A joint? He could not be certain. He began to feel increasingly hungry, then ravenous. It was several minutes past one, and he always ate at one. Mrs Abercrombie had not even offered him a drink or a cup of coffee.

When eventually, at twenty-two minutes past one, Justin was once more outside the house, his first thought was to find a restaurant. But then he decided to return to the Palm House and the girl. He would give her his business card – how stupid of him not to have done so before rushing off! – and he would tell her that he would be only too happy to help her, that there were a number of properties on the firm's books which might be suitable for her, that he could of course accompany her to view any of them that might interest her.

But, sadly, the Palm House was empty. However, a wheelbarrow, full of tools, still remained at the place where they had met. She must, he decided, be planning to return after her lunch. How long would that be? He looked at his watch. At two-thirty two clients would be awaiting him outside an empty house in Parsons Green, to which he was carrying the key in his briefcase. He could not afford to be late, he must be on time for them. Eventually, he took out one of his cards from his wallet, hastily scribbled on it: 'So sorry I had to rush off – do get in touch if I can help you', and left it in the wheelbarrow. Would she act on it? With a terrible sense of regret, he decided that probably she wouldn't.

As the train carried him back into London, that regret remained with him. Since his wife had left, he had been feeling increasingly lonely. It would be nice (that was the adjective he used to himself) to show the girl flats in Fulham, Battersea and Acton; to reach a stage of intimacy when he could invite her to lunch or tea or even dinner; and eventually to – well, what?

Once again he looked at his watch. Thank God, the train had arrived at Kew Station so soon and there had been no subsequent hitches with it. It should reach Parsons Green in seven or at most eight minutes. From Parsons Green Station the house was only five, no, perhaps six minutes away by foot. He had time, lots and lots of time, oceans of it.

Suddenly he stopped thinking about the girl. Suddenly he felt happy.

Panama

Below the tiered balconies of the hotel, Lake Bled, usually so placid, fretted and frothed as gusts of wind whipped at it. Conrad put up a hand mottled with age – senile purpura, that was what members of the medical profession like himself called those reddish-brown and purple areas, caused by not merely blood but life itself imperceptibly seeping away from tiny vessels damaged because of loss of elasticity in the skin – and clutched at his panama hat, as he felt the wind tug at it. Then, with a disgruntled sigh, he jerked off the hat and, swivelling in the cast-iron chair into which he had lowered his aching body, he chucked it away from him, through the door open to the bedroom. Good shot, good shot! Floating like a discus, the hat eventually landed on the double bed which he knew, with the melancholy resignation of old age, that during this week of the conference no one would ever share.

On the far side of the lake, in the shadow of the rocky hill on which the fairy-tale castle was precariously perched, an eight was skimming towards the fairy-tale church perched no less precariously on its rocky islet. Grimacing at a twinge in each of his hips, he got up from the chair and leaned over the concrete balcony. If only he had remembered to bring his binoculars, then he might have been able to examine the rowers in detail. As it was, he could only squint down at a far-off blur.

Once, in the immediate aftermath of the last War, he had stroked the Oxford crew to an ignominious defeat. But his interest was now not in rowing, but in those rowers.

In the bar downstairs, Karen, the Swedish woman who seemed far too young to be a delegate at a conference like this, sipped at her coffee, then tilted her chair backwards and stretched out her bare, shapely, shiny legs in their espadrilles. 'Thank God he's not

[115]

taking the chair this afternoon. I know he's the doyen of the profession but, frankly, he's past it.'

'It's the deafness,' Anna, the plump, middle-aged Italian with a fuzz of peroxided down above her long upper lip, said.

'Yes, the deafness,' one of their Slovene hosts, Marko, agreed. 'Half the time he hasn't any idea of what is being said. He's just guessing. But what could we do? We had to ask him to take the chair for at least one session. After all he is the doyen. But for him, we should all be treating angle-closure glaucoma in a totally different way.'

'He's sweet,' Karen said, sipping again at her coffee. 'When he was young he really must have been something.'

'He is still handsome,' Anna said. '*Distinto, insigne.* That is how we describe him in Italian.'

'I so much like his elegance,' Louis, a far from elegant, middle-aged Frenchman in a boldly checked blouson and rumpled pale blue linen trousers, took up. 'That suit, beautifully cut.'

'Raw silk,' Marko gave as his opinion. 'Savile Row, I am sure.' Marko had done some postgraduate research at Moorfields. He knew about Savile Row.

'And the hat, that hat!' Karen cried out. 'Don't you love that panama hat?'

As, with a barely audible groan, Conrad lowered himself on to the seat beside Karen in the horse-drawn carriage, Anna raised her hand, her charm bracelet jangling, up to the brim of the hat. 'Dr Franks, may I tell you something very personal?'

'Certainly ... Oh, by the way, it's not Dr Franks. It's just Mr Franks.' Conrad had long since wearied of explaining to foreign colleagues the quaint English snobbery which decreed that Fellows of the Royal College of Surgeons were called plain Mr and not Dr. 'So what is this very personal thing you wish to tell me?'

Briefly she placed a hand over his. 'I love your hat. So elegant.' Unnecessarily, since, so close to her, he could hear her perfectly, she was at pains to raise her voice.

'It's a panama.'

Louis, seated opposite, his knees all but touching Conrad's, asked: 'From Panama?'

'Well, no, actually no. From Ecuador. That, suprisingly – and not from Panama – is where the best panama hats come from. I've had this one for, oh, donkey's years. Twenty, twenty-five. I actually bought it in Ecuador, you know. I went out there as a guest of the university, to demonstrate, er, one or two techniques.'

Anna noticed how his hands were trembling as they rested, splayed out, with those reddish-brown and purplish blotches, on his bony knees. She would not care to have him perform an iridectomy on her, even if he was the originator of the technique which she herself now used.

'Is it true that you can fold up a panama?' Louis asked.

'Yes. That's how you know a *real* panama from a phony. Look!' Conrad removed the hat and, watched by the other three occupants of the carriage, began to roll it up. Then he was distracted. Half-rolled, the hat rested between his blotched hands.

Bicycling towards them, in the shortest of shorts and nothing else, was that brusquely unsmiling young waiter who would slam down plates before the guests as though he were in half a mind to break them. One would never have guessed, when he was in his uniform of white shirt, black tie and greenish-black jacket sheened with age, that he had the remarkable physique, shoulders broad and torso heavily muscled, that was now revealed to Conrad's surreptitious gaze in thrilling near-nakedness.

'Isn't that one of the waiters from the hotel? Anna asked.

'Oh, is it? I didn't notice.' Then Conrad swivelled round and peered. By now the waiter, failing to acknowledge a wave from Karen in the carriage behind, was about to disappear around a corner.

'He is so rude, that one,' Anna said.

'Maybe he is shy,' Louis suggested.

'Shy!' Anna emitted a derisive snort of laughter.

On one occasion, sauntering past her in the corridor to her room, the waiter, carrying a breakfast tray, had begun to sing 'Volare' in a high, nasal parody of an Italian tenor, while grinning impudently at her.

Once again Anna put out a hand and touched the brim of the hat. 'Is it intended to be so yellow?'

'*Intended*?' Conrad smiled in gentle mockery as he repeated the word. Then he said: 'No, not intended, not really. It's the passing of time. That discoloration comes with the passing of time.' Like the senile purpura on the back of my hands, he added to himself.

'I like that darker yellow,' Louis declared. 'Chic. *Très distingué.*'

The next day the morning session had gone on so long that they were more than half an hour late for lunch. The waiters in the special dining-room set aside for the members of the conference were far from pleased. Alojz ran a hand over his brush of closely cropped blond hair and then reached over to the table beside him, plucked a bread-stick out of its vase-like glass container and munched on it. 'What the hell has happened to them?'

'It's always like this at these fucking conferences,' another, older waiter said. 'They should be told that, if they're not on time, that's it. They can go out to a restaurant. After all, they're here at a special price. The hotel makes almost nothing from them.'

Fragments of bread-stick scattered from between Alojz's large, white teeth, and stuck to the greenish-black jacket, too tight across the swelling pectorals and too long in the sleeves, which had been passed on to him from a predecessor.

'Oh, here they are!' another waiter announced, straightening himself up from the wall against which he had been leaning, while contemplatively picking his long nose.

Conrad, glimpsing Alojz, at once veered away from the table towards which he had been walking and, smiling, advanced on the boy. He was surprised when Alojz, usually so offhand, at once pulled out a chair for him. Then the boy extended one of the hands which, their wrists thick and their nails savagely bitten, Conrad always found so attractive. 'I take your hat, sir?'

'Oh, thank you. Thank you very much.'

Alojz placed the hat on a chair which stood, its seat a bird's-nest of broken cane, against the wall. He grinned at Conrad. 'Safe,' he said. Then he added: 'Beautiful hat.'

Soon Conrad was drawn into conversation by an energetic American – he was always about to swim, play tennis or golf, walk round the lake or up to the castle, or had just finished doing so – with a lazily drawling voice. The American wanted to boast to Conrad of his success with laser treatment for macular degeneration. Recently he had cured – yes, he thought it could

[118]

be called a cure, without any exaggeration – a well-known senator.

As the American's voice, so deep and so slow, flowed on and on like some sluggish river, Conrad kept watching Alojz. After that brief grin, the boy's face had resumed its expression of morose sulkiness. At another table, Anna smiled up at him as he poured out some water for her, her peroxided vestige of a moustache catching the light. But she received no smile in return. The boy moved purposefully, his thick eyebrows drawn together in a frown, snatching up plates, banging down others. When an elderly Finn tried repeatedly to catch his attention, even clicking his fingers and calling out 'Garçon, garçon!', to order some beer, the boy deliberately ignored him until at long last, in his own time, he came across and said: 'Yes, sir? You wish something?' The back of his neck was raw with sunburn and his forehead was slightly flushed with it. At once violently stimulating and painful, a memory jabbed at Conrad, of the boy, in nothing but those shortest of shorts, weaving his bicycle into now the shadows and now the sunlight of the narrow, tree-canopied road which lassoed the quiet lake.

'Tell me, Dr Franks, did you ever imagine, when you started out on your career, that one day lasers would play such a major part in surgery of the eye?'

Conrad restrained himself from saying yet again that he was Mr, not Dr, Franks. 'What? No, of course not. How could I have? My surgical experience extends back into Prehistoric times.'

'Oh, not as far as that! Though I guess you are our doyen.'

Doyen! Conrad thought: When people call one the doyen of this or that, it means that one is already far advanced on the way to putrefaction.

Conrad lingered over his fruit salad, while one by one the other diners left. The American excused himself – he was going to play tennis with an English tourist, met by chance in the pool that morning, who had once reached the last sixteen in the men's singles at Wimbledon. 'I have a hunch I can beat him.'

'Well, good luck!'

Alojz swooped from table to table, stacking plates and placing them on a trolley. Conrad watched him; but, perversely, the boy seemed determined not to return his gaze.

One of the Slovenes called from across the room: 'Oh, Dr Franks don't forget we start on the excursion in five minutes!'

Conrad had no wish to visit some caves which he had seen on a previous visit many years before. But his sense of duty was strong. He owed it to his hosts to board the bus at the time designated – unlike the young American, said to be a brilliant surgeon, who had blithely opted for his tennis match instead.

Conrad rose from the table and looked around for the waiter. But the boy, along with all the others, had now disappeared. Disappointing. Alone in the dining-room, Conrad had hoped to say something to him, however brief, however trite.

It was as he was leaving the room that he heard the ringing voice: 'Sir! *Sir!*'

He turned. The boy, with a mischievous expression on his square, sunburned face, was hurrying towards him. 'Sir! You forget! Your hat! Your hat!'

'Ah, yes! My hat, my panama hat ... How foolish of me!' Conrad extended both hands, smiling as Alojz approached. 'Thank you. Many thanks! I shall need it on our expedition. At least, until we reach the caves ... The sun is so bright ...' He pointed towards the high windows at the far end of the room, half their panes iridescent with an upwardly slanting dazzle reflected off the lake.

Then, on an impulse, as he took the hat in his left hand, he put his right hand into his trouser pocket and drew out a bill. One dollar, five dollars, ten dollars? He did not know, he did not look, he did not care. When travelling he always kept an assortment of dollar bills in that pocket. People were just as happy – sometimes even more happy – to receive dollars as the native currency; and such trivial extravagance always helped to oil the wheels – as he himself would put it.

'For you,' he said. 'You work so hard to see that all of us have what we want.'

The boy stared down at the bill. Yes, it was for ten dollars, Conrad could see that now. Far too much! But in that case, all the better. If one was going to oil the wheels, then one should do so liberally ...

The large hand eventually went out. 'Thank you, sir. Thank you.'

Conrad placed his hat on his head. He patted it down, he tweaked at the brim. Then he smiled: 'You deserve it. Oh, absolutely.'

'Thank you, sir.'

The boy repeated the words with a mixture of bewilderment and half-suppressed joy.

'This dripping water will ruin your hat,' Karen said.

With a small grimace, Conrad swept it off.

'You don't want that to happen. Such a beautiful hat,' Anna said, her voice again unnaturally raised, as always when she spoke to him, so that he wanted to snap at her: 'I'm not *that* deaf, you know!'

'Oh, it's really very old. Some day I really must replace it.'

'It's beautiful. Old things can be beautiful.' Karen, who was wearing shorts and a scanty halter-neck blouse which exposed her midriff, put out a hand. 'Let me help you up.'

'Thank you, thank you. Most kind. But I can manage perfectly well on my own. If I take my time.'

These steps from one cave to a higher one were steep and slippery. Without his hat, he could feel drops of moisture spattering down on his head, penetrating the sparse, white hair which he now took so many pains to plaster across his skull, and chilling his scalp. But far worse than that, he could feel a grinding pain in his chest as he toiled up and up in the rear of the party.

'Why not rest for a moment?' Anna suggested with concern. She could hear his laboured gasping behind her.

'No, no. Really. I'm fine. Fine.' He gulped for air and gulped again. 'It's only this wretched asthma of mine. I forgot to bring my nebulizer.'

Each morning he woke early. Uncovered except by a sheet – they were now in the middle of a heat wave which caused even the most formal of them to appear in the most informal of clothing – Conrad would lie out on his bed and listen to the birds twittering in the ivy which hung down in huge, dusty sweeps, like bedding put out to air, from the tiered balconies. Then, prompted by his aching bladder, he would slowly raise first his head and then his torso, before swinging his legs to the ground and limping towards the bathroom. Dressed, he would make his way down through the hotel, deserted but for an occasional cleaner, out towards the lake.

It took him exactly fifty-five minutes to circle the lake. Each morning he clocked himself, taking pride in that time and, so far from ever attempting an improvement, sticking obsessively to it, not a minute more or less. A few cars would pass him on the road immediately above the footpath, he would pass a few solitary men already out fishing. Otherwise he would be alone. He liked that. From time to time, he would halt and, hands on hips, would draw a number of deep breaths as he gazed out at the lake or up at the trees on the hills behind him. Sometimes he would take out his nebulizer and insert it in his mouth, eyes half closed and an expression of intentness on his face.

That morning there had been a small, flat, greyish-green cloud, like a lump of lead, tilted at rest immediately above the castle. He had thought nothing of it. As though snagged by it in their erratic passage, other clouds had soon nudged against it, eventually to coalesce. The air had grown increasingly heavy and sticky, so that, under the panama, Conrad had felt the sweat collecting, as it was also collecting under his armpits and in the small of his back. Repeatedly he halted and puffed at the nebulizer, even though he knew that he should not dose himself with it more frequently than every three or four hours. Suddenly he was coughing, his mouth filling with phlegm. He startled some ducks, a mother with her brood, as he spat into the undergrowth by the lake.

There was a flash of lightning, followed by a crackle of thunder. Soon the rain began to fall, the first of his present stay, whereas on his previous one it had never stopped raining for a whole week on end. It fell with a malevolent persistence straight downwards out of a sky which now seemed extraordinarily dark and close.

Conrad began to hurry, a cough repeatedly rattling in his chest from the extra exertion, and his spectacles misting over. Then he heard a motor-cycle behind him, a squeal of breaks.

'You want lift?'

It was Alojz, in jeans and a rain-soaked T-shirt sticking to that heavily muscled torso of his.

Conrad laughed in sheer joy. 'A lift? But how?'

'Come up.' The spikes of his close-cropped blond hair glistening with diamonds of rain, he indicated the pillion behind him. 'Come! Safe, very safe, easy.'

It was years since Conrad had been on a motor-cycle. But he had no hesitation. Taking off his sodden hat, clumsily rolling it up and placing it in one of the side-pockets of his jacket, he clambered astride the pillion.

'OK?'

'Fine.'

'OK! We go!'

Conrad had his arms around the boy's waist. So sodden was the T-shirt, it seemed as if he was making contact not with its fabric but with the living flesh beneath it. He moved first one hand and then the other, in a pretence of changing his hold. He felt the hardness of the hip bones under the no less sodden jeans, and then the muscles below the ribs. On a crazy impulse he then raised his arms and placed them tightly around the boy's torso, hugging him to him. Meanwhile the rain streamed down on them, and splashed up over them from the road each time that they roared round a bend.

In an area behind the hotel, into which Conrad had never penetrated, one side of it lined with giant garbage-containers and the rest crammed with cars, trucks and motor-cycles, Alojz brought them to a halt. 'We arrive!' he called out in a loud, elated voice as he dismounted.

'Thank you! Thank you! You saved my life.'

Conrad now drew out another ten dollar bill from his pocket. It was damp from the rain which had penetrated the fabric of his suit. 'Please.'

Vigorously the boy shook his head, scattering drops of rain.

'Please!'

'No, no! No!'

'Oh, very well.' Reluctantly Conrad replaced the bill in his pocket. Then he ventured: 'Tell me your name.'

'Alojz.'

Conrad repeated it. 'I've never heard that name.'

The boy shrugged. 'Usual in Slovenia. Not strange.' He put a hand on Conrad's shoulder and patted it. 'You?'

'Conrad.'

'Dr Conrad.'

'No. Just Conrad.'

Puzzled, the boy frowned. Then he began to move off. He turned, raised a hand. 'Goodbye.'

'Goodbye, Alojz.'

'Goodbye, Dr Conrad.'

*

The next day, Conrad walked to the farthest extremity of the lake, selected a bench, overhung by rowan trees, on the hillside, and waited. He waited in total composure. He knew, knew for an absolute certainty, though he could not have said why, that Alojz, coming to work, would pass below him and would see him. He listened for the approaching roar of the motor-bike and, as he did so, he seemed once again to feel the sodden fabric of the T-shirt and the jeans under his hands and, beneath that fabric, that flesh, muscle, bone. He adjusted the panama, he coughed, coughed again.

When Alojz appeared it was not on yesterday's motor-cycle but on the bicycle of three days before. He was weaving in leisurely fashion from side to side of the road, as though he had the whole day before him; and as he approached, head tilted, he was whistling 'Volare' slightly off pitch.

Suddenly, as though Conrad had succeeded in willing him to do so, he turned his head round and up and saw the bench and its occupant. 'Hi!' He halted the bicycle and jumped off.

'Hi!' It was not a word that Conrad would ordinarily use.

Resting the bicycle against a tree, Alojz began to hurry up the slope.

Conrad patted the bench beside him. 'Join me.'

The boy looked at the obviously cheap watch which he wore on a frayed fabric strap. Then he shrugged. 'I must not be late. Manager angry.'

'Oh, let him be angry!'

Seated beside Conrad, the boy leaned forward and gazed at the lake. 'Beautiful weather! No rain! Sun, sun, sun!' He gave a loud, joyful laugh.

'Yes, beautiful.'

The boy scrabbled in a pocket of his jeans and brought out a crushed pack of Slovenian cigarettes. He shook one out and extended the pack.

'Thanks. I don't smoke. No longer. Bad for you,' he added.

'Yes, bad, bad!' Alojz laughed, then extracted the cigarette and brought out a throw-away lighter from the same pocket. He pulled on the cigarette greedily, holding it between index finger and middle finger of his left hand. Conrad noticed that there was a rusty rim of blood around the savagely bitten nail of the middle finger.

As Alojz now leaned back on the bench, screwing up his eyes

against the glare, Conrad extended an arm along it, extended it further, rested it on a massive shoulder. He pressed the shoulder, pressed it again. Alojz made no move, sucking yet again on the cigarette.

'Where do you live? Far from the hotel?'

'Seven, eight kilometres. There!' The boy pointed across the lake and up towards the hillside opposite.

'You live with your family?'

'With mother. Only mother. Father dead. Sister married. Ljubljana.'

As they talked, Conrad again stroked the shoulder. Then steeling himself, he lowered his hand, put it on Alojz's thigh, stroked the thigh, gripped it, stroked it again. Alojz went on talking about the new municipal swimming-pool – just constructed, better than that of the hotel, Conrad should try it, one of the biggest and best in Slovenia – while dragging greedily on the cigarette which was now little more than a pinched, sodden fragment. It was only when Conrad moved his hand yet higher, higher again, that all at once, with an impatient exclamation, Alojz broke off. He grasped Conrad's hand in his and firmly removed it. Then he burst into laughter. He raised his right forefinger and, with a mock frown, shook it back and forth. He might have been playfully admonishing a mischievous child who had attempted to do something which it knew full well to be forbidden. 'No,' he said. 'No, no, no! Bad!' Again he shook the forefinger, again he gave that mock frown. Then his laughter rang out, as before.

'Sorry.' Conrad turned his head away.

Now the boy began to ask Conrad about himself. Was he American? Did he have children? Was he married? He was clearly amazed to receive the answer No to each of these questions.

'One day I wish to visit England. My dream.'

'Then come and stay with me. I have a large house in the centre of London, and no one to share it with.'

The boy shrugged, then smiled pensively, gazing out over the lake while biting at the nail of his forefinger. 'Maybe,' he said. 'Yes.'

'Let me give you my address.'

But as Conrad said this, the boy looked at his watch and jumped to his feet. 'Late, late, late!' He stretched, extending his

[125]

arms above his head and drawing in his diaphragm before emitting a prodigious yawn. Then he said: 'Today I cannot give you ride.'

'Yes, where's the motor-bike?'

'Not mine. Cousin. Cousin work today.'

Conrad watched while Alojz scrambled down the hillside and mounted the bicycle. Alojz did not look back. But Conrad watched him intently as, growing smaller and smaller, he emerged now after one bend and now after another and now after yet another, of the narrow, ceaselessly winding road. He could still see him, a mere speck, as he turned into the entrance to the hotel.

The next day was Conrad's last at Bled. He rose even earlier than usual, completed all his packing, and then set off on his walk round the lake. He reached the bench of the previous day and composed himself on it. In preparation for his flight back to England, he was wearing not the suit of beige raw silk but a worsted one. He took off the panama hat and wiped his forehead with a handkerchief. Then he replaced the hat. He was certain, as he had been certain yesterday, that at any moment now Alojz would appear.

But the minutes passed and there was no sign. There were other people, on bicycles and motor-cycles; there were cars and trucks and even a party of Austrian or German hikers, in shorts and mountain-boots, with rucksacks on their backs and guttural voices which reverberated back and forth across the lake. The boy must have the day off. That must be the explanation. Unless, of course, he was ill.

Eventually, glancing at his watch, Conrad realized that, if he were to have breakfast before catching the bus which was taking the participants of the congress to Ljubljana airport, it was time to return. He sighed, adjusted his hat, rose with an audible groan.

He had never before felt this tiredness while circling the lake. It was all he could do to put one foot in front of the other; each gentle slope upwards caused him to pause, hands on hips and head lowered, as though in preparation for some demanding feat. What had happened to Alojz? He had failed to exchange addresses with him, he would never see him again. Unless of course – why not? – he merely sent to the hotel a letter addressed

[126]

to 'Mr Alojz'. But there might be other members of staff with that name – a common one, the boy had said.

He was once more passing the duck with her brood when suddenly he heard, like the sound of a fretful midge, a whirring behind him. Then he felt something plucking the hat off his head and heard a burst of laughter. There, in front of him, on the bicycle, weaving from side to side just out of his reach, was Alojz. The boy turned his head, now bicycling so slowly that he all but capsized. He held out the hat. 'Your hat,' he called. 'Hat, hat, hat!' Now he was singing it out. 'Fetch! Fetch!' It was some absurd kind of game, such as one might play with a dog or a child.

'Give it to me!' Conrad called. 'Please!' He put out a hand, lurched forward, stumbled on the root of a tree, all but fell.

'Come! Fetch! Come!' Again the boy held out the hat. The bicycle wobbled dangerously. 'Hat! Beautiful hat! Come!'

Yes, it was all a game, a game! The boy was laughing and Conrad now laughed too, as he once more broke into a near-run, hands outstretched.

For a long time it went on like that, the boy and the hat always almost within Conrad's grasp and both of them laughing. Then, suddenly, as though tired of playing, the boy's strong legs worked furiously at the pedals and he was away. Conrad now really began to run. 'My hat! My hat!' he wailed. 'Give it back to me!'

At the top of an incline, Conrad panting at its bottom, the boy braked, halted, turned. Then he raised his hand and flung the hat away from him, into the wind, down towards the lake. Once more like a discus, the hat floated, floated, floated, on and on over the lush grasses and, beyond them, the sharp reeds. It plunged and soon was lost to sight. The boy again raised the hand, this time in farewell. 'Goodbye, Dr Conrad! Goodbye! See you! See you again!'

Then, over the brow of the incline, he had vanished.

It was at that moment that Conrad felt a terrible agony, as though some giant tooth were being extracted from the middle of his chest. He staggered over to a bench and first sat on it, his body hunched over, and then lay out on it. His last despairing thought was, My hat! My hat!

Everyone was agitated. If the coach did not start at once, they would miss the plane. Eventually, after Karen had said that from her balcony early that morning she had seen Conrad setting off for his daily walk round the lake – 'I knew at once that it was him because of his hat' – Marko volunteered to take his car and go in search, while the others set off on the coach. As soon as he had found Conrad, he would bring him to the airport.

Karen at once said that she would accompany Marko. Though they were both happily married, they had been carrying on a discreet affair throughout the conference.

'What could have happened to him?' Karen said as they set off. 'I hope nothing bad.'

Marko bit his lower lip and shook his head.

'He's such a sweet old man. It's not like him to be late for anything. When he took the chair for that session, he arrived *hours* before anyone else.'

At first they thought that, dappled with the sunlight slanting through the rowan trees, Conrad was asleep. 'He looked so peaceful, so incredibly peaceful,' Karen was later to say, and Marko was to add: 'What a wonderful way to go – in a moment, with no struggle at all, beside the lake he so much loved.'

The three Bosnian refugee children with the dog now trampled over the reeds and now waded in the water. Their faces were sharp and set. Their ball had ricocheted off a rock and plopped down somewhere here.

Then one of the two girls saw the panama hat floating on the water beside a clump of bulrushes. She pointed, let out a screech. The boy, her older brother, pushed her aside. The water reaching up over his ankles, he bent down, picked up the hat, shook it vigorously.

He put the hat on his head. It came down over his eyes to the tip of his nose. Water trickled to his chin and spattered his shirt. The girls pointed at him. He took off the hat and, with a sweep of it in one hand, the other hand on his hip, he bowed to them in a parody of aristocratic courtliness, pirouetted forward, pranced now to this side, now to that.

Bent double, grubby hands on bare knees, the girls squealed with mirth.

[128]

Beakie

Lauris squinted balefully out of the kitchen window at the smug, corpulent pigeons strung out along the fence separating her narrow Campden Hill garden from the even more narrow one of her neighbours. The neighbours, a childless couple called Donoghue, fed the pigeons, emptying out on to their dishevelled lawn not merely scraps of bread but lard, chicken carcasses and glutinous mounds of rice or spaghetti. Lauris had first spoken to them and then, when she and they were no longer on speaking terms, had dashed off to them a number of increasingly acrimonious notes, which she would give to her eleven-year-old daughter, Charmian, to push through their letter-box on her dragging way to school. 'Are you sure you delivered that letter?' she would ask when no response came and yet more garbage appeared in the next-door garden; and Charmian would then answer in a voice pitched high by wounded feelings, 'Yes, of course, Mummy! What *do* you think?'

'Wretched birds, wretched people,' Lauris muttered, turning away from the window and seating herself opposite to her mother, Mrs Greene, at the kitchen table, the tea set out between them.

'Isn't Charmian going to join us?' the older woman asked. She often suspected that her daughter – so possessive of people until, on a sudden impulse, she jettisoned them as though they were clothes which, however serviceable, now bored her too much for her to go on wearing them – deliberately kept her and her granddaughter apart from each other.

'Homework.' With her sleek head, Lauris indicated the dining-room next door. 'She never drinks tea, as you know. But I'll put this macaroon aside for her.'

'And a piece of this chocolate cake.' Mrs Greene again bit into the slice which her daughter had cut for her. 'Delicious.'

It irritated Lauris to have to watch her mother guzzle (as she thought of it) almost as much as it irritated her to have to watch the pigeons do so. But she said, with genuine warmth: 'Oh, it *is* nice to see you, mother. I wish you came more often.'

'I wish you came to us more often. You know how hard it is for me to leave your stepfather.'

'And you know how hard it is for me to leave the shop.' To the family it was a shop, to the world a boutique.

Mrs Greene sighed. Then she murmured: 'I wonder if I might have just another teeny . . . It's so good.'

'Of course.' Lauris cut another slice, not teeny but thick, and held out the plate.

'Oh, that's far too big!' Mrs Greene protested as her hand went out. Having masticated for a while, her head on one side – it was extraordinary how much like one of those fucking pigeons she looked, Lauris thought – she at last ventured: 'Is Eddie in?' Eddie was her grandson, Lauris's nephew.

Lauris shook her head. 'Never at this hour. You know that, Mother.' Then she said: 'I've been thinking – I'll really have to give him the push.' It was, in fact, the first time that she had thought it; but having thought it, she was the kind of woman who at once took action. Thus on similar impulses she had, in turn, given the push to a travel journalist husband who had come increasingly to confine his writing to descriptions of his journey deeper and deeper into the wasteland of alcoholism; to a moony, etiolated Old Etonian business partner; and, most recently, to her jolly, dirty Irish char, Mrs Rooney.

'Give him the push! But why, Lauris, why? He's such a dear – and he can't be any trouble.'

'Well, frankly, Mother, he stinks. Literally, I mean.'

'Stinks! He always strikes me as being, well, as clean as anyone of that age is ever likely to be.' Eddie, a music student, occupied what Mrs Greene called, because of its size and with no *double entendre* in mind, 'the fairy's room', in return for some lackadaisical, inexpert help in the garden.

'He never changes his underclothes and it's all I can do to get him to change his sheets – even though the washing-machine is there, costing him nothing. He never opens the window in that room, even in a heat wave – too lazy to do so. He wears the same terrible pair of sneakers day after day.' Lauris cut herself a piece of cake and picked it up and examined it. 'He pees in the basin,' she concluded.

'Oh, I'm sure not!' Mrs Greene was shocked. 'You must be mistaken.'

Lauris smiled mirthlessly. 'Well, I admit I've not seen him do it. Not actually. But often he disappears into that lair of his as soon as he's gobbled his supper – no attempt to help me clear the table or stack the dishwasher, of course – and then doesn't crawl out until the following morning. So one can only draw one's conclusions. Admittedly, it may be that he pees out of the window instead of into the basin. Those geraniums were stunted this year, no doubt of that.'

'Lauris!' Mrs Greene screwed up her face in feigned disgust. Then: 'Eileen will be awfully cross if you ask him to go,' she said. Eileen was her other, favoured daughter, married to a farmer in Devon.

'Let her be cross. Since she's in a perpetual state of crossness about something or other, that doesn't really matter.'

'I wish you both got on better.'

'I wish she hadn't married someone so dreary. Mine was no better, admittedly, but at least I had the guts to give him the push.'

Soon Mrs Greene arose from the table, daintily dabbing with a lace-fringed handkerchief at a crumb lodged in one corner of her mouth. 'If I'm going to get your stepfather to the doctor, I'd better be off.'

'Oh, do stay a little! I could run you back.' It was not so much that Lauris wanted her mother with her as that she could not bear to think of now surrendering her to the invalid fractiously awaiting her in Harrow.

Mrs Greene shook her head. 'Sweet of you, darling. But you know how he frets and pines for me – even when that nice Major Mallory has come by for a game of chess.'

'It's so nice that you find everyone so nice.'

'Well, most people are,' Mrs Green said, meaning it.

Through the half-open hatch between dining-room and kitchen, Charmian had been listening to the adults instead of getting on with her homework. What her mother had said about giving Eddie the push had appalled her, even though it had not been unexpected. But with the precocious canniness of years spent largely in the company of her capricious, self-willed

mother, she knew that to protest would only produce a harden-
ing of resolve, followed by a hastening of execution. She rose to
her feet, a bird-like figure, with bony legs and arms, a beaky
nose and an upswept crest of hair, screwed the cap on to her
fountain-pen while deciding whether to go out or not, and then,
at Mrs Greene's 'Charmian! Charmian dear!' from the corridor,
eventually emerged.

'I'm off, darling.'

'I'll walk with you to the station.'

'No,' Lauris intervened. 'You must get on with your homework.' She did not want to accompany her mother herself but
she hated the idea of anyone else, above all her own and only
daughter, doing so instead.

'But I've awfully little for this evening. Miss Parker forgot to
give us anything and Mrs Strachan is ill.'

'Oh, very well. But come back quickly. I don't want any
wandering round the streets.'

Charmian, who was fond of her grandmother, slipped an arm
through hers as, side by side, they descended the steep steps.
Lauris frowned down at them from the half-open front door.
Then she called: 'Goodbye, Mother. Love to Pop.' She had never
been able to bring herself to call her stepfather 'Daddy' or even
'Father'.

'Yes, dear. Of course.'

As the child and her grandmother walked arm in arm down
Hornton Street – 'I'm afraid I have to take my time,' Mrs Greene
said, as always on these occasions – Charmian could no longer
restrain herself. 'Do you really think that Mummy means to give
Eddie the push?'

'Oh, Charmian! Were you eavesdropping?' Mrs Greene tried
to sound reproachful.

'I just couldn't help hearing. The hatch was open, you see.'

Mrs Greene sighed, her grip tightening on the child's arm as
she carefully negotiated a dip in the pavement. 'When your
mother decides to do something, then she does it. Doesn't she?
Look what happened to old Mrs Rooney. Here today, gone
tomorrow.' She might have said: 'Look what happened to your
father.'

'And only because she put away the saucepans without
washing them properly.'

Mrs Greene tried to change the subject. 'You must get Mummy
to bring you out to see us soon. Grandpop would so much enjoy

that. Next Sunday perhaps.' Lauris rarely brought Charmian with her on her visits to Harrow.

'It's not true,' Charmian persevered.

'What's not true?'

'What Mummy said about Eddie. About his peeing in the basin or on to the geraniums. He can go for hours and hours. Really. Honestly.'

'Mummy gets these ideas.'

'It's the wrong idea.'

Mrs Greene sighed again. 'Well, if she makes up her mind to a thing.'

'It's so unfair!' Charmian was on the verge of tears; and, realizing this, Mrs Greene dipped into her bag and produced a pound coin, as they entered the arcade of Kensington High Street Station. 'Buy yourself something with this, dear.'

Charmian shrank. Her mother was always telling her how badly off Granny and Grandpop were and Granny herself was always remarking that she had to 'count the pennies'. 'Oh, Granny, I couldn't, I couldn't!'

'Of course, you can. Don't be silly! I'm sorry it's not more. Grandpop told me to give it to you,' Mrs Greene lied. 'He got an unexpected cheque this morning – a dividend.'

Reluctantly Charmian took the coin and slipped it into the pocket of her anorak.

'Now don't lose it!'

'Oh, no, Granny!'

Charmian stood, hands in the pockets of her anorak, and watched her grandmother as, handbag dangling from one wrist and a Marks & Spencer shopping-bag dangling from the other, she edged her way through the barrier. Turning once to call out, over the heads of the people behind her, 'Bye, darling!', Mrs Greene disappeared from sight. But Charmian stayed on, her shoulders hunched and her eyes peering astigmatically from behind the glasses which her mother was always telling her that she really must give up for contact lenses.

Mr Donoghue emerged on the crest of the next wave of passengers and gave Charmian a little nod of the head, as though he were one of the pigeons pecking at some offering in his garden, and a murmured 'Good evening' before he hurried on, a briefcase, ER II stamped on its cracked leather in faded gold, swinging from a hand. He and his wife were always saying that they had nothing against that wretched, downtrodden child, it was the mother who was such a pain in the neck. Two school-boys, in identical blue blazers with gold buttons, stopped beside her on the pretext of staring into the window of a shop selling handbags. One of them then turned and said something to her, which, by willing herself not to hear, Charmian somehow managed to make inaudible. She tossed her head to one side, blushing. Both boys giggled and sauntered on.

At last what she had been waiting for happened. Eddie appeared, with the shabby black case containing his flute under one arm and his tweed jacket over the other. He was wearing a cap with a peak which seemed far too big for the wan, triangular-shaped face beneath it, a striped shirt fastened at the collar with a stud but tieless, and extremely narrow trousers supported by braces.

'Oh, Eddie!' Charmian cried out.

'What are you doing here?' he asked, not really interested in knowing.

'I came down here with Granny. She was sorry to miss you, she was asking where you were.'

'She knows I'm always at school on a Thursday afternoon. Today I'm back home earlier than usual.'

'Oh, I hoped you'd be. I hoped you'd be!' Charmian wanted to tell him; but instead she asked: 'Did you have a successful day?' It was what her mother used to ask her father when he got home, until it became clear that none of his days, passed in one Fleet Street pub after another, could ever be successful.

Eddie shrugged. 'Oh, a day like any other day. I'm going to a concert tonight,' he volunteered, as they now emerged from the arcade. 'Susie managed to get two free tickets out of her uncle. The Barbican. I don't know if I can really bear to hear the Elgar Cello Concerto for the umpteenth time but they're also going to do . . .'

Charmian had ceased to listen. Susie! Though she had never met her, she hated her. Perhaps, if Mummy persisted in her idea of giving Eddie the push, he and Susie would then live together. Susie's parents were rich, her uncle was a famous pianist. Susie could pay the rent for the two of them.

'Mummy seems to be in one of her moods,' Charmian said. This was the nearest she could get to mentioning the actual threat.

Eddie seemed not to hear her, as he trudged on up Hornton Street, always a little before her, his head bowed under that ridiculous cap of his, his jacket now swinging by its tab from the crooked middle finger of his left hand, and a soft whistling emerging from between his pursed lips.

'Mummy seems to be in one of her moods', Charmian repeated.

He turned. 'Oh, is she? Well, we'll soon charm her out of that.' The sad thing was that Eddie had no charm; and, though she loved him, Charmian was precocious enough to know it.

Charmian lay stretched out on the bed, now stripped of its bedclothes, and, eyes fixed on the damp-stain which darkened the wallpaper in front of her, cried and cried and cried. Tugging off sheets and blankets earlier that day, Lauris had exclaimed, 'God, what a smell!' But that smell, lingering on in the fairy's room despite the window which Lauris had thrown open, now only intensified Charmian's grief. It was Saturday, her mother was at the shop.

Charmian remembered another, no less poignant smell in this room, after her father had first been banished to it and then been banished from it to the Notting Hill Gate bed-sitter which had become merely a staging post on his way to the hospital in which he was now confined. 'May we go and see Daddy?' Charmian had at first asked persistently; and, stonily obdurate, Lauris had always, in effect, given the same reply: 'No point. He no longer recognizes people. That's what drink does to the brain in the end.'

Daddy, Eddie: would she ever see either of them again? Charmian put out a hand and, with the nail of the forefinger, scratched at the damp patch until it achieved the colour and consistency of wet, yellow blotting-paper. Her mother, when she noticed the mess, would be furious; but she would think Eddie to have been responsible.

'Why, why, why does he have to go?' Charmian had demanded; but the intensity of her concern had, as she had all along feared, only served to confirm her mother in her resolve. Lauris had answered: 'Because it's better for him and better for us.' 'How better?' Charmian had demanded and Lauris, at a loss to answer that, had said: 'Now Charmian! That's enough. Quite enough.'

It was the first time that Charmian had lain on that bed since Eddie's arrival, though she had often lain on it in her first desolation at the departure of her father. In all the months of

Eddie's occupancy, she had never even sat on it, as he would do, preferring it to a chair despite all Lauris's protests that he would ruin the springs. At the sound of the flute, Charmian would gently knock and then open the door before being told to do so. 'May I listen?' she would ask of him, as he looked up at her, in the striped flannel pyjamas which he wore at home even in daytime, the flute between the fingers which to Lauris always looked grubby and greasy. 'Listen to what? I'm only doing some boring old exercises.' He would go on with the exercises, as though she were not there, and she would stand, her hands resting against the lintel of the half-open door and her slack body resting against her hands until they grew numb. Sometimes, if she were at home, Lauris would eventually call out irritably: 'Oh, do shut that door, Eddie! I can do without that noise. I'm trying to work at my VAT,' and then Charmian, glad of the pretext, would slip into the narrow, high-ceilinged room, which had been built on, with the cloakroom below it, as an extension to the original late Victorian cottage.

'I'd like to learn the flute,' Charmian ventured on one occasion.

'Hopeless. You've no ear, no ear at all,' Eddie retorted loftily. 'You can't carry the simplest tune. Like your mother.'

'But I like music.'

Eddie shrugged.

'The kind of music you make,' Charmian qualified. 'It's like – like a bird singing.'

Charmian would often linger on in the kitchen, a morsel of bread still on her plate and a finger of cold tea still in her cup, and would wait for the sound of Eddie emerging from his room. She would be late for school but she did not care. Lauris was already at the shop. 'Are you leaving, Eddie?' He would grunt in answer. 'Then I'll walk with you,' she would volunteer. 'Oh, all right, in that case you can carry these shoes for me. I have to take them to be mended. Your mother's always telling me that the sole is coming loose on the left foot.'

In this room, grey and damp, Eddie had lain coughing and sneezing. 'Don't go near him!' Lauris had ordered Charmian. 'It's just this flu which everyone is getting. He can look after himself. I don't want you to get it and to give it to me.' But when Lauris had set off for the shop, Charmian had prepared a tray. 'Here,' she had said, 'I've made you a pot of tea and some toast. I could boil you an egg if you wanted one.'

'No, I don't.' At that, he sneezed so violently that a projectile of catarrh spattered the wall beside his bed. 'Oh, Christ!' He dabbed at it with a handkerchief already too damp to be effective. 'What I'd really like is something to drink. Some of the hard stuff, I mean.'

'Whisky?'

'Why not?'

Lauris kept the drinks cupboard locked, from a habit acquired when her husband was still around; but Charmian knew that the key lay under some luggage labels in one of the small drawers of her secretaire. She fetched the key – oh, God, don't let Mummy come back yet! – unlocked the cupboard and, with a trembling hand, poured out the whisky. 'Super!' Eddie exclaimed, having gulped at it. Later, Lauris commented that old Mrs Rooney seemed to have been up to her old tricks again, helping herself to the booze.

Charmian herself got the flu soon after Eddie was up and about again. He once put his head round the door of her bedroom to ask how she was. Otherwise he never came near her.

'Where are you going to live now?' she had asked.

'Well, to begin with, I'm going to join up with some friends in a squat in Clapham. Students. A couple.'

Well, at least he was not going to live with Susie, as she had feared 'I wish ... I wish Mummy hadn't decided to turn this room into a garden-room.' That was Lauris's excuse for giving the push to Eddie: she had always planned to make the fairy's room into a garden-room and now, with business picking up since she had given the push to that Old Etonian twit, she found that she could just afford to do so. Charmian shrank from telling Eddie that this was all a lie; she did not wish to cause him any hurt.

'It won't get any sun. Faces north,' Eddie said. 'Look at the damp.' He pointed to the patch at which Charmian would later scrape with a fingernail in tearful desolation. 'I only put up with a hovel like this because I got it rent-free.'

'May I visit you in Clapham?'

'It's a long way,' was Eddie's only answer.

... Charmian was still lying on the bed, her cheek pressed to the mattress and one hand trailing to the linoleum-covered floor, when Lauris returned from the shop. 'Charmian!' Lauris called. She was in a good mood.

'Yes, Mummy!' Charmian scrambled off the bed; but she was not quick enough in leaving the room.

'What on earth are you doing in there?'

'I was looking to see . . . to see how it would become a garden-room.'

Lauris laughed, her sturdy legs apart and a hand on her hip. 'It's not really going to be a garden-room, lovey. But I didn't want to hurt poor old Eddie's feelings or annoy your dear Aunt Eileen more than I do in any case.'

Curiously, Lauris was soon missing Eddie, as she had never missed her flushed, stumbling, incoherent husband after giving him the push. 'It seems odd not to have Eddie around,' she said a few days later, as she and Charmian sat facing each other at supper, with no Eddie silently wolfing his food between them.

'The house doesn't seem to be the same,' Charmian concurred, feeling herself to be on the verge of tears.

Lauris rallied herself. 'No, thank God!' she exclaimed. 'Though the stink, like the melody, lingers on.'

Charmian wanted to jump up from the table and flee to her own room; but she controlled the impulse. 'It's . . . lonely.'

'Lonely!'

'For me.'

'That's a nice thing to say, when you have your mother for company. Lonely! Yes, that's a nice thing to say.'

In the bleak days which followed, Charmian would often venture into the fairy's room when her mother was out; but she never again threw herself on to the bed and she never again succumbed to that first wild, noisy paroxysm of grief. Instead. she would stand in the doorway, a hand on the doorknob, and she would will herself to see the narrow, bony hands holding the flute and to hear that shrill, exciting, slightly eerie sound which bubbled out of it.

'It's funny that Eddie never comes to see us.'

'Not funny at all. People are like that, most people. All those months with us and now we might have never existed. People, young people, have so little gratitude. Of course I'm expected to forward his letters, that goes without saying.'

'Perhaps we could go to see him in Clapham one day? On a Sunday or a Saturday afternoon.'

'I doubt if he'd thank us for that. Not even your aunt has ever visited him in that squalid squat of his. A squat! As though he

didn't have a grant and your aunt didn't keep sending money to
him. A scandal, I call it.'

One autumn day, instead of returning straight home from school,
Charmian wandered with a school-friend, an Indian girl
immensely tall for her age, into Holland Park. The friend was
hoping to meet a boy from the comprehensive and when she at
last saw him in the distance, with a group of other boys, she
raced off from Charmian with barely a word of excuse or
apology. Charmian wandered on by herself, by narrow, erratic,
mud-choked paths, deeper and deeper into the heart of the park.
Suddenly she came on a shabby, gaunt, middle-aged man, with
an old-fashioned hearing-aid dangling a wire to his shoulder,
who was feeding the birds from a brown paper bag. She halted
and watched him. First a small bird – a blue tit, though she did
not know that – swooped down on to his outstretched palm;
then, all at once, he was covered with pigeons, with one even
perched on his balding head, an eye glittering sideways at her, a
sharp chip of mica. She walked over to the man and in a soft,
timid voice asked him: 'May I try to feed them?' But, not hearing
her, the man made no response other than a vague, distant smile.
    The next day, when school was over, Charmian set out with a
bag of her own full of breadcrumbs. Once again she passed the
deaf man, covered with his pigeons, and then pressed on even
deeper into the woods. She took a handful of crumbs out of the
bag, held out her palm as she had seen him doing, and then
waited with a combination of excitement and dread. A robin
perched on a branch not far from her, its head on one side. It
hopped to another, nearer branch and then to another. Finally,
with a noisy flutter of wings, it descended. For a moment she
felt it, as light as a ping-pong ball, near the fleshy base of her
thumb. Then it was gone, a crumb in its beak. An extraordinary
joy flooded into her. Other birds came both on that day and on
all the days which followed, but she never again experienced
precisely the thrill of that moment.
    Soon, she had her own place in the park, just as, she had
noticed, the deaf man and a number of other people each had
their own places too. If someone – a small child with a girl who
was either his mother or his minder, an elderly, cross-faced
woman, a giggling couple, arms around each other's waists –
trespassed on her place, she felt a furious resentment.

She had not merely her own place but also her own birds, like the sparrow, instantly recognizable, one of the tail-feathers of which was as white as a swan's.

It was as she was feeding 'her' birds one chill November afternoon that a tall woman, looking like some nineteenth-century grenadier in her sweeping loden cape and her shako of a hat, stalked past, with two golden retrievers on leads. She halted, shortsightedly screwing up her eyes under sandy eyebrows. 'Do you catch birds?' she asked in a hoarse, actressy voice. The approach of her dogs, panting and slavering as they tugged at their leads, had frightened away all but one bold pigeon.

Charmian shook her head. The woman's tone sounded to her as accusatory as her mother's when, returning tired and fretful from the shop, she asked: 'Have you been at those biscuits yet again?' Then she added: 'I only feed them.' She held up the brown paper bag.

'Well, there's a bird by the pond over there and the ducks seem to have made up their minds to kill it.'

The woman marched on, clearly believing that she had done her duty.

Charmian deliberated, a hand outstretched with some crumbs on it. Then she walked towards the pond, milkily calm beneath its overhanging branches. The ducks were quacking tumul-tuously, as they did when a middle-aged, gypsy-like woman, in a dirndl skirt and with a red, woollen scarf wound round her narrow head like a turban, used to approach to feed them. But the woman was not there. Charmian peered. The ducks were clustered round the farther rim of the pond, where the path did not reach, now trampling on and now pecking at what seemed to be no more than an agitated ball of mud. Charmian eventually managed to scramble over the wire fence separating the pond from the path; but, in doing so, she gave her shin a jagged scratch from which the blood soon began to ooze. Her feet sank deep, until she could feel the chilly mire oozing over a shoe on to her instep. She made her way round, arms extended and body tilting from side to side, as though, inexpertly and fearfully, she were negotiating a tightrope.

'Go away! Shoo! Go on!' The ducks retreated a short distance, still quacking, their necks extended, and shaking their tails. She stooped, she scooped up the ball of mud. At first she did not know what to do with it, as she stared down at it. Then she shoved it into the brown paper bag and returned back along the marshy rim of the pond. Having once again scrambled over the fence to regain the path, she set off briskly for home. In her hand, the bird had lain so still that she had wondered if it might not be dead; but as she hurried along under the giant chestnut trees of Duchess of Bedford Walk, she felt a tremor and heard a rustle in the bag. She stopped, opened a corner and gingerly peeped in. The bird, clearly famished, was pecking at the crumbs which still remained.

Since her mother was so often away at the shop, Charmian had her own key. As she turned it in the front door, Lauris called out: 'Charmian!'

'Yes, Mummy.'

'Eddie's here. He called by. Happened to be passing on the way to a concert in Leighton House.' Lauris did not sound pleased.

'Eddie!' Charmian hurried down the basement stairs, taking them in twos and threes, and raced into the kitchen, the bag in her hand. Her mother and Eddie sat facing each other over cups of tea.

Except that his hair was much longer than she remembered it, falling almost to his shoulders, and that he had a gold stud in one ear, Eddie looked unchanged.

'Oh, Eddie!' Charmian cried out.

'Hello.' Eddie did not get up. He raised his cup in both his hands and gulped from it.

'I've rescued a bird! It's here – in this bag. The ducks were trying to kill it in Holland Park. By the pond.'

'Oh, Charmian!' Lauris exclaimed in reproof. Then she and Eddie both peered into the bag, as Charmian held it out for their inspection. Eventually Eddie inserted a hand – 'Take care! Don't hurt it!' Charmian cried out – and withdrew the throbbing, bedraggled creature. He rubbed off some mud with the thumb of the hand on which it was now resting. 'A budgie,' he said. 'Fancy that. It must have escaped from somewhere.'

Lauris tugged off a length of paper towelling and began to dab and scrape. 'Poor little thing!' She was now delighted, not annoyed, as at first.

'Can we keep it? Charmian asked.

'It must belong to someone,' Lauris answered. 'The question is who?'

'Probably at this very moment some little girl is crying her eyes out for it,' Eddie said.

'Or an old-age pensioner is frantic.'

Charmian, who did not care about some little girl or an old-age pensioner, persisted: 'Can't we keep it, Mummy?'

Eventually, Lauris rang up the police and reported the find. But the man to whom she spoke was offhand, almost rude: no, no one had reported the loss of a budgie, but he would make a note of Lauris's name, address and telephone number.

Charmian took heart. 'Where shall we keep it?' she asked.

Lauris surveyed the bird, which had now fluttered off Eddie's palm and had perched itself on top of the eye-level grill. 'It's awfully pretty, now that one can see it through the mud. Sweet. We'll need a cage.'

'Let's go to the pet-shop,' Charmian said. 'You know, the one in Abingdon Road. Where Indira bought her gerbil. Oh, do come with me, Eddie!'

Eddie looked at his watch. 'OK.'

'What would a cage cost?' Lauris asked.

'Ten pounds?' Eddie suggested.

'At least that.' Lauris picked up her bag from the kitchen-dresser. 'Here's fifteen.'

In the event, the cheapest cage cost sixteen pounds fifty and, since Charmian had only thirty pence on her, Eddie paid the difference. Then there were seed, grit and a piece of cuttle-fish bone also to be purchased. Eddie paid for those too, resolving that he would get the money back from Lauris as soon as they returned. The efficient girl assistant gave them a free leaflet with instructions – 'Your Budgerigar and You.' Eddie commented jocularly that the title seemed to have got its priorities wrong.

'I wonder if it's a boy or a girl,' Lauris said, when she, Charmian and Eddie had pursued the increasingly terrified bird around the kitchen and, with an unexpectedly athletic leap, Eddie had at last managed to grab it, trapped against a pane of the window on to the garden, and to manoeuvre it into the cage.

Eddie shrugged, his narrow shoulders rising and falling as his breath came fast. 'There's some way of telling from the beak. The experts can do it. Can't they?' He was not sure.

'What shall we call him?' Charmian was convinced that the bird was a male, and not even one of Lauris's friends, a woman who had kept budgerigars and who expressed doubts, could subsequently persuade her to the contrary. She stooped, her hair screening her face, and called: 'Beakie! Beakie! Beakie!' Beakie became his name from then on. She was so interested in the bird that she was hardly aware of Eddie's departure for his concert. He had to dash, he said, or Susie would give him a rocket.

In the weeks which followed, Charmian used her pocket-money to buy Beakie a variety of playthings. These included a bell encrusted with seed, a pink plastic swing and a mauve-and-pink plastic staircase. Beakie would sometimes jerk perfunctorily back and forth on the swing and he would sometimes distractedly race up and down the stairs from nowhere to nowhere, just as Lauris would distractedly race up and down the stairs of the house when she kept forgetting things in her hurry to arrive at the shop by opening-time, but what really engrossed him was to gaze longingly through his bars – his cage was on a low table below the window of Charmian's bedroom – at the pigeons strung out along the garden fence. 'If they could get at you, they'd peck you to death,' Charmian told him, but still he gazed out.

Charmian would sit by the cage or would stoop over it, calling out: 'Beakie, Beakie, Beakie!' or 'Good morning, Beakie!' or 'Good evening, Beakie!' in her clear, high-pitched voice. But, disappointingly, the bird showed no inclination to talk, though he would often sing, looking out on to the pigeons beyond his bars. Lauris's friend who had kept budgerigars said that she thought that he was probably too old to learn.

Lauris would come into Charmian's bedroom and they would let Beakie out, watching him as he fluttered from cornice to cornice or perched himself on the head of the teddy-bear propped against the mantelpiece and then placed his beak against the reflection of his beak in the mirror which hung above it. At first, Lauris seemed as fond of the bird as Charmian.

But then it began to annoy her that, as soon as she had come back from school, Charmian would at once race upstairs to see how the bird was doing. 'Aren't you even going to greet your mother?' Lauris would ask. Beakie would now perch on Charmian's forefinger, her shoulder or her head; but he would rarely stay with Lauris. 'He seems to feel that he belongs only to you,' Lauris said. 'He obviously doesn't realize who it is who pays for his food.'

Soon after that, Lauris was complaining about the mess that the bird made. 'But it's quite dry, Mummy,' Charmian would say, scraping away with dustpan and brush; but to that Lauris would retort that it was insanitary to have that sort of muck falling everywhere, particularly in a room in which one slept.

One day, when she was in the room, Lauris suddenly cried out: 'Oh, my God!' and pointed to the wallpaper above the window.

'What is it, Mummy?'

'That wretched bird' – he was no longer Beakie to her – 'has been pecking at that lovely William Morris paper. Oh, really, it's too bad! You must keep his cage shut in future.'

Charmian wailed: 'But he must get out sometime! He can't spend all his time in a cage as small as that.' She went over to the cage and stared at Beakie; he stared back at her, his eyes unwinking. 'That leaflet – the one the girl gave us – says that, if budgerigars don't get exercise, then their life expectancy is shortened.'

Lauris told old Mrs Greene on her next visit: 'That beastly little budgerigar is making absolute havoc of this house.'

'He keeps Charmian happy.'

'She wastes far too much time on him. She ought to be getting on with her homework.'

'I suppose we could give him a home,' Mrs Greene said doubtfully. 'But it would break Charmian's heart not to have him around.'

'Nonsense! She gets these crazes. You know what children are like.'

One day Charmian came home and found her bedroom window open and the cage empty. Her mother was still out at the shop but a used plate and knife, a half-drunk cup of coffee beside it, showed that she must have been home for a snack at midday. The child searched all over the house for the missing bird and then went out into the garden and even into the street, calling in a high, forlorn voice: 'Beakie! Beakie! Beakie!' People stared at her but, usually so self-conscious, she was impervious to them.

Mr Donoghue, working in his front garden, looked up to ask: 'What's the trouble?' When she told him about Beakie's disappearance, he said that he would keep an eye open for him. He was sure that he could not have gone far.

By the time that her mother returned, Charmian was distraught. 'Who left my window open?' she demanded.

'I expect you did,' Lauris retorted, her mouth grim.

'I'd never have left the window and the door of the cage open both at the same time.'

'Your room has to be aired. Perhaps Edna left it open.' Edna was the char who had succeeded Mrs Rooney.

'But Edna doesn't come on Fridays.'

'Well, I really don't know. I have enough to worry me without that wretched bird. Now don't make such a fuss. I dare say he'll fly back.'

'A cat may have caught him.'

'I doubt it. Unless the cat has wings.'

That evening Charmian laboriously wrote out a number of notices: 'MISSING – LOST. Blue-green budgie, answers to name of BEAKIE. Reward of £2 for safe return.' She added her name, address and telephone number. She went out and stuck the notices on trees, lamp-posts and pillar-boxes in the surrounding neighbourhood. Then she rang the bells of the houses in the street and in those on either side of it. Everyone was sympathetic but no one had seen Beakie.

'You haven't done your homework,' Lauris said.

'I can't, can't, can't!'

'Oh, don't carry on so!' The child was being even worse than when Lauris had given the push to her drunken father.

Beakie did not return. The next day, Charmian would eat nothing. 'You're being very silly,' Lauris told her. 'Such a fuss about a miserable little bird.'

Charmian did not answer. Tears formed along her lower eyelids, which were inflamed from lack of sleep.

Lauris said: 'He's probably quite happy. In another home.'

Charmian put the back of her hand to her nose and gave a loud sniff. Then she began to sob: 'It's so lonely without him!'

'Well, really! That's a nice thing to say. All that fuss about Eddie, now all this fuss about a bird. Haven't you got me?'

The days limped by. When not at school, Charmian wandered Campden Hill, peering over fences and railings and up into trees, in the hope that, by some miracle, Beakie would suddenly be visible to her. Then she resigned herself to the loss. But she did not forget him.

A few days before Christmas, Eddie arrived with two clumsily wrapped presents from his mother and one, for Charmian, from himself, in return for the two handkerchiefs which she had already posted to him at the squat. His present was a jigsaw puzzle, so simple, a mere two dozen pieces or so, that it was clearly intended for a much younger child; but Charmian was touched, laying it out on the kitchen table and putting some of the pieces together there and then. Lauris, who thought that he might have brought her something too, after all those months of hospitality, asked him what he was doing for Christmas and was obscurely satisfied when he answered that he would be spending it with Susie and her people in Norfolk.

Charmian, who had not fed the birds in the park since her rescue of Beakie, suddenly abandoned the jigsaw puzzle, got up and took a crust of bread from the bread bin.

'What's that for?' Lauris asked sharply.

'I thought I'd go into the park and feed the birds. They can't find much to eat at this time of year, with this frost.'

'Well, don't bring back another Beakie,' Lauris said, half in joke and half in earnest.

'Come with me,' Charmian said to Eddie, more a command than a request.

'Eddie's hardly finished his tea.'

But Eddie got to his feet. When Charmian had said that 'Come with me,' she had sounded disconcertingly like her mother.

The cousins walked along Duchess of Bedford Walk in silence. Then 'Depressing time of year,' Eddie muttered at last. He kicked out at a dead branch which lay in his path. 'How I loathe Christmas!'

'But you'll be with Susie.'

'Their house is like a refrigerator. Hell, absolute hell.'

He did not sound happy about the visit. Charmian was glad.

The park was all but deserted, with mist clinging like cobwebs to the branches and the air damp and chill. 'Is the flute going all right?' Charmian asked.

'Not bad. I won a prize at college. Did I tell you?'

'No . . . It's so long, ages and ages, since you came to see us.'

'Well, your mother doesn't make one feel precisely welcome.'

Charmian knew she ought to protest but she could not do so. 'I miss it,' she said.

'Miss what?'

'Your playing the flute.'

'Nonsense!' He laughed derisively. 'You've got no ear for music. You know that.'

'The house seems lonely without it.'

'It got on your mother's nerves. She's got no more ear than you have.'

'This is where I used to stand to feed the birds. Always the same place, my place. But I haven't been here for, oh, ages. I expect they've forgotten me.'

The cousins stood in silence, side by side, under the vague, dripping branches and then Charmian slowly inserted a hand into the brown paper bag and drew out some crumbs. Eddie hunched himself inside his anorak, drawing in his pointed chin. Charmian held out a palm. 'Come, come, come!' she called, quietly and yet with such intensity that Eddie, staring down at the frost-hard ruts of the path, gave a little shudder, though he did not know why. Out of the darkening sky first a robin, then a tit and then five plump, awkward pigeons descended. 'They've remembered me!' Charmian cried out in mingled joy and wonder. 'Look, look! They've remembered me!' There was now a pigeon on her shoulder and another in the crook of her right arm.

Eddie hugged himself inside the anorak. A bead glittered, as though it were a diamond, on the tip of his reddened nose. His back was aching.

Charmian looked up into the trees, her palm still upraised. Then all at once she cried out piercingly: 'Oh, look, Eddie! Look! There he is! There's Beakie!'

Eddie craned his neck. He screwed up his eyes. He could see nothing.

'Up there! High, high!' She pointed. Then she called: 'Beakie, Beakie, Beakie!' She raised her palm higher, her oblation on it.

She lowered her palm. Softly she said: 'He's gone. He's flown off. Perhaps he didn't see me. Perhaps he didn't hear me.'

Suddenly Eddie felt a strange tremor, not of the body but of the spirit, such as, in the past, he had only experienced when listening to music. On an impulse, he drew his hands out of the pockets of his anorak and then placed his right arm around her shoulder. He had never touched her before, he hated touching people or himself being touched; even with Susie he had to steel himself for contact. He drew the gauche, bird-like body against him. 'Well, there, you see! Beakie's quite capable of surviving on his own. You don't have to worry about him. He's got all this way through the winter. You don't have to worry about him. He's free and he's happy.'

'Yes, he's free and he's happy. Yes.' She gazed up into the misty branches, her eyes wide and a hand to her lips. 'Yes. Yes. Yes!'

The Cloven Hoof

'Darling, I feel so *bad* about leaving you over Christmas,' Mummy exclaimed yet again, as Laura said goodbye to her and Daddy at the airport before they flew off to Naples to board their ship. 'I shouldn't have dreamed of going away if my arthritis hadn't given me such hell all this month. But you'll have lots of friends to see, won't you?'

'And you can always go to Aunt Iris,' Daddy said.

'Or the Cudlipps.'

Daddy told Laura to drive home very, very slowly. He was thinking at least as much of the BMW as of her.

'Oh, and pet, you will take the greatest care of my poor little Poochie, won't you? You must now think of yourself as his second mother.' The poodle was scratching himself with an air of rapturous concentration on the end of a rhinestone-studded lead, which Laura was holding in the hand not holding Mummy's crocodile-leather make-up box. Laura nodded and Mummy went on: 'Don't, dear, please don't let him do his business, big or small, on the lawn. Daddy would be awfully peeved if, after that reseeding, he were to come back to find it covered in those horrid orange patches once again. I know it's a nuisance to have to rush home in your lunch-hour but I'm afraid there's nothing else for it, is there?' Again Laura nodded. 'And bones, dear – bones. You will remember what bones do to his tum?' Laura said that of course, yes, she would remember what bones did to his tum.

When at last they had vanished from sight into the departure lounge, Laura felt none of the relief that she had promised herself. Poochie might caper about at the end of the jewelled lead, even attempting to cock a leg against some luggage abandoned in his path; she herself felt so far from capering about that she had to force herself not to cry.

*

[148]

'There's that yappy little dog,' their neighbour Mr Purdy boomed good-naturedly at her when, on her return, they came face to face – his flushed and hers wan – in the hall of the mansion flats overlooking Regent's Park. Mummy called him 'a vulgar little man', though in fact he was enormous. Daddy merely returned his greetings with a nod ever since that time when a male guest at one of his all-night parties had used the garden, *their* garden, as not even Poochie was allowed to use it, leaning over the balcony for this purpose.

But Laura had secretly admired and envied Mr Purdy for a long, long time. Certainly he was at least fifty and therefore some fifteen years older than herself; and no less certainly he was grossly overweight, ungainly and often drunk. But there was something jolly, amiable and, yes, even sexy about him; so that it was not really surprising that a succession of young girls should have taken up residence with him, albeit each for no more than a week or even a weekend at a time.

Laura smiled at him and then halted – both things she would not have done if Mummy and Daddy had been at hand.

'I thought you'd gone away for Christmas,' he said, and then belched audibly behind a pudgy fist. 'I saw you loading up the BMW. With all those suitcases I guessed that you might all be emigrating.'

Laura explained that Mummy and Daddy had left on a three-week Mediterranean cruise, but that she herself had been unable to go too because of her work.

'And what do you do? I've often wondered.'

'I'm at the Foreign Office.'

'How very glamorous!'

Laura did not explain that to be Sir Andrew's secretary was far from being glamorous. Instead, she looked down at Poochie, whimpering for his dinner at the end of his lead, with a shy, furtive smile.

'Well, you must come in for a drink sometime. Especially as you're now enjoying your freedom.'

'I'd love that. I'm – I'm told that you have some really lovely things.'

'Good God! Who told you that?'

'Mr Roberts.'

Mr Roberts, the porter, enjoyed gossiping to the residents about each other.

'He must be off his nut.'

*

The days dragged by and Christmas crept nearer and nearer; but the invitation for which Laura continued to wait with so much eagerness never materialized. She glimpsed Mr Purdy from time to time. Indeed, she herself more than once precipitated an encounter, lurking behind the net curtains of the sitting-room until she saw him approach the block and then running out. But though he boomed 'Hello there!' or 'Beastly weather!' in the friendliest fashion, he never said anything further.

Laura blamed the French girl, so often now to be seen swinging from his arm, her triangular, kittenish face upturned to his square, bovine one.

Eventually there was a terrible night when Laura was woken by thumps and bangs, as of furniture being overturned, and the crash and clatter of breaking crockery, all interspersed with shrill cries and deep bellowings in a mixture of English and French. "elp! 'elp!' she had heard at one moment; but, cowering under the bedclothes, she did not think of either offering or summoning 'elp.

The next day Laura saw Mr Purdy dragging himself heavily up the steps, a bag from the off-licence round the corner dangling from either swollen hand. There was a piece of sticking plaster puckered across the bridge of his nose, and an aubergine-coloured bruise darkened one side of his dimpled chin.

Laura hurried out into the hall, pulling on her overcoat for appearances. 'Have you had an accident?' she asked disingenuously.

'You might call it that.'

'A fall?'

'A fall? Yes, you might call it that too. One tends to return to reality with a nasty thump.' He hunted in his distended pocket for his keys. 'What a Christmas! And on top of it all my job has folded up.'

Laura had long since learned from Mr Roberts that Mr Purdy wrote a weekly column on dining out for a newspaper which Daddy and Mummy would never have dreamed of having delivered to their flat. In consequence she bought it every Thursday to read in her lunch-hour.

'You've been made redundant!'

'If you want to use that euphemism. I'd prefer to say that I've had the boot.'

'Oh, I am sorry! I love your pieces. You make one feel that one's actually eaten all those meals.'

'Yes, food *is* interesting. And satisfying. I sometimes think that there's really nothing quite so interesting and satisfying in the whole world. Even better than a good . . .' He broke off with a guffaw. 'Come in and have that drink I promised!' He indicated the upstairs with a jab of the keys in his hand.

Laura, who had for so long been looking forward to this moment, now felt an overwhelming panic. He was all too clearly drunk; and last night she had heard him roaring 'Slut! Slut! Slut!' at that French girl, after which there had been the sound of a slap and a scream of piercing shrillness. No, she could not face it, not all alone. So, quickly, nervously, she said that she was sorry but she was just going out to do some last-minute Christmas shopping.

'To hell with Christmas!'

Laura, scurrying to St John's Wood High Street, cursed herself for having been such a coward.

But the next evening, returning late from work, she was bolder. Glimpsing Mr Purdy as he was about to march into the pub at the corner of their street, she slipped in behind him. 'The usual,' he was saying. Then, catching sight of her, 'Hello, my pet! Never seen you here before. You *are* getting bold. What can I order for you?' It was obvious that the double whisky being set down before him was not his first of the day.

But Laura, who had always had such a fastidious horror of drunkenness and drunks, now strangely did not care. Indeed, all the symptoms of his condition – the slurring of the speech, the heaviness of the eyelids, the loud and unfocused *bonhomie* – in some way had even started to excite her.

They sat down in a corner and soon he was telling her how at first he had thought her a God-awful toffee-nosed little bitch but now he realized that he just couldn't have been more wrong. It must be those parents of hers. For Christ's sake, what had she done to deserve such parents? In other circumstances Laura would have leapt to their defence; but, like all the other symptoms of his drunkenness, this rudeness about Daddy and Mummy now only gave a sharper edge to her excitement.

Then he began to talk about Christmas: how he always loathed it and how this year he was going to loathe it even more than usual, now that that little tramp had walked out on him and that two-faced little shit had grabbed his job; how he had a good mind to get pissed and retire to bed until the whole bloody pantomime was over; how turkey and plum pudding and mince pies always made him want to puke . . .

It was then – the excitement surging up within her, an irresistible tide – that Laura swallowed hard, cleared her throat and came up with her invitation: 'I'll also be on my own. So why don't we both. . .?'

Mummy, who was a good, plain cook, had never allowed Laura to do anything in the kitchen other than wash up, prepare the vegetables and scrub the floor when the Portuguese 'treasure' was away – as she was now. But, having committed herself to a Christmas dinner, Laura now realized that she would have to search through Mummy's cookery books for a dish both elaborate enough to please an expert ('Not, for Christ's sake, *not* a bird!' he had admonished) and simple enough for her to produce with success. After reading cookery books through almost a whole night, she eventually decided – seduced chiefly by the instruction 'Preparation for this dish to begin three to four days before it is required' – on a *Boeuf estouffade d'Avignon*.

The next day (since only four days now intervened till Christmas) there was a long quest during her lunch-hour for the sprig of rosemary required for the marinade and an equally long contemplation of Daddy's wine racks before selecting the claret to be used for the same purpose. The day after that, again in her lunch hour (Sir Andrew scolded her for her lateness in returning) she went in search of some pickled pork, arrowroot and coriander seeds. On Christmas Eve she reread the recipe and realized, to her horror, that she had omitted to procure a pig's trotter and had no idea where to find one. It was only after she had trailed the whole length of the North End Road, on the advice of a colleague who lived in Fulham, that she at last tracked one down.

Everything was now ready. The three pounds of fillet steak had been marinated; she had even practised, the previous evening, making some of the pastry with which the recipe said that the lid of the casserole must be sealed. Again she had read the final instructions: 'The cooking, which must be very, very slow – the slowness can hardly be overemphasized – should, for best results, take six to seven hours . . .' She had set her alarm clock for six on Christmas morning.

'What a marvellous smell!' Mr Purdy – who had asked her to call him Willy in the pub – exclaimed, as he marched into the flat, a bottle of Lafite Rothschild in either hand and a Camembert cheese tucked precariously under an arm.

'I hope it'll be all right. It's the first time I've attempted this particular dish.'

'What is it?'

She told him and he whistled. 'Thank God it's not a bloody bird. I can see this is going to be a real gastronomic adventure, Laura my dear.'

Each time that Laura tried to lure him into the dining-room he insisted on yet another glass of Daddy's Manzanilla Pasada; but at last, when it was almost four o'clock, there he was slouched at the other end of the table, in excited if groggy anticipation, his napkin tucked into his overtight collar, and there she was, saying nervously, 'I didn't prepare anything for starters,' as she carried in the French earthenware casserole.

'Christ – what an odour! One can't call it a smell. Laura, my sweet – I can see that you know your way to a man's heart. A Cordon Bleu cook – like my late but not otherwise lamented wife!'

Laura cracked the pastry round the lid, baked to the consistency of clay in a drought; and then, with a palpitating heart, she raised the lid itself.

What looked like a sediment of semi-liquid mud was caked at the bottom and on the sides of the casserole. Embedded in it, bleached and bare, was a single cloven hoof: all that was left of the pig's trotter.

'Christ!'

'What's happened to it? What's *happened*?'

'The pastry couldn't have sealed the lid. Evaporation, my dear. Or maybe the oven . . . Perhaps you left it in too long.'

For a few seconds Laura was frozen in horror. Then she snatched up the casserole, burning the ball of her thumb as she did so, rushed into the kitchen and clattered it down into the sink. Oh, hell, hell! It was his fault for having drunk on and on and on; and it was her fault for not having given him a shove. With furious, stricken eyes she stared out into the garden, where Poochie was straining at his business in the middle of the lawn.

She flung up the window. 'Poochie!'

Terrified by her tone, he cringed over to her.

'There you are! Take that! See what that does to your tum!'

She picked the pig's trotter out of the casserole and hurled it not so much to him as at him. Now not merely the ball of her thumb but all the tips of her fingers were burning.

Slowly she went back into the dining-room, feeling her finger-tips still burning, burning, burning and tears pricking at her eyes.

Mr Purdy – Willy – was guzzling a biscuit piled high with the Camembert he had brought. 'Not to worry,' he told her airily, waving the remainder of the biscuit back and forth before his face. 'This claret is first rate. And this Camembert has achieved just the right degree of ripeness. Here. Have some. A real treat.'

Mechanically she cut herself a sliver of Camembert, took a biscuit from the barrel, and then placed the first on top of the second.

She bit into the biscuit. The dry crumbs filled her mouth; but somehow she could not swallow them. It was as if all the dust of her thirty-four years with Daddy and Mummy had suddenly exploded behind her teeth and in the back of her throat, to suffocate her.

'Have a sip of this, old girl.'

He held out, not her glass, but his own, the claret glinting in it.

She shook her head, her mouth still parched with biscuit and the tears still pricking at her eyes.

'Try some. It's a cure for all disappointments. None better. Go on.'

Slowly she put her lips forward to the glass he was uptilting to her. She gulped and gulped again; and then suddenly, miraculously, the dust had gone.

She smiled across at him.

'See? What did I tell you?'

He put a swollen, purplish hand over her bony, pallid one. Then he splashed some more wine into his glass and once again held it up to her lips.

This time she drained it greedily.

Have You Had a Nice Day?

It was the rainy season. Grey-green rods of rain pierced the towering foliage, hammered the deliquescent track over which the ancient Cadillac was slithering and bumping, and made it all but impossible for Clare, hunched forward over the wheel, to see out.

High up here in the mountains, it was also the landslide season. 'Listen!' Ruth exclaimed and, straining to do so, Clare could hear a rumbling, as of a distant earthquake, followed by a crash.

It was crazy to attempt such a journey. Clare had already told Ruth that twice already, and so checked herself from telling her it again. Ruth would often remark: 'I hate complainers.' Sometimes she would add: 'That's what I like about you. You never complain. So many Brits never stop complaining.' Ruth was Australian, married to a professor at the same university in Kobe at which Clare taught. The black eye-patch over one eye gave her square, seamed, jowly face a piratical look. The empty socket covered by the eye-patch was the reason why Clare, not she, was driving. The Cadillac belonged to Ruth's husband, whom she tended to refer to as 'the *sensei*'. Because 'the *sensei*' was suffering from shingles, Clare had been persuaded to drive Ruth to the Naked Festival in a car far larger and far more powerful than she had ever driven before.

Ruth was writing a book about Japanese festivals. Neglecting his students and his book, already years in gestation, on Lafcadio Hearn's Japanese years, Ruth's grey and patient husband drove her to innumerable festivals. No doubt it was only through illness that he could escape from the dictates of his wife's relentless will. Now it was Clare who had to submit to those dictates.

'Shit!' Ruth suddenly exclaimed. 'What's going on?'

Only a few minutes before, Clare had remarked: 'Everyone is

constantly telling one that Japan is overpopulated, and yet we must have driven for at least half an hour without seeing a house or even a single person.' Now, ahead and below, where the road precipitously dipped, there snaked a queue of trucks, with countless people, looking like insects under their umbrellas, scurrying around them.

'Some sort of hold-up,' Clare said.

'Oh, shit!' Ruth repeated. Hold-ups of any kind drove her to frenzy.

Clare halted the Cadillac at the end of the line of vehicles. 'Ask someone what's going on,' Ruth commanded. But it was hardly necessary to do so. There had been a landslide and, at the bottom of the dip down which they had just jolted, the road had tumbled into a ravine. Ruth reached back for her raincoat and, having jumped out of the car, struggled into it. Clare followed her, opening a waxed paper umbrella given to her by one of her students.

'The road has vanished,' Ruth said.

'They're repairing it.' Another statement of the obvious.

Men in baggy cotton trousers and shirts, soaked with rain, were heaving up huge logs, with sudden, concerted yelps, and then lugging them to the place where instead of the road there was a jagged wound of mud, rocks and serpentine tree-roots.

'Ask them how long it's going to take. We're already behind our schedule.' Ruth often used the word 'schedule', pronouncing it in the American manner. She had a schedule for most things in her life.

Clare, wishing, not for the first time, that she spoke no Japanese, squelched over the mud to someone in a peaked cap who looked like the foreman.

He shrugged; said: 'One hour, two hours, maybe three hours'; shrugged again. Then he shouted out something to the gang of men and strode off.

Clare translated for Ruth. Then she said: 'No use in getting wet. We might as well wait in the car.'

'You could first tell them to get a move on.'

'I don't think there'd be much point in doing that.'

Back in the car, Ruth produced a Hershey bar, broke it in two and gave Clare the smaller half. 'Unless they get a move on, we'll never make it to that inn before nightfall.'

'Then we'll have to find another inn.'

[156]

'If another inn exists ... Ah, well, it won't be the first time I've bedded down in the Caddy.' Munching at another bite of the chocolate, she went on: 'Isn't it odd that not one of all these men has shown the smallest interest in us?'

'Is it?'

'Well, suppose we had been held up like this in some remote spot in Australia or the States or even in England ... The only women among a horde of truck-drivers ... You can bet your bottom dollar that we'd be the centre of attention. There'd be a crowd around the car.'

'That's what I like about Japan.'

It clearly wasn't what Ruth liked about Japan. 'Well, I like to be noticed. I like to feel that I exist.'

One hour passed. A second hour passed. Ruth said: 'You'd better ask that man how much longer we'll have to wait.' The rain had now ceased. Saffron-coloured, the sunshine of early evening filtered down through the branches.

'There's not much point. He probably doesn't know.'

'Oh, go on!'

Clare got out of the car. And as she did so, she saw a young man, in jeans and a shiny black blouson, walking towards her. His close-cropped hair was glittering with raindrops. He smiled and, in quaintly formal English, said: 'Excuse me, please. You are American lady?'

'English.'

'*So deska?* May I please talk English with you?'

'Well, not really at this moment. I'm going to ask the foreman how much longer we have to wait.'

He drew in his breath with a hiss: 'Long time.' Whether he meant that they'd already waited a long time or that they would still have to wait a long time, wasn't clear. 'Sorry.'

Ruth now clambered out of the car. 'You speak English.'

'A little.'

'How much longer are we going to have to wait here?' She spoke crossly as though the young man were to blame for the landslide and for the delay in erecting the temporary bridge across it.

Again he drew in his breath with a hiss. 'Many men working.'

'Yes, I can see that.'

'You travel far?'

'We're going to the Naked Festival – the *Hadaka Matsuri*,' Clare answered.

[157]

Eyebrows raised in his handsome face, the young man looked astonished: 'You are interested in such things?'

'Yes. Aren't you?'

Ruth's question embarrassed him. He giggled, hand to mouth.

'Aren't you?' she repeated.

'Such things are things of past. Old Japan.'

Ruth snorted. She began to give him a lecture, familiar to Clare, about the folly of the Japanese in gradually abandoning their unique way of life for a 'rubbishy' one imported from the West. Clare wondered how much the young man, now looking apprehensive, understood. Probably not much. Certainly not the word 'rubbishy'.

At the end of the lecture, Clare asked how far it was to the small town to which they were travelling.

'Two, three hours,' the man replied. 'Maybe four in this weather.'

'Well, that's nice and precise!' Clare hoped that Ruth's sarcasm was lost on the man. With the Japanese, sarcasm usually was. 'We were recommended this inn – this *ryokan*,' Ruth went on, using one of the few Japanese words which she had learned. 'A Japanese colleague of my husband told us about it. Not at all luxurious, of course, but *clean*. We were planning to spend two nights there – tonight and the night of the festival.'

'Maybe you will only spend tomorrow night there.' The young man laughed. Ruth scowled.

Were there any other, nearer inns? Clare asked. The young man was dubious.

Ruth clambered back into the car, a clear indication that, for her, the conversation was over. Clare and the young man exchanged smiles.

'Which is your truck?'

'Over there.' He indicated a mud-spattered vehicle seemingly without a load. 'I come back from Osaka. I carry wood from here to Osaka, Kyoto, Kobe. My job.' He took a packet of cigarettes out of his breast pocket and held it out to Clare. 'Marlboro,' he said. 'American cigarette. Better than Japanese.'

Clare shook her head. 'I don't smoke.'

'I smoke much, too much.'

They continued to talk. 'Excuse me,' he would begin, and then he'd ask her some question about her life or life in general in England.

'You like Japan?'

'Yes, I love it, I fell in love with it the moment I got here.'

He shook his head, frowning, as he drew deeply on yet another cigarette.

Suddenly the foreman was approaching, waving an arm and shouting.

'What is he saying?' The man's accent, so unlike the Kansai accent to which she was accustomed, made it difficult to understand him.

'Bridge is ready. He is asking you to come.'

'Us?'

'He is asking you to come first.'

'But why?'

'You are foreigners. It is polite for you to come first.'

The foreman was gesticulating and shouting again.

Was politeness to foreigners truly the reason? Or did the foreman think that in trying out his makeshift bridge, it was foreign, not Japanese, lives which should be risked?

'Frankly, the thought of driving across those logs terrifies me. I'd rather see someone else do it first.'

'I will drive!'

'You?'

'If you are . . .' He hesitated for the word she had used. 'If you are *terrified*.'

Ruth opted not to be in the car – 'There's no point in our *all* being killed.' The logic was irrefutable, but Clare didn't think that she too could quit.

The young man frowned in concentration as, on the wrong side of the road, he coaxed the Cadillac past the long line of waiting trucks. The car arrived at the makeshift bridge, stretched like a fragile plaster over the jagged wound of the landslide. The man smiled at Clare in reassurance. Such was her fear, she couldn't smile back. If only they were not in this monster of a car but in something smaller and lighter. She shut her eyes. With a creaking of the logs, the Cadillac bumped across. Every other truck-driver seemed to have gathered round to watch.

When at last they were over, the Japanese turned to her with a smile. 'Easy! No danger!'

Cursing loudly each time that she nearly slipped, Ruth had meanwhile been negotiating the crumbling hillside.

'Why didn't you use the bridge?' Clare asked.

'It might bloody well have collapsed, that's why!'

The young man was looking at his watch. Then, shaking his

head: 'Too dangerous to drive to inn in dark. Maybe road has fallen in other place. You sleep my house.'

Ruth didn't in the least care for the suggestion. 'If we press on, I'm sure we can arrive before nightfall.'

But Clare, usually so submissive at each clash with Ruth, held out against her. And there was another reason for her opposition. She was attracted by the young man. She wished to talk more to him. She wished to see his home.

After some argument, Ruth snapped: 'Oh, very well. Have it your own way.'

The young man, who was called Masa, lived with his parents in an untidily thatched little house by a brook. At intervals all through the night, Clare was to hear that brook, beyond the paper screens, its low murmur insinuating itself into her dreams.

Masa's mother, so stooped and lined that one might have mistaken her for his grandmother, carried in the simple meal and laid it out on a low table. The two foreigners had been given the main room of the house, clearly seldom used. It was damp, with cobwebs stretching across one corner of a ceiling covered in yellowish-brown stains.

After the woman had bowed her way out, Masa entered.

'Excuse me! May I talk to you while you are eating?'

Ruth gave a deep sigh. 'Why don't you eat with us? Why don't you all eat with us?'

Embarrassed, he gave no reply. He edged round the low lacquer table and lowered himself to the floor. Clare suddenly noticed that he had three books with him: a pocket dictionary, its leaves curling and crumpled as though from constant use; some kind of primer; and what looked like a photograph album. He consulted the dictionary. Then he said, with difficulty: 'Primi-tive.' He looked up and smiled, not at Ruth but at Clare. With more confidence he repeated: 'Primitive.'

'Primitive?'

'Life here. Life in my house. Life in the mountains.'

As they ate, he spoke haltingly, with frequent recourse to the dictionary, not merely of the primitiveness but of the tedium of this life. In California, he had an uncle, well, not really an uncle, a cousin of his mother. The uncle had suffered in the War, he had been interned, his citrus farm had been taken from him. But now he was very rich. Masa wished to go to California to join him. Maybe soon, very soon . . . That was his dream. He would apply for a visa and then . . . He was suddenly eager and hopeful.

He opened the photograph album. This was his uncle. This was his uncle's son and his daughter. Americans! They looked like Americans, didn't they? Here was their house. As she shovelled rice into her mouth with her chopsticks, Ruth hardly listened or bothered even to glance at the photographs. But it was to Clare that Masa was really trying to convey all this, and she was totally attentive. Over and over that one word recurred: Dream, dream, dream. Her dream, as a student, had always been of Japan. His dream was of the West.

Eventually, the meal long since over, Ruth said: 'Well, I don't know about you, but I'm bushed.' Then she turned to Masa: 'I think that it's time we turned in.'

'Turned in?'

'Slept.'

'Yes, yes . . . But first, first I must show you . . .'

He opened the third of the books he had brought with him. The primer. Clare decided it must date from before the War, so yellow were the pages, so old-fashioned its illustrations and typeface. 'From here I learn my English. This is my – my key. My key to my dream.' He turned the pages over. He laughed. Then he read out: '"Have you had a nice day, Mrs Jones?" "Thank you, yes, I have had a very nice day. The weather was fine and I had a visit from my daughter, my son-in-law and my two grandchildren."' He laughed again.

'Perhaps you could bring us the *futon*,' Ruth said sharply. As Masa left the room, she remarked: 'Oh, what a bore! Perhaps we'd have done better to have slept in the Caddy.'

'Well, at least you've had a good meal.'

'Not good. Ample.'

Driving back from the Naked Festival two days later, they passed the little house by the brook. Clare would have liked to stop, to have seen Masa again. But Ruth was anxious that they wouldn't reach Kobe in time for a committee meeting of the local branch of the Japan Animal Welfare Society.

Gazing out through the windscreen at the rods of greyish-green rain once more slanting down through the trees, Clare thought of the festival. It had seemed incredible that so many young men could crowd into the small temple compound, packing themselves tighter and tighter, naked flesh on naked flesh. Some had climbed up on to the roof of the temple, to hurtle downwards on to the bodies below. Some were actually walking over their fellows. She seemed once again to hear their mass chanting, like the mating-call of a wild animal in rut. From time to time temple attendants splashed water on to the milling bodies. And then there was the same hiss of shock from those on whom it fell; the same cloud of steam rising from the chaos of jostling, overheated flesh. It had been frightening and exciting. And, yes, primitive.

Suddenly Ruth exclaimed: 'Oh, shit! It's happened again.'

'What's happened?'

'A landslide! Another bloody landslide! Can't you see? And there's no one there. Not a soul. We're well and truly stuck until someone comes along.'

Clare stopped the car. She got out. Afterwards she persuaded herself that she already knew what she would see.

Far off, at the bottom of the ravine, lay the wreck of a mud-spattered truck, with logs scattered, like matches, all around it. Logs had also jammed against tree-trunks as they had tumbled out during the fall. She thought there was a body spreadeagled on some brushwood. There was a cheap suitcase, miraculously unharmed. Beside it was a primer. Suddenly, she heard Masa reading from it:

'Have you had a nice day, Mrs Jones?'
'Thank you, yes, I have had a very nice day.'

A Lost Opportunity

Reynolds yawned and yawned again in anticipation. You must get it into your heads that conversation is like a game of tennis. It's not enough to get your racket to the ball, you must, I repeat must, somehow hit it back across the net. He yawned again. He had given this advice to these Japanese and to so many Japanese before them, but it was seldom that the ball did anything but fall inert to the ground after it and the racket of one of them had met.

The director of the Institute called it a conversation class. But how could one teach conversation in a foreign language to people who could not conduct it in their own? He got up and fidgeted with the chairs, the three sitting-room ones supplemented with others from the dining-room, the kitchen, his bedroom and even the bathroom. Why not follow the example of his French colleague and let them squat on the floor? After all, as the Frenchman had said with one of those contemptuous shrugs of his, the students were more used to the floor than to chairs.

At exactly four o'clock there was a ring at the bell. At exactly four fifteen Reynolds's maid, hunchbacked, her greying hair coiled into a loose bun at the nape of a neck which had the appearance of crumpled-up brown paper, would come in with the tray clicking with glasses of Coca Cola. 'You spoil them,' the Frenchman said. But to provide a few bottles of Coca Cola, so much sweeter in Japan than in the West, was a cheap way of spoiling.

With one or two exceptions, the students would all arrive together, the early arrivals waiting for the latecomers outside the gate. One of the exceptions was always Miss Nishikawa, who invariably rang the bell either five minutes before or five minutes after everyone else, as though deliberately to assert her difference from them.

[163]

When Reynolds opened the front door, the students, as always, giggled, looking anywhere but at him. Was there something irresistibly comic about his appearance or behaviour? There was more giggling on this occasion when, instead of his usual 'Hi! Come in!', he gave a mock Japanese bow and cried out '*Dozo!*', with a wide sweep of one arm to invite them to enter. Heads lowered, they then scuttled in, the men in most cases preceding the women. Once they were all herded together in the tiny hall, they stooped to remove their shoes, neatly placed them on the racks by the door, and then thrust their feet into the slippers provided.

Conversation is like a game of tennis. To ensure that in this weekly game of tennis the ball at least got off the ground, Reynolds had got into the habit of giving his students a topic in advance. Cheating, his French colleague said – the point about conversation was that it must be impromptu. But if each impromptu was at best merely a few breathless words and at worst a sigh, a giggle and a silence, then cheating was surely justified.

'What was it that we were going to talk about this afternoon?' Reynolds seldom remembered the topic set the week before. He did not remember now.

An elderly woman, wife of a famous physicist, who was both one of the most intelligent and one of the shyest people in the class, held out her notebook towards him.

'No, no, tell me! I don't want to read it.'

But this was something that she was clearly not prepared to do. The notebook still extended, so that he could see the minuscule writing covering the two open pages, she gazed imploringly first at the tousled boy on her left and then at the young housewife on her right.

It was the young housewife who eventually said, on an upward note of vague interrogation: 'A Lost Opportunity.'

'Yes, that's it. Right.' Now why on earth should he have chosen that, of all subjects? Perhaps one of the class had suggested it, although it was difficult ever to get them to suggest anything at all.

It was at that moment that Miss Nishikawa entered, having presumably been let in by the maid, who edged in behind her with the tray of Coca Colas.

Reynolds was glad to see 'Miss N', as he referred to her when talking about her to his French and other colleagues. Of all his students, she was the one about whom he talked most often, so vividly idiosyncratic was she in comparison with her fellows. She often missed classes and, when she did so, the hour seemed to stretch far longer than when she was present.

'Good afternoon, sir,' she greeted him. A woman of about thirty, still unmarried, she all too obviously dressed, as few Japanese women dressed, to excite attention. Her unusually short tartan skirt – when Reynolds had once remarked jokingly that he had never before realized that she belonged to the Stuart clan, she had screwed up her face in offended bewilderment – revealed sturdy bow-legs, encased in pale green tights. Her shiny black hair, parted in the middle, was gathered by ribbons, of the same pale green shade, on either side of her jolly face.

'Good afternoon, Miss Nishikawa.'

'The late worm gets the bird,' she remarked as she motioned to one of the two youths on the sofa to shift over for her. Was she attempting to be witty? Or had she merely got the proverb mixed up? As always with Miss Nishikawa, Reynolds could not be sure; and not being sure, he felt vaguely uncomfortable.

Reynolds waited until everyone had a glass of Coca Cola. Then he repeated: 'A Lost Opportunity. Now what have you all got to say about that?' (Bloody little, he decided privately, if one was to go by previous experience.)

There was a lengthy silence, during which all of them, sipping at their glasses, seemed determined to avoid his gaze.

'Well?' Silence again. 'Mrs Muto.'

The young housewife looked down at the exercise book open in her lap. Then she looked up and put a forefinger, Japanese-fashion, to her nose. 'I?'

'Yes – you.'

She began to read in a voice so faint and an accent so appalling that it was difficult to understand anything at all. Her lost opportunity seemed to have been the opportunity to visit a cousin of hers, married to a diplomat, in Kampala.

'Kampala? Many people might think that you were lucky to miss that opportunity.'

'Please?'

Reynolds shrugged, deciding to let it go.

The next student on whom he called, the tousled youth, had learned his speech off by heart. He screwed up his eyes under a tangle of hair as he began to recite. His lost opportunity had been the opportunity to learn Esperanto from a female Australian missionary neighbour.

Reynolds's attention wandered; and as it did so, he suddenly became aware that Miss Nishikawa, plump legs crossed at the ankles and no less plump hands folded in her lap, was staring at him. Why did she so often stare at him? He had once put the question to his French colleague, who had answered: 'Women usually stare at men for only one reason.'

Reynolds was not physically attracted by Miss Nishikawa, but he liked her. Secretary to the dean of the law department at the university, she struck him as unique in Japan in dominating her boss, instead of being dominated by him. How had she achieved this? Could it be that the small, frail professor was in love with her? Or had she discovered some secret which she now used for blackmail?

Other women in Japan dominated their bosses, Reynolds's French colleague had once argued. Every office and every university department had its éminence d'ivoire. But not openly, not openly, Reynolds had protested. It was the blatancy of her domination that set Miss Nishikawa apart from all those female moles, invisibly burrowing their way to unacknowledged power.

As the youth went on reciting, his face screwed up as though in an agony of regurgitating what his memory had digested, Reynolds remembered his conversation with Miss Nishikawa at a concert on the previous Saturday. She had arrived, as the musicians were already filing on to the stage, at the row in which, fortuitously, he had also had his seat.

'Reynolds-san!'

He had risen to let her pass, as had the elderly couple between him and the empty seat which was presumably hers. Heedless of the elderly couple, she faced him, her back to the seat in front of his and their knees touching, with a smile of delight irradiating her face. 'I am happy to see you, so happy. I did not know that you like classical music. I thought you like jazz.'

'I like jazz, I like classical music. It's possible to like both, you know.'

She appeared to be dubious about that, as he once again felt her knees against his.

'I think these people are waiting for you to pass,' he said.

'We will talk in the interval. You will buy me a Coca Cola – like we drink in your home.'

[166]

It was extraordinary that a Japanese woman should be so forward. No wonder that the other members of the conversation class seemed either to distrust or actively to dislike her.

In the interval he bought her the Coca Cola.

'Do you think that the soprano is glamorous? Reynolds-san – be frank!'

'I hadn't really considered the matter.' Nor had he.

She laughed. 'I think that you are lying! Every young man must consider such a thing.'

'Not at all. What matters is whether she can sing well or not. Unfortunately, she can't.'

'But she is a very sexy lady. Reynolds-san, do you agree – she is a very sexy lady?'

He shrugged, smiling down into his half-drunk glass of Coca Cola.

'Yes, yes! You are smiling! You agree, you agree!'

'Not at all!' But in fact she was right. He had found consolation for the inadequacy of the American soprano's voice in her sturdiness, her air of physical well-being and the beauty of the blonde hair worn loose almost to her waist.

'Reynolds-san, now I will ask you a question I have wanted to ask you for a long time.'

'Yes?' Oh, lord, what was it going to be? That roguish smile, her head tilted to one side and the tip of her tongue peeping out of one corner of her small mouth, signalled an embarrassment.

'In England do you have a girlfriend?'

'Of course! Many, many girlfriends!' He laughed. But there was no mirth in his laughter. His one girlfriend had only the previous week married the managing director, several years her senior, of the publishing house in which she had been working.

She looked at him, head still tilted to one side, with a disbelieving, misty pity in her eyes. Then she nodded. 'And in Japan, Reynolds-san? Do you also have many girlfriends in Japan?'

'Of course! Many, many!' But again he was lying.

After that it was a relief when the gong boomed out to announce that the interval was over.

... At last the tousled young man had finished. As though after some tremendous physical effort, he lay back in the sofa, arms trailing on either side of him, face pale and glistening with sweat, and mouth agape in what appeared to be an effort to gulp more air.

[167]

'Thank you, Mr – er – Morimoto. I mean, Mr – er – Morikawa.'
Reynolds always had difficulty in remembering the names of his
male students, never those of his female ones. 'Very interesting.
Has anyone any comment on that?'

No one had.

'This is a *conversation* class, you know. As I constantly tell you.
We don't want isolated statements. Things must be linked.
So . . .' He felt a sudden, ineluctable weariness, such as all too
often overcame him in the course of his teaching. But he pushed
it aside, as though it were some cumbrous, leaden object in his
path. 'Has anyone here ever studied Esperanto?'

No one responded.

'Has anyone ever thought of studying Esperanto?'

After a long silence, an elderly man, employed in the Post
Office, reluctantly put up a hand.

'Yes?'

The man said nothing but kept his hand raised.

'Why did you think of studying Esperanto?'

'No, no, I am sorry, Reynolds-san. I wish only to go to toilet.'

It was with relief that eventually Reynolds turned to Miss
Nishikawa. 'Well Miss Nishikawa, we've not yet heard what you
have to say on this subject of a Lost Opportunity.'

'I think that I have something interesting to say.' The other
members of the class fidgeted, glanced at each other and then
stared down at the carpet. Clearly they disapproved of the
immodesty of the claim.

'Good. Then say it.'

Miss Nishikawa neither recited nor read. Hands clasped in her
lap, she leaned forward to Reynolds as though, the others absent,
she were speaking to him alone. 'A funny story, a sad story,' she
said.

Again the other Japanese showed their disapproval and unease
by fidgeting and glancing at each other. Plainly each was
wondering what was about to emerge from this woman so unlike
any other Japanese woman known to them.

Miss Nishikawa gave Reynolds a slow, happy smile. Her eyes
held his. Then she launched into her narrative.

Travelling, the previous summer, from Kobe to Kyoto, she had
found herself sitting opposite a man 'not young but glamorous,
very glamorous, with little, little moustache and romance-grey
hair, cut long, long.' They had got into conversation, they had at
once liked each other – like music, perfect music, me high notes,

he low notes, perfect!' The man was married, he had three children. Each year he came to Kyoto from his home on the island of Shikoku, in order to attend a meeting of the sub-managers of the company for which he worked. At Kyoto she and he had left the train together. The man had one hour to spare before the meeting. 'We went – ' Miss Nishikawa gave a loud, clear laugh, not raising a cupped hand to her mouth, as most other Japanese women would have done. 'I will not tell you where we went! But we have a good time, happy time.' What did she mean? Had they merely been for a walk in one of the parks or sat in a café or sake-bar? Or had they taken a room in one of the innumerable *maisons de passe*, their tariffs displayed on their entrances, in which the area around the station abounded? Reynolds sensed that all the other Japanese were wondering the same thing. He also sensed their growing embarrassment, and then their growing annoyance with Miss Nishikawa for causing that embarrassment.

'We are together only one hour. Then he must go to his meeting. But he tells me that each year, on the first Tuesday of June, his company has such meeting.' She drew a deep sigh. 'Then we make a promise to each other, a very romantic promise. Next year, on the first Tuesday of June, we will meet again. Same time, same place. Maybe same happiness? Who can say?' She looked around at the others, but none of them looked back. Then she looked at Reynolds. Her eyes were sparkling with what he could only assume was mischief. 'Well, what do you think I did when that day comes? I go back or not go back?'

No one answered the question.

'Reynolds-san – I go back or not back?'

'From what I know of you, Miss Nishikawa, I think you went back.'

Everyone nodded approval of his answer.

'Wrong, wrong, wrong!' she cried out. 'I do not go back. A Lost Opportunity? Maybe. Reynolds-san must tell me.'

'How can I say?' He turned to the class. 'What do all of you think?'

But what they thought, they were none of them prepared to disclose.

Reynolds concluded the class ten minutes before the hour was over. All at once he found that, with so little co-operation, he could no longer ask another question or make another comment. Even Miss Nishikawa had fallen silent after her account, her eyes

uncharacteristically dreamy in a face that was no less uncharacteristically still.

While the others exchanged their slippers for their shoes,
Reynolds noticed, with foreboding, that Miss Nishikawa was
hanging back in one corner of the hall, her hands clasped before
her and her head bowed.

When all of them were ready, they surged together to the
door, calling out in ragged unison: 'Goodbye, Reynolds-san!
Thank you! See you again!' When they had passed beyond the
gate, he heard one of them – the tousled boy, he thought –
laughing loudly. Then the rest of them began to laugh. Were
they laughing at him? Or at Miss Nishikawa? Or at something
wholly different?

He turned. 'Well, Miss Nishikawa . . .'

'Did you like my story?'

'Yes, I thought it an interesting story. Revealing. Odd. But
whether it was precisely the sort of story to tell on this
occasion . . .' How priggish that sounded! He felt a not unwonted
disgust with himself.

She smiled from the dark corner in which she was still
standing. 'But I do not tell the story right,' she said. 'Not quite
right.'

God! Was she now going to tell him explicitly about the sex-
hotel to which she and her pick-up had adjourned?

'Not quite right?'

'I lie. I lie about the date. I say first Tuesday of June. Really it
is first Tuesday of April.'

'Oh.' The lie hardly seemed to be of importance.

She looked into his face. Then she burst into laughter. 'Reynolds-san – what is today?'

'April the second.' Still he did not get it.

'What day?'

'Tuesday, isn't it?'

She nodded. 'Yes, Tuesday. The first Tuesday of April. You
understand?'

He began to understand. 'Then you mean. . .?'

'This afternoon is the afternoon of my rendezvous. Yes.' She
nodded vigorously. 'Yes. I do not go. I do not go. Do you know
why I do not go, Reynolds-san?'

'Perhaps in retrospect he seemed less attractive than you'd
thought him?'

She shook her head. 'No. No. I do not go because I wish to be with someone else . . . I wish to be with you.'

'With *me*?'

Again she nodded vigorously, her small eyes glittering out of a face that now seemed extraordinarily white in the gloom of the corner. 'With you.'

'But you can always come to my classes.'

'I wished to see you. This afternoon. Now. That was more important than anything else.'

The telephone had begun to ring. Thank God, thank God! 'Excuse me,' he said. 'I must answer that. Your shoes are over there.' He pointed at the rack. Of course she would know where she herself had placed her shoes. The invitation to go was all too obvious.

When he returned from the telephone, she had got into her shoes.

Embarrassed, hardly looking at her, he opened the door.

She edged towards it, her umbrella dangling from a wrist. All at once she looked despondent, weary, afflicted. He had never before seen her look like that.

'Then I go,' she said. 'That was my Lost Opportunity. Now you know. Reynolds-san. See you again!'

'See you again!' Since he had taken up residence in Japan, he had become accustomed to echoing the idiotic phrase.

She descended sideways from step to step, like an old woman afraid of falling, while he looked down at her. Without once turning, she made for the gate.

Slowly he closed the front door. Then he raced up the stairs to his bedroom, the window of which overlooked the bus stop at which he knew that she usually waited for the bus which would take her to the suburb in which she lived. He stood behind the net curtain and gazed down at the empty street.

When she appeared, she had raised the edge of the tartan skirt and was tugging at a thread – presumably loose – in its hem. She no longer looked weary, despondent, afflicted. She now looked as she always looked. Had that been a true story? Or had she made it up? He would never know.

Her hair shone in the late spring sunlight. In that sunlight the skin of her arm also shone, as she raised it to pick a blossom, small, crumpled and white, from the hedge of the next-door house. She raised the blossom to her nose and sniffed at it.

Suddenly she was laughing. As with the others earlier, he wondered if she was laughing at him.

Still standing at the window and still looking down at her – now she was motionless, gazing up the road for the bus – he thought, with a sudden hurt and anger, of the girl who had married the publisher so many years her senior.

The bus had arrived. Miss Nishikawa was skipping – yes, there was no other word for it – aboard.

The Interment

'Are you sure you don't want to come?'

'Quite sure. Once was enough.'

'It's a damned nuisance, another rehearsal at an hour like this.'

Carol lay outside the bed, in nothing but pants and brassière, the shiny pale blue bedspread tacky against her skin. She was doing nothing and she wanted to do nothing – except smoke a cigarette; but that was the one thing that she must not do in Ian's presence. He had brushed his teeth and then he had gargled with Listerine and now, dressed but for the jacket draped over the back of an upright chair, he was alternately humming and clearing his throat in that irritating way of his, while he checked that he had his music, his extra-strong mints and his throat-spray in the attaché case that she had given him the previous Christmas. She had had his name engraved on its lid; but that had been a mistake. 'Don't you think that's just a wee bit ostentatious?' he had asked, since he was modest about his modest fame. But how many people would connect the name with a singer whose reputation was still merely a national one?

'Why are you watching me like that?'

'Watching you? Am I? I suppose because there's nothing else to do in this ghastly city.'

'You could have gone out. Shopping. Or sightseeing.'

'There's nothing cheap enough to buy or interesting enough to visit.'

He shrugged. Then: 'Promise me one thing, darling.'

'Yes, I promise. I won't.'

They both of them laughed.

'If you must do it – '

'Yes, I'll go down into the lounge or out into the street. I know.'

'Sorry to be so faddy but you know how – '

'Yes, yes! I know!'

He was as anxious about his voice as a Don Juan about his sexual equipment: a roughness was the equivalent of a dose of clap, laryngitis of impotence. Due to stand in for an ailing and ageing but still world-famous tenor at the Colón, he was like some small-town philanderer suddenly and unexpectedly summoned to the bed of an Eva Perón. It was, as his agent had said, an opportunity in a thousand; and it would be a disaster if the small-town philanderer could not 'rise' to that opportunity. His care for his voice was like that of a parent for a sickly and therefore abnormally cherished child, and it filled Carol with a mixture of irritation and pity. For that child, every sacrifice must be made, not only by him but also by her. Cigarettes were bad, but sex was even worse. Yes, he knew about those rumours of how Melba would 'irrigate' her voice before a major performance and of how the ailing and ageing tenor whom he was now replacing once told a gossip-columnist that he only gave of his best if he had spent the afternoon 'loosening up' with someone in bed. (He had not specified the sex of that someone, but the gossip was that it must be male.) 'But I'm just not like them, darling. Somehow sex drains me, *bleeds* my voice. The tone whitens.'

He stooped to kiss her, first on the forehead, then on the side of the neck, and then, for seconds on end, on the mouth. It was his way of making up for not having agreed to allow his voice to be 'bled' during the afternoon siesta that, out of boredom, they had prolonged until, with the descent of the wintry dusk, they had heard the central heating come on with a curious gasping, chugging noise, as though far below them in the basement of the small elegant hotel some antiquated steam-engine was gathering itself to set off on invisible rails.

'Shall I wait for you for dinner?'

'Not if you're hungry. I may be hours.'

'Well, I am hungry.'

'Then don't wait. Simple.'

'I *hate* eating alone.'

'Why? You might have some adventure.'

'I've made up my mind that I'm the kind of person to whom adventures never happen.' She took his hand. 'I hope it goes well.' She meant it, knowing how important this 'opportunity in a thousand' was to him and knowing, too, from her own observation at rehearsal and not from anything he would admit, that he was uneasy with the domineering black American prima

[174]

donna, each of whose dresses was like some voluminous tent, with the Spanish conductor, who spoke to him so peremptorily, and, above all, with the emaciated, waspish French director, who at moments of exasperation – and there were many – would run both hands back through his thick tangled hair and scream, 'Merde!'

'I hope so, too.' The tone was rueful – because he knew, as she knew and as his agent knew, that he was not really at home in that gilded railway station of an opera-house, almost twice the size of Covent Garden, and that he was not really at home in early Verdi. But there it was – that 'opportunity in a thousand' – and he could not turn it down. Yet each time that his voice, that cherished sickly child, seemed to stagger and all but faint as he pushed it out towards a receding desert of old gold and plush, he would experience a terrible despair. The small-town Don Juan was indeed impotent.

After Ian had gone, Carol continued to lie there for a time on the bed. She thought of the children and decided that, no, she would not ring the parents yet again to ask if all was well. Ian had said that it was absurd to do so night after night, at such an appalling expense, when, if anything were wrong, they would hear soon enough, God knows. She thought of the garden, wondering if, in a summer so remote from this Argentine winter and probably much colder, the neighbours had remembered to hose it from time to time. She thought of the familiar shops and the familiar cooker and the familiar sink. Odd! She thought of them with regret and a mournful longing; and yet she had always resented their daily tyranny.

Eventually she got off the bed, with the voluptuous laziness of a gorged cat, slipped into a dressing-gown and then, smiling at herself, took a packet of the forbidden cigarettes and a lighter out of her bag, hesitated a moment, and then lit up. The bathroom or the windowsill? He always detected the reek of smoke, however faint, on towel and face-flannel. The windowsill was better, even if the temperature was falling. Cigarette smouldering away between two fingers ('I do wish you'd use a holder; those stains are so ugly'), she struggled with the catch of the window and eventually slid it open. Far down below there was the courtyard of some government building, and in the dimming evening she could make out foreshortened men hurrying diagonally across it, most of them with briefcases. They arrived late, they went home early, she noticed – unlike the hotel staff, who must sleep on the premises, so constant was their presence.

She inhaled deeply, enjoying the contrast between the vitalizing smoke and the numbing air on her bare throat, forehead and hands. From the room next door she could hear angry English voices, male and female. She had seen the couple, a tall young man and an equally tall young woman, who had a way of walking down the corridor hand in hand, their sharp-featured faces turned to each other, slightly smirking. They were so lovingly decorous in public that it was hard to believe that, only a short while before, they had been shouting those crudities at each other in private.

When the cigarette had been sucked to its last bitter scorching gasp, she threw it, unextinguished, down into the courtyard, watching it shower sparks as it fell. Pretty. She would have liked it to have alighted on the head of one of those hurrying men with their briefcases, but no such luck. Another? Better not. No, definitely not. She began to dress. It was early to dine in Buenos Aires, but she was feeling hungry after the sandwiches and coffee that had made up their early lunch. ('Things are so expensive; we'll just have to make do with one main meal a day.' It was as though Ian knew that the unprecedented sum that he was to receive for his performances would never be repeated.)

The avuncular, and not the cheekily flirtatious, porter was at the desk and, on an impulse as she handed in her key, she asked him if he could recommend a restaurant. He got out a map – though he had already given her one only two or three days before – and carefully put a cross for the hotel on it and then, his head so close to hers that she could smell his sweet and pungent hair-oil, he ran the tip of his pen up one street and down another and then put in another cross. He wrote on the map 'San Bernardino', saying: 'I think you will like. All foreigners like. Not too expensive.' As she took the map with a smile and a thank-you, he went on: 'But it is very early.'

'Yes, I know. But I'm hungry, you see.'

He laughed uproariously at that, as though she had made some joke. She had noticed that, just as the British tended to regard sex as intrinsically comic, the Argentines had the same attitude to food. 'Hungry! Hungry!' She might have said that she was feeling randy, from his reaction. The wizened old man who carried suitcases up to bedrooms, summoned taxis and was perpetually mopping over the tiles whenever it was raining enough for the clients' shoes to dirty them joined in his mirth.

Flat – yes, that was the word that best described this city, even if it did bristle with skyscrapers. She had not ventured beyond its centre; but she had a sense of the narrow canyons of its streets radiating symmetrically around her, without any hills or any hollows, and then petering out in featureless suburbs, which in turn merged into plains as monotonous as oceans. Despite the grid system, she often got lost, because every street seemed to look precisely like every other street. Oh, yes, she would tell herself, it must be left turn here for the hotel, because there is that chemist's shop with those mysterious pink coils of rubber attached to a black box in its window; and now it must be right turn, because there is that statue of a general with his nose eroded as though by tertiary syphilis.

This flatness seemed to apply to the people, too. But that, of course, could only be an illusion: it was not that a people so excitable were not exciting but merely that she had mysteriously lost the faculty of getting excited by them. Ian was perpetually exclaiming, 'They really are stunners!' when they passed some group of young girls emerging from a school, a shop or an office.

To follow the route marked for her by the porter, she had, at one point, to negotiate some slithery planks that covered an excavation. Some people had told her that the excavation was for an underground car-park; others, for a subway. She thought it odd that even natives of the city seemed not to know for sure. Alone like this, she felt perfectly safe, as she always felt perfectly safe when wandering about this city, whatever the hour. Yet there were people, not foreigners like herself and Ian, who never felt safe. At any moment they could disappear as completely and as disastrously as if her foot were now to slip, the hand-rail were to crumble, and she were to plunge, unseen, into the dark abyss beneath her.

This must be the restaurant. She looked through the plate-glass window and saw the huge bed of a charcoal fire, with a boy in an outsize apron, no more than a child, blowing at it with a pair of bellows almost as large as himself. There were other aproned figures, adult and in most cases heavily moustached, lugging about vast haunches of meat or hacking and sawing at them. Their sweating faces were lurid in the flames that leaped up from the charcoal grid as the boy pumped at it.

'Yes, madame.' The elderly head waiter, the menu in its stiff leather folder tucked under one arm, might have been a civil servant taking a confidential file to his minister. How had he guessed that she was either English or American?

'For one, please.'

'For one . . . Yes, madame.' He spoke with a faint hesitation and a frown, as though she had asked for something difficult; but at that hour the restaurant, which stretched far back under its white vaulted ceiling, was all but empty. There were some red-faced American men, who might well have been there since lunch, slumped morosely around their glasses and bottles of Bourbon; a family celebration of some kind, composed of grandmother, her grey hair twisted into a number of stiff whorls, portly mother and father, three prettily nubile girls in court-shoes that looked too tight for them and almost identical white cashmere dresses, and a bored supercilious youth with a loud braying laugh; and an elderly man drooping over a *café filtre* and a newspaper with a fatigue so extreme that it made Carol feel tired just to look at him.

The head waiter drew back a chair for her at a table against a wall, saying, 'Please' with a small, slightly ironic bow. Carol was still struggling out of her coat. When she had done so, he took it from her, folded it neatly and, instead of carrying it away, placed it over the back of the chair opposite to the one that he had drawn out for her. After she was seated, he handed her the menu and left.

Minutes then passed, during which no one took any notice of her. A number of waiters, all in evening-dress, clustered negligently around the cash-desk, chattering to the youth – no doubt the son of the proprietor – perched on a high stool behind it. An oriental, in a white jacket stained with blood, hurried past, bearing a carcass on his shoulder. The boy in the overlong apron continued to work his bellows.

At last she heard a voice behind her: 'You wish to order, madame?'

As a child, she had once said of a bus-conductor, 'Isn't he beautiful, Mummy?' to be told: 'Women are beautiful, dear, men are handsome.' But 'beautiful' was the only word adequately to describe the man who now moved forward; and that it should be the only word was all the more astonishing because he must be at least in his fifties. From the tips of his gleaming patent-leather shoes to his crisp grey curls, he had the sleekness of a champion at a dog show. The pale grey eyes, set wide apart,

[178]

were startling above the black moustache and under the sweeping black eyebrows. He held himself erect, his cleft chin slightly
uptilted and his chest thrust out. If one had met him at a Buenos
Aires party, one would have assumed him to be an army colonel,
perhaps even a general, in mufti – no doubt already planning the
coup that would bring him to supreme power.

'Yes ... Thank you ...' She looked again at the menu. 'Have
you any avocados?'

He smiled indulgently, revealing perfect teeth, and shook his
head. She remembered now that avocados could be bought here
for a few pence a kilo and that they would therefore be as out of
place in a restaurant of this kind as faggots and mashed turnips
at Claridge's.

'Well, then I'll just have a T-bone steak. And a salad.'

'Tomato? A green salad?' His English was far better than that
of either of the two porters at the hotel.

'A mixture of both.'

'Certainly, madame. And to drink?'

She hesitated. 'Oh, some red wine.'

'You wish to see the wine-list?'

Again she hesitated.

'Will madame leave it to me?'

She nodded, relieved. 'But only a small quantity. Not too
much.'

'Of course, madame. Not too much.'

He began to laugh, and his laugh was exactly like that of the
hotel porter and his wizened satellite when she had confessed to
being hungry. Involuntarily, she herself joined in.

When he had given the order to one of the sweating cooks, he
picked up a table-cloth from a stack on a corner of the counter
beyond the cash-desk, shook it out, and approached her table
once again. Since the table-cloth before her was clean, she
wondered what he was going to do with it. Without looking at
her – it was as if, deliberately, he were avoiding her gaze – he
carefully placed the table-cloth over her overcoat on the chair
opposite to her, twitching it now on one side and now on another
to make sure that it lay in precisely symmetrical folds, and then
stood back for a moment to confirm that no mistake had been
made. Still not meeting her gaze, he walked off.

She was puzzled by this interment of her ordinary grey
woollen coat under the dazzling napery. But when she gazed
about the cavernous restaurant – it had now become much fuller

[179]

– she saw that at other tables other table-cloths had been draped, admittedly not with similar care, over discarded coats. In some cases, where the party was a large one, these coats, piled on top of each other and then surmounted by the cloth, looked like some slumped Arab woman under a voluminous veil.

She had been foolish to order a T-bone steak, since meat in such quantity and so little disguised always induced in her a vague nausea, even while she told herself how tender and delicious it was. Soon, as she cut sliver after sliver from it, it was standing in a pool of pinkish blood, 'Everything all right, madame?' the waiter asked, as he hurried past her, balancing at shoulder level a vast silver salver on which a profusion of meats – liver, steaks, chops, kidneys – had been piled high. Perhaps he had guessed from her expression that all was not precisely right. 'Yes, thank you,' she answered; and soldiered on.

Soon the wine, the heat – though so distant, that vast bed of charcoal seemed to be breathing directly at her – and the noise, echoing in the white vault of the ceiling, had begun to make her feel vaguely giddy and confused. She pushed aside her plate, the steak barely half-consumed, jabbed at some more lettuce and tomato with a fork, and then pushed aside that plate, too. She took her cigarettes and her lighter out of her bag and again she lit up.

'Was everything to madame's satisfaction?'

'Yes, thank you. It was excellent. But far too much. I'm not used to such vast quantities of meat.'

Again there was that laugh. 'In Argentina we eat too much meat.' He went on to ask if she would like some sweet – a *bombe surprise*, a Mont Blanc, a cassata? – but at each suggestion she shook her head, her eyes fixed, not on those remarkable pale grey eyes, but on those no less remarkable teeth. Some coffee, then? Yes, some coffee.

As she sipped the coffee, she watched him moving about the restaurant. Unlike some of the other waiters, who shouted their orders, snatched up dishes, and all but ran between the tables, he never gave any impression of hurry; and yet, miraculously, he forestalled all requests. A woman would be about to ask for some oil and there, just as she was raising a plump hand and opening her mouth, he would appear beside her, the cut-glass bottle in his hand. A man would want a toothpick and, even before he had started to look around for one, the waiter would arrive, setting down the holder with a flourish. When Carol herself had decided that the time had come to ask for the bill, he was already asking: 'Would madame like something else?'

There was a service charge of twenty-five per cent, but nonetheless she left a tip far in excess of what Ian would have given. The waiter showed no particular gratitude or surprise, merely bowing as he murmured: 'Thank you, madame.'

As she got to her feet, he whipped the table-cloth off the chair opposite, with some of the exuberant triumph of a sculptor unveiling what he is sure will prove his masterpiece, folded it deftly and placed it over another chair. Then he took up her coat and helped her into it.

'I hope madame enjoyed her meal?'

'Very much. Very much indeed.'

'But there was too much meat!'

'Yes, too much meat, much too much!'

They both laughed.

As she made her way back along the board-walk above the excavations, she clutched tightly at the hand-rail. Though it was totally irrational, she had a panic certainty that at any moment the planks would collapse and she would hurtle down, among splintered fragments of wood, into the darkness and dankness far below. But eventually, with a gasp of relief, she had come to the end and emerged out on to the pavement beside a busy thoroughfare.

As she walked on at a faster and faster pace, hands deep in pockets, she began to think of the sleek military-looking waiter. Yes, beautiful, beautiful. That was the only adjective that described him. Now, what would a man like that be doing in a job like that? It seemed so improbable. She was passing a small public garden, with iron hoops set in the ground to fence this area of quiet darkness off from the bustle and brightness of the street. She had seen a bench, and in order to reach it she stepped over the hoops, instead of walking round to the gate. There was no one else in the garden – no doubt because to any Argentine such a night would seem far too cold for loitering. She would smoke one more cigarette out here, in the dampness and gloom, before she went back to the hotel. 'Old enough to be your father . . .' She could hear her mother say it of a middle-aged vet, who had been a neighbour of theirs and with whom she had been briefly infatuated, hurrying round to his premises, a schoolgirl of fifteen, to help him with sweeping out kennels or feeding ailing cats and dogs. In his innocence, he had never realized that it was not with animals but with him that she was in love.

Well, she'd better get back to the hotel.

When she opened the bedroom door, she found that, surprisingly, the light was on and Ian had returned before her. He sat slumped in the one armchair with a plate of sandwiches and a glass of their duty-free whisky before him.

'You're already back! If I'd known you'd be so quick, I'd have waited for you.' She took off her coat and put it over the back of the chair beside the bed, remembering how those broad hands, their nails buffed to a pinkish shine, had covered it so oddly and so deftly with that table-cloth.

'Oh, it was the usual cock-up. They didn't want me at all. Why they couldn't have telephoned . . .'

They were all inconsiderate with him, because they knew that he was not the sort of person who had to be considered. He was not like the majestic black soprano, who was perfectly capable of announcing that she was 'indisposed' and must cancel her opening night performance, or like the no less majestic Russian bass, who bellowed with rage and thumped anything handy, if anyone tried to thwart him or criticize him.

Carol went to Ian and put her arms around him, lowering her cheek to his.

'Have you been smoking?'

'Of course. But not in here.'

'Your hair smells of it. Filthy habit!' But he was joking.

He began to loosen her hold, putting up his hands and gripping her arms above the elbows. Then he reached for another sandwich, peered at it, and finally took a bite. 'Dry. Dry bread, dry ham. I bet you had a lovely dinner.'

'Yes. Yes, it *was* rather lovely.'

She removed her coat from the chair and went towards the cupboard to hang it up. As she placed it over a coat-hanger, there came back to her the image of those coats each interred under a white table-cloth all about the restaurant.

It was several nights later when she saw the waiter again. By then Ian was about half-way through the fourteen performances that he had contracted to give. In general, the critics had been polite but unenthusiastic: he had 'courageously' taken over the role at short notice; he showed an admirable musicianship; the voice was 'light but well-focused'. All this was what both Ian and Carol had expected and yet both were disappointed that their expectations had not been confounded.

Carol had been having a drink and coffee after an early dinner – not at the San Bernardino but at a cheap snack-bar recommended by the wife of someone at the Embassy. It was ten o'clock and the opera, which did not begin until nine and was interrupted by intervals so long that it would almost be possible to eat a three-course meal during one of them, would not end until long after midnight. Even now those women glittering with far too much jewellery and wearing furs despite the warmth would be promenading with their black-tied escorts through foyers that flatteringly gave them back their own reflections from mirrors framed in elaborate gilt.

Suddenly, as she raised her glass and looked about her, she realized that the waiter from the San Bernardino was staring at her intently. He was seated with a group of men of the same age as himself but not of the same impressiveness – oh, far from it – all of them brooding silently in their chairs as though bored with each other. They might have been a group of businessmen, who had concluded whatever transaction they had had with each other and now merely out of politeness did not immediately separate and go their different ways. He was in a dark blue pin-stripe suit, with a stiff collar and the kind of tie that, in England, would indicate that he was proud of having gone to some minor public school. His feet were on the chair opposite to him, his ankles crossed, and his chin was sunk low on his chest.

Their eyes met again, and this time he gave a half-smile of seeming recognition; but she at once looked away. Soon, the intentness of his gaze had become almost insolent; she was aware of that but she resisted the impulse to meet his eyes again. His companions seemed totally unconscious both of her and of the scrutiny to which she was being subjected, as they made desultory remarks to each other, eyed the women who passed, often arms linked, beside their table, or sipped from their drinks. Yes, he was beautiful, beautiful; and she thought of Ian's firm, slim, white body and the gentle way in which he had repulsed her earlier that evening, putting her aside from him, when she had gone into the bathroom as he was towelling himself down and placed her arms round his shoulders.

Eyes still averted, she gulped at her drink and gulped again.

A young man lingered briefly beside her table, looking down at her in a bird-like way as though he were about to peck her; but, receiving no encouragement, he eventually moved on, hands deep in pockets as he whistled 'Don't cry for me, Argentina'. The musical was forbidden and yet everyone seemed to have heard the music.

Still the waiter stared, chin resting on his chest and the strange pale grey eyes fixed on her from under the black sweeping eyebrows. Had that half-smile really been one of recognition, as at first she had assumed? Or was he merely staring at her because she was a woman by herself and he was a man bored with the exclusively male companions with whom he found himself? She began to feel self-conscious and clumsy. When she poured some more coffee out of the silver pot on the tray beside her brandy – the handle was so hot that she had to wrap a paper napkin round it – she slopped some into the saucer; and when she raised the cup, she had to hasten to wipe away, with the same napkin, the drips that splattered her blouse. Suddenly, she began to shiver, though overhead electric bars were radiating their warmth over those customers who had opted to sit outside in this Argentine winter evening as warm as many an English summer one.

When she next had an opportunity to do so, she asked for her bill. There were innumerable noughts at the end of the figure; but by now she had got used to them and they did not cause her the same alarm as when first she had arrived. Even so, the sum was an absurdly high one. A glass of the local brandy and a pot of coffee and she was paying out over five pounds.

She got up, her chair scraping back on the pavement and the nape of her neck suddenly feeling the heat of the electric bar above her, and began to walk away slowly, without looking at him. She had forgotten to ask for some cigarettes as she had intended, from the bar, but even at this hour there were countless little kiosks and tunnel-like openings in walls where she could get some. A wan youth leaned against a lamp-post, hands in pockets and one foot, shod in scuffed suede, crossed over the other. She remembered that she and Ian had passed him at exactly the same place long after midnight when returning from the opera-house. That he did not even glance at her with his lacklustre eyes, in a country in which every male seemed to glance at a woman of her age, seemed to confirm Ian's verdict ('But how on earth can you know?') that he must be a male tart.

[184]

Beyond him, she saw one of the tunnel-like openings and entered. She pointed at a packet of Benson & Hedges and the frail old woman with arthritic hands in mittens reached up and got it down for her. But as she fumbled for her purse in her bag, a hand came out from behind her and held out a note between forefinger and middle finger. Curiously, though she had been totally unaware that he had followed her into the shop and even that he had been walking behind her, she felt no surprise. She knew whose hand it was and she knew why he was paying for the cigarettes. She took the packet and, without looking at him, walked past him and out of the door.

He caught her up and, beside her now as she continued to walk down the street, took her arm lightly. 'You are always alone.'

'Not always. But . . .' No, she would not tell him about Ian.

'It is sad to be a foreigner alone in a strange country.'

'Oh, I don't feel sad. I rather like it.'

'You are always smoking. That is because you are sad.'

'How do you know that?'

She had meant 'How can you say with such certainty that I am sad?' but, misunderstanding her, he replied: 'In the restaurant – five cigarettes. This evening, how many? Three? Four?'

She laughed. 'I've no idea. I didn't count.'

'Why did you never come back to the restaurant?'

'Because I went to other restaurants. Cheaper ones.'

'Was that necessary? You look rich.'

'I'm certainly *not* rich!'

'You look rich. Expensive clothes. Expensive perfume.'

'Well, I'm not.'

It was a strange conversation and yet nothing in it surprised or disturbed her. There was a rhythm to it, unfamiliar yet potent, like the rhythm of some dance that one has never attempted before and yet immediately masters; and there was the same rhythm to this walk, side by side, very slow, their gaze never meeting, through this canyon of the city. She had no wish to ask him about himself – Are you married? Where did you learn such excellent English? Why do you work in a restaurant? – and he seemed to be similarly devoid of any curiosity about her. Her only curiosity now was a sexual one. How would he look stripped of that pin-stripe suit and that shirt with the stiff collar, and of the vest and pants beneath them? And how would he make love to her – gently or violently, noisily or in silence, approaching her by stealth or with the snap and lash of an uncoiled spring?

They arrived at the hotel and it seemed perfectly natural that they should mount the steps together and that he should stand behind her as she asked for her key. There was a bar on the first floor and she had already decided that the porter would suppose merely that she was taking this guest up there for a drink. Ian and she had entertained some of his colleagues from the opera-house in its dim-lit, slightly clammy luxury more than once.

But to her horror, he greeted the cheekily flirtatious porter as though he were a friend. 'Hey, Alfredo!'

They spoke for a while in Spanish, the porter's gold fillings glittering as he threw back his narrow close-cropped head and laughed repeatedly. She had no idea what they were saying to each other. She hoped it was nothing about herself.

The bedroom was – as always at this hour – far too hot, and, curiously she could still smell the cigarette that she had smoked before she had left it. It was as though she had acquired Ian's sensitivity. The waiter said nothing. He merely approached her and began, deliberately and expertly, to undress her as though she were some mannequin in a shop-window. The pale grey eyes were blank. Eventually she stood naked before him, feeling no vestige of shame under that steady gaze that gave away nothing and seemed to ask nothing. He put his hands on her breasts, the coldness of them making her give a brief involuntary gasp, and then gripped them with sudden force, which made her gasp again. Then he gently began to massage the nipples. She put her hand down to feel him but he said, 'No,' shaking his head. He led her to the bed and laid her down on it. Face turned up to the ceiling, she waited, without looking at him. She heard first one shoe and then the other fall to the floor. She heard a rustle, then another rustle. That click must have been a cuff-link. A rustle again.

At last he clambered on top of her; the pale grey eyes looked into hers. There was a crucifix round his neck and she could feel it, like a sharp sliver of ice, against her throat. For a second, she had a strange fantasy of its cutting, painlessly but deep, into the carotid artery, so that all at once her life would be spurting out of her, while he continued to look down into her eyes in total indifference.

She put her hand down again; and this time he made no protest. 'Beautiful,' she murmured. 'Beautiful.' As she said the word, the central heating started that panting and throbbing as though, somewhere far below, a steam-engine was about to start out on a journey. She could feel, with an amazing hyperaesthesia, each hair on his chest, his forearm and his thigh; each drop of sweat on his shoulder; each breath that he drew. 'Beautiful.'

When they had ended, he got off the bed and went into the bathroom. She heard the water running into the bidet and called out, 'For God's sake use the towel on the left and not on the right!' He did not answer. She heard him clearing his throat and expectorating. Then – he must have found Ian's bottle of Listerine – there came the sound of gargling. Finally, he was urinating. It was odd, she thought, to use the bidet first and then to urinate. not the other way about. All at once she felt soiled – not by the semen trickling out of her, and not by his saliva and sweat, but by this whole elaborate ritual of cleansing. It was as though he regarded her as a whore, who might transmit some disease to him, which he in turn might transmit to his wife.

He came out of the bathroom and, without looking at her, began to dress. She watched him, marvelling yet again at that beauty; but he never once glanced at her, as he hurriedly pulled on vest, shirt, pants, socks and then went over to the mirror to tie his tie before pulling on his trousers as well and reaching for his jacket. Dressed, he turned to her and at last gazed down at her for a moment before opening the door. The pale grey eyes looked even paler than usual and still they were devoid of any kind of expression. She had seen that same kind of blankness in the eyes of a girl at school after she had had one of her attacks of *petit mal*.

'Are you going so soon? Let me give you a drink.' She raised herself on an elbow, drawing the sheet up about her in a sudden access of modesty that she had not for a moment felt until now.

But silently and swiftly he had gone, answering nothing, promising nothing, acknowledging nothing.

'Oh, you've used my towel! How often have I told you. . .?'

But Ian was too tired, and too much discouraged by a performance that he knew to have been deteriorating night after night, to notice much. 'And my Listerine. . .,' he grumbled at one moment; and at another: 'You do manage to get an awful lot of water on to the floor of this bathroom!'

When at last he was nestling down beside her – he was too

done in to want to eat, he said – he asked her: 'Why so early to bed?' Since they had arrived in Argentina, they had got into the habit of retiring long after midnight.

'I was bored.'

'Yes, I'm afraid it is boring for you. Never mind. We'll soon be home. Only another nine days.'

'Nine days!'

After five of those nine days, consumed by a restlessness that manifested itself in a number of trivial ways – she scratched and tore with each forefinger at the skin around each thumb-nail, she snapped at Ian, at the lethargic negligent maids and at an uncommonly stupid clerk in the post office, she took long walks up and across and down the grid of the city, she was perpetually washing her hair, her own and Ian's hairbrushes, their under-clothes – Carol resolutely made her way to the restaurant. It was about the same time as when last she had visited it; the huge bed of charcoal still glowed, as the sweating boy in the overlong apron exerted himself at the bellows; the head waiter showed the same worried irresolution, as he looked around the almost deserted restaurant, before guiding her over to precisely the same table at which she had sat before. Obviously, it was not a 'good' table, so near to the cooking area and to the cash-desk; but, then, what single woman was ever regarded as a 'good' customer? Again she took off her coat and again the head waiter carefully folded it and put it over the back of the gilt chair opposite to her, before he handed her the menu and disappeared.

She waited, her eyes fixed on the Spanish words, in total composure and total certainty that it would be he, the beautiful one, who would eventually come to take her order.

'Is madame ready to order?'

Yes, she had known it all along.

She now looked up and, as she smiled, the pinched, slightly disagreeable expression of her face was irradiated with a happiness that made her look almost as beautiful as the man standing above her. 'Hello!'

He nodded, with a polite irony, as any waiter might do to an eccentric female foreigner who greeted him so familiarly. 'Good evening, madame. Would madame like to order now or shall I come back later?'

She could not believe it: it was as though he were now seeing her for the first time. But then she decided that probably he was frightened of gossip if he were seen talking intimately with her – after all, she knew nothing about him and he might be married and even related by that marriage to the proprietor or the head waiter or one of the other waiters – and so she replied quietly but with a slight tremor in her voice: 'No, I'm ready to order now.' She ordered precisely what she had ordered on the previous occasion, with each of them repeating, almost word for word, their exchanges about what kind of salad she would have and what kind of wine.

'Thank you, madame.' He bowed and withdrew.

She was waiting now for something, the next stage of this curious ritual; but at first she could not remember precisely what it was. But then, as she glanced round the restaurant, her chin cupped in the palms of both her hands while her elbows rested on the table, she saw those strange mounds of starched whiteness at every table: the overcoats covered with their table-cloths. But he brought no table-cloth to cover hers.

Well, it must be an oversight, she decided; it was too trivial to worry about and certainly not something to which to draw attention. A young couple, also obviously not deserving of a 'good' table, were ushered over in her direction by the head waiter. The girl, who was tall, pale and not unattractive, slipped out of a shabby woollen coat, one button of which was hanging loose from a thread; the boy, who had a simian look, with unusually long, dangling arms, removed an overcoat spotted with oil at the hem. For them the waiter took a table-cloth from the heap, shook it out, brought it over and arranged it symmetrically. Then, as though aware all along that Carol had been watching him, he looked over to her, even while giving the table-cloth a final tweak, and for the first time smiled. But it was not a smile of love, friendliness or complicity, but of a contempt so blatant that it was as though he had come over to her and slapped her across the face.

Soon after that, she asked him in a low voice, as he was hurrying past the table, to bring her the bill. She had hardly touched the steak, which was congealing in a pool of blood and fat; she had swallowed only a mouthful or two of the salad. Only the wine she had finished, gulping it down, despite its slightly salty, slightly brackish taste, as of blood.

'The bill, madame? Certainly, madame.'

He put the plate down beside her and she carefully counted

out from her purse the precise sum asked. She was being mean, she knew; but she wanted to be mean.

He picked up the plate. 'Thank you, madame.' Totally indifferent.

He did not help her on with her coat; and, though she knew that the head waiter was watching as she struggled to get an arm into a sleeve, neither did he.

'Thank you, madame,' the head waiter said. The other had vanished.

It was their last night in Buenos Aires, and Ian said that they must have a celebration, even though there was nothing to celebrate but their imminent return to England and a cheque that, because of various inexplicable deductions for tax and stamp duty, was for far less than they had hoped.

'What about that steak-restaurant you told me about? I feel like a large juicy steak.'

She hesitated for a moment and then thought: Why not? There was nothing to lose, since everything had been lost already.

Although the restaurant was thronged with people when they arrived – it was almost ten o'clock – the head waiter at once hurried forward when he saw them. 'This way, please.' He sidled between tables at which, chairs thrust back, flushed diners shouted at each other in between gobbling chunks of bleeding flesh. Yes, this table was a 'good' one, set far away from the cooking area and the cash-desk and far from the door, in what was almost an alcove. The head waiter helped her off with her coat, as he had not done on either of the previous occasions, and then took Ian's coat from him, too. He neatly folded both coats over the back of the chair between the two on which they were about to sit and then, when they were seated, handed each of them a menu.

'Are you ready to order, sir?'

She did not have to look up to know who it was.

'Yes, I think so. Yes.'

'May I recommend the mixed grill?'

'That sounds an excellent idea. How about that, darling?'

Carol remembered the silver salver, piled high with meats, that the waiter had carried at shoulder-level through the restaurant to a party at the farthest end. She nodded and answered: 'Why not?'

Eventually, without having given her a single glance, the waiter went off to deliver the order. While Ian babbled on about a telephone call that he had received about two possible engagements at Glyndebourne – his career seemed to consist largely of possibilities that never got realized – Carol watched the athletic figure in the beautifully cut dinner-jacket as it moved about its tasks.

Now the waiter had gone over to the pile of table-cloths. He raised it at one corner, as though he were in search of a table-cloth even more dazzling and even larger than any on a table in the restaurant. He at last jerked one out, and then gave it a shake, so that it opened out like a parachute before him. He hurried over with it.

He still did not look at Carol as he placed it, in that curiously reverent ritual, as though he were draping some altar, over their coats. As on that first occasion, he tweaked at a corner, stood back to examine the result, and then tweaked at another. The folds fell stiff and symmetrical to the floor. The overhead light glittered harshly on the chalk-like blankness. It glittered so harshly indeed that, as though she were staring out over the sea on a day of brilliant sunshine, she felt herself screwing up her eyes and then, slowly, a headache forming between them.

Satisfied at last, the waiter gave a friendly smile to Ian and then moved off.

'What a weird idea!'

'Yes, isn't it? But you must have seen it before. They often do it.'

'Not in the kind of cheap eating-places where *I've* been keeping body and soul together!'

'But you must remember, in that place which that conductor man took us to . . .'

She broke off, oppressed almost beyond endurance by the sight of the strange white shapes, dotted like so many grave-stones all over the cavernous restaurant. When her plate was at last set down before her, it brought a strange relief to cut deep into a kidney and to see the beads of blood ooze out, as from an ox still alive.